DRESSED
TO KILL

Books by Lynn Cahoon

The Tourist Trap Mysteries:

Dressed to Kill
If the Shoe Kills
Mission to Murder
Guidebook to Murder

DRESSED TO KILL

A TOURIST TRAP MYSTERY

LYNN CAHOON

LYRICAL PRESS
Kensington Publishing Corp.
www.kensingtonbooks.com

LYRICAL PRESS BOOKS are published by

Kensington Publishing Corp.
119 West 40th Street
New York, NY 10018

All Kensington titles, imprints, and distributed lines are available at special quantity discounts for bulk purchases for sales promotion, premiums, fund-raising, educational, or institutional use.

Special book excerpts or customized printings can also be created to fit specific needs. For details, write or phone the office of the Kensington Sales Manager: Kensington Publishing Corp., 119 West 40th Street, New York, NY 10018. Attn. Sales Department. Phone: 1-800-221-2647.

Lyrical and the L logo are trademarks of Kensington Publishing Corp.

First Electronic Edition: June 2015
eISBN-13: 978-1-60183-415-7
eISBN-10: 1-60183-415-2

First Print Edition: June 2015
ISBN-13: 978-1-60183-416-4
ISBN-10: 1-60183-416-0

Printed in the United States of America

To my mother for teaching me to follow my own path.

ACKNOWLEDGMENTS

The last few years have been crazy busy with a lot of learning and growing as an author and as a person. When I look back at my life, I've realized that all my years have led me right to where I belong. Every decision, every mistake, every trial in some part has made me the person who I am today. My mom is one of those people who taught me to always believe in myself.

Big thanks as always to the Kensington/Lyrical crew who believed in South Cove and Jill's adventures. Especially Esi Sogah, my editor, and Ellen Chan who helped me understand the world of book promotion.

CHAPTER 1

Sometimes what you see is not what you get. The small building had its doors flung open, looking more like a gaping mouth posed to devour us than the entrance into South Cove's newest and only clothing business, Vintage Duds. Pots of flowers lined the sidewalk, giving the store what should have been a homey look. My aunt nudged me, and I took one halting step closer. I, Jill Gardner, owner of Coffee, Books, and More and South Cove's business community liaison to the city council, knew a trap when I saw it. And this tastefully decorated store selling upscale designer clothing at a ridiculous price for used threads was definitely a snare.

"What is wrong with you?" Aunt Jackie snapped. "Just because Greg was married to the woman doesn't mean the two of you have to be sworn enemies."

Yep, the new store owner was my boy toy's ex. Small towns are alike. You have to learn to forgive and forget because the person you fight with—or divorce—just doesn't move away. It's more than likely you'll run into them at the grocery, or the diner, or even at a meeting you're running. Life is messy that way. I turned away from the door, ready to sprint back to my shop down the street. "Maybe I don't have to attend every Business-to-Business meeting. You could say I was sick."

Jackie gently turned me around, linking her arm in mine. "You can do this. It's just a two-hour meeting. You can do anything for two hours."

As soon as we entered the store, I knew my aunt was dead wrong.

A hostess greeted us and gave us a swag bag. Aunt Jackie cooed and opened the silk ties. "A scarf, bubble bath beads, a coupon for a free glass of wine at Darla's winery, and"—she pulled out one last item—"jewelry."

The high school student grinned. "Keep digging. There's a little something from every store in South Cove."

"Except ours. Total waste of marketing money. You're preaching to the choir with this group," I muttered. Aunt Jackie quickly closed her bag and grabbed mine, as well, tucking them both into her purse.

"We'll save those for later." She smiled at our greeter and led me deeper into the store. Two chair-massage technicians had their area set up against the wall next to an eight-foot-square portrait of Marilyn Monroe. People lined up for their turn.

Bill Sullivan, our meeting chair, waved us over to where he waited in line. Bill was a member of the city council along with running South Cove Bed-and-Breakfast with his wife, Mary. "Great meeting, don't you think? Sherry went all-out."

"Is this a meeting or a party?" I waved away another high school student who had a plate of black caviar on crackers.

"Relax, Jill. We have plenty of time to get through the agenda." He glanced at the now empty chair. "Looks like it's my turn. You should get in line. You could use a massage."

"What's that supposed to mean?" I started to follow him, but again, I felt my aunt's hand on my arm.

"Leave it alone. There are enough rumors going on about you and Sherry. Can't you just pretend to enjoy yourself for a few hours?" my aunt asked, her voice low.

I took a deep breath. Jackie was right. No use getting upset. Sherry had been nice enough to volunteer to host this month's Business-to-Business meeting. Of course, when she'd offered, I'd expected her to serve cookies and coffee and for a freaking meeting to actually happen instead of this cocktail party. Apparently, I'd been delusional.

"I'm so glad to see you. I was beginning to think I was at the wrong place." Sadie Michaels came up on my right side and gave me a hug. She'd opened Pies on the Fly a few years ago, renovating her garage into a small bakery. Between Diamond Lille's and the coffee shop business, Sadie made a good income for the part-time-at-home venture. She was also one of my best friends.

I glanced around the room. Sherry had taken the entire clothing inventory out of the main showroom for our meeting. Two tables sat in the middle of the room, apparently for our use once we got done with our massages and caviar. White lights lined the room, giving the entire room a festive glow. A short runway in the center of the showroom featured models wearing designer gowns sold in the shop. If Sherry wasn't the owner, I would be enthralled with her collection. I saw some classic Chanel as well as a good dose of Michael Kors, the early years. Even though you couldn't tell it from a survey of my wardrobe, I loved watching designer trends. Just not buying them.

I focused on the conversation.

"So, I may be a little short on the pie order tomorrow, but you'll be caught up on Wednesday." Sadie smiled like she'd just solved a third world problem. "I'm going to grab some coffee."

"I don't understand. What happened to the pie order?" I called after Sadie, but my words were lost in the din. Or, more likely, she was ignoring me. I looked for my aunt but she'd stepped away. Scanning the room, I found her drinking a flute of champagne and talking to Kent Paine. Kent was dressed in a tailored black suit and looked more like a financial mogul than a small branch manager. His too-white teeth and salt-and-pepper hair added to his almost-perfect actor looks. He and Sherry had been dating for a few months now and gossip was they were made for each other. Both shallow and petty to the core.

Sherry floated into the conversation, took Kent by the arm, and moved him over to the side of the room. Aunt Jackie returned to our group. "You get dumped?" I teased.

She polished off the champagne and traded it with a full glass off the tray of a waiter she'd motioned over as she approached. I waved the guy off. I didn't need alcohol in my system this early in the day. "Just mingling. Kent's such a charismatic person, I don't understand what he sees in Sherry."

Raised voices from the side of the room had us turning to watch Sherry and Kent. ". . . keep it in your pants for an hour?"

"I was just being nice . . ." Kent grabbed Sherry's arm and they disappeared into a doorway, away from the crowd and blocking their next words.

"Looks like there's trouble in paradise." I nudged my aunt. "Maybe you have a shot?"

Her face turned beet red and she took a sip of her champagne. "Stop teasing. I feel bad for the guy, that's all."

"Looking for a new dancing partner?" Sadie rejoined the group, sipping a cup of coffee. "I thought you and Josh were almost exclusive."

Hearing his name, Josh lumbered toward the group in his normal attire, black suit, white dress shirt. He owned Antiques by Thomas and was Jackie's new beau. Josh looked as confused at the meeting events as I felt. He didn't say a word as he took a protective stand next to my aunt.

"Anyway, back to this week's order. Sherry came in with a last-minute order for the meeting. I just couldn't turn her down." Sadie led me toward the runway area, looking back at my aunt and Josh. "I almost put my foot in my mouth back there. I didn't know he was so close."

"When Jackie's around, Josh is never too far away. The man's besotted." I frowned, mentally calculating what Pies on the Fly product we had left at the shop. "I hope we don't get a tour bus stop, we'll be wiped out."

"Stop stressing. You'll have your order, just not tomorrow."

"I just can't win today," I muttered, allowing myself to be swept into the crowd. After a ten-minute show, Sherry walked out on stage to the thunderous applause of the group. She even bowed, as if she'd created each and every dress instead of the famous designers she stocked.

"I'm so blessed you all have opened your arms to welcome me and my little store into your community. When Greg told me how happy he was here in South Cove, I knew I was destined to become part of this amazing town." She paused, glancing through the crowd until she found me. Her smile widened. Instead of a woman, I saw a barracuda getting ready to attack her prey. "And now, I'm sure Bill wants to start the meeting. I've had coffee and pie set up at the main table. You'll find a place card with your name. Sue me, I love party planning."

The crowd laughed with her, turned, and found their way to their seats at the table. Typically I get maybe ten of the invited businesses to attend. Sherry's count seemed to be at least thirty. I didn't think I had thirty people on my invite fax list. My list of reasons why I hated Greg's ex-wife was growing by the minute.

When I sat down in front of my nameplate, I added two more reasons. Sherry had sat me on a corner of the table, next to Josh and

Lille. Josh sighed when he saw me. I put on a council business smile and greeted the two. "Good morning."

I turned toward my left and Lille was scowling at me. She wore catlike frames today, making her eyes look larger than normal. "Figures I'd get stuck at the loser table."

Lille owned the other food establishment in town, a diner called Diamond Lille's. She also had been dating the town bad boy and thought I'd had a role in sending him up the river. Or whatever they called prison life these days. I guess she didn't think his dealings with the local motorcycle gang and being an accessory to the last murder in town actually should count against him. I squared my shoulders and made my smile even bigger, then lied. "I asked Sherry to seat us together. I think it's long past time to mend fences, don't you?"

Lille's eyes widened and she looked like she was going to tell me what I could do with my fence work when Bill Sullivan called the meeting to order.

"Quiet down, people, this is a meeting after all." Bill took a sip of champagne and waited for everyone to settle.

"Could have fooled me," I uttered a little too loud. Everyone turned their attention from Bill to me, then swiveled to see Sherry's reaction. *Shut up, shut up, shut up.* Aunt Jackie shook her head, warning me, again.

Kent Paine stepped up, blocking the icy stares between Sherry and me. "I'd love to stay for your little meeting, but the auditors are coming in and they'll be upset if I'm not there to welcome them." He glanced around the table. "Although if I'd known how much fun you have at these meetings, I would have come before."

Not like I hadn't personally asked him several times to attend or at least send a representative. I'd even brought cookies three times to tempt him. I guess all I'd had to do was put on a circus clown costume and promise him a good time.

I watched him exit the building, and then saw a woman follow him out. Probably one of the servers. No, most definitely one of the models, tall with long dark hair, the woman was gorgeous. I heard the tap of a gavel. The meeting was starting.

"Jill's right." Bill tried to smooth the waters. "It's more than time to get started. First up, a report from my Mary on the results of the Christmas Festival." He smiled down at his other half.

Mary Sullivan had rounded up the troops to pull together the decorations at the last minute for a true South Cove Christmas after the mayor's wife had dumped the project. Then she'd run the entire festival, scheduling carolers, school visits, and setting up a Santa's workshop on the lawn of City Hall. The woman was amazing in my eyes. Mary stood, her warm smile enveloping me. She seemed to know exactly how I felt. "Repeating the brief I gave last month, we had a terrific festival. Every business owner I talked to saw an increase in profits over last year this time. I know our bed-and-breakfast is still working bookings we got during December." She passed out a stack of folders. "This is the final report for the festival numbers and accounting. At the end, there's a questionnaire for you to complete with ideas for our next festival. Please be honest. Many hands make light work."

When I got my folder and opened it, my eyes widened. Not only did she have an executive summary I could forward to the council, daily revenues were listed along with a description of the festival activities so we could see what brought in the visitors. At first glance, the Santa visits were high-profit days. Mary needed to be doing this analysis full-time rather than serving breakfast muffins to her guests.

"This is amazing." Holding the book open to one of the pages for the table to see, I pointed. "Mary's broken our store traffic down to events and times. We can use this to make staffing decisions next year rather than just guessing."

Bill beamed at his wife. "Mary used to be in market research before we moved here."

I didn't know that. Why didn't I know that? I thumbed through a few more pages. "We should do this for all of our festivals. We could get a grant from the city to pay for her time. This insight is promotion gold."

Mary's cheeks turned a bright pink when I gave her my usually-reserved-for-chocolate grin.

"My store isn't listed in the book." Sherry slammed her copy of the report back on the table. She looked toward Bill. "She didn't include Vintage Duds."

I didn't wait for him or Mary to speak. Have mouth, insert leg is my motto. "That's because your store hadn't opened yet. She's not a mind reader, Sherry."

Tension flowed down the table as Sherry turned toward me. If the girl had any supernatural power, I'd be stone now, holding purses or necklaces, forever stuck in this three ring circus she called a shop. Instead, I got the evil eye. Compared to the glares I got from my aunt at times, Sherry's scowl had no power on me.

Bill must have been concerned we would jump on the table and give the group a version of a catfight from the women's prison. He coughed, then continued like Sherry and I hadn't even spoken. "Mary, do you want to respond to Jill's suggestion?"

The woman's eyes got as big as two saucers. "What suggestion?"

"That you could do this for the business community. Maybe you and Jill should talk after the meeting and iron out a proposal. Then we'll vote on it here and take it to the council." He patted his wife's hand. "Next order of business"—he glanced down at the paper—"Josh Thomas would like to discuss the amount of trash floating around the streets." Bill waved his hand toward Josh and he took it for his cue to stand.

Josh Thomas moved his antique business, Antiques by Thomas, to South Cove last year. Since joining the Business-to-Business group, all he'd done was complain. Okay, he did call the police and save my life last year, but typically, getting involved was not his forte.

He passed out pages of blown-up pictures of trash, flyers, and mostly cups, including a few with Coffee, Books, and More's logo, on the streets of South Cove. Unfortunately for me, the amount of trash also showed my customer base compared to Lille's. Her cups outnumbered mine at least two to one. More drinks equaled more revenue, and the hope to make my store profitable on the long term.

"That's my car," an artist who ran his own minigallery sat up straighter. Conner McBride was his name, but his Irish ancestry was in doubt, as his accent only came out for the paying customers. "You took a picture of the inside of my car."

Josh shrugged. "It was disgustingly dirty. You are leaking this trash all over South Cove every time you drive that rattrap."

"Uncool, man. Way uncool." The artist shook his head sadly then leaned back, his large sunglasses covering his eyes. If the meeting had been back at the shop, I would have bet money that the guy was asleep behind the sunglasses. Power-napping through the day. It's a good model. And there's plenty of mentors in our little town.

Bill's shoulders were coming close to squeezing his ears off his head. The meeting wasn't going well, even with the relaxing massage and wine. "Look, Josh. Let's not start a fight over a little thing like trash. We're all in the same lifeboat and we can't be having people punching holes in the bottom of it."

"He started it." Josh pointed at Conner.

The young man popped up out of his chair. "I can finish it."

A hand gently pushed him back in his seat. "So can I."

Greg King, South Cove police detective and my hunky boy toy, stood behind Conner. He caught my eye and winked. Then he went back to saving Josh's life.

"Man, I wasn't going to hurt the dude. I'm not that type of guy." Conner glowered at Josh. "He needs to stop putting his nose into things where it doesn't belong."

"If you can't calm down, you'll have to leave." Greg's voice was calm, but his words hard.

Conner's hands flew up in mock surrender. "Like I wanted to be at this stupid meeting in the first place. I just came for the paycheck, man."

Greg stood back and let the tall, skinny artist stand up and step away from the table. Conner glanced at Sherry, who nodded some answer to an unspoken question.

This was curious. I didn't think Conner even knew Sherry. And what did he mean by a paycheck? Maybe Conner didn't own the gallery and his silent partner sent him to the Business-to-Business meeting this month.

Greg watched him leave the store, then slipped into Conner's chair. He picked up the photocopied picture of the inside of the artist's car, frowned, then folded the paper and slipped it in his front shirt pocket.

Leaning over the table, I whispered, "What are you doing here?"

Confusion clouded his face, but he leaned toward me and tapped my hand with his. "I'm on the agenda, remember?"

I shook my head. "No, you're not." I'd typed up the agenda last weekend. Bill, as chair of the business group, ran the meetings, but I set up the agenda and did the paperwork for the council. Nowhere on the agenda did it list Greg King to speak on anything.

"If we could continue?" Bill visibly shook off the stress the altercation had caused. "Maybe we should table the trash discussion to next month and let our invited guest talk about the viability of a city position for dog catcher."

I narrowed my eyes at Bill, but he turned his head away. This subject had definitely *not* been on the agenda I'd sent him. The lack of a central number for pet control was one of Josh's pet peeves about South Cove. He wanted to round up the homeless cat or two that hung around the shops. Aunt Jackie, on the other hand, couldn't help feeding the strays.

Sherry stood and took over the meeting. My eyes were almost slits now. What was going on?

"I know Josh has been trying to shine light on the problem of stray cats and dogs roaming the streets of South Cove for months. With Bill's approval"—now she paused to shoot a look at me, making sure the table knew I'd been pushing off Josh's request for meeting time—"I invited Greg to come and talk to us."

Wait, what? It was then I realized my aunt had been wrong. There was no way I was going to survive two hours without killing someone.

As Greg stood, Josh folded his arms and fake-whispered to everyone within earshot. "Finally, someone who can get things done around here. Maybe we need a new business liaison?"

It took all my willpower not to stand up and resign on the spot. I consulted my watch. Less than an hour left then I'd be home free. As long as I didn't open my mouth.

CHAPTER 2

I threw Emma's ball into the backyard, not looking at Greg. "I can't believe you let Sherry bamboozle you that way."

Greg closed the grill. Dinner consisted of steak, corn on the cob, and a cheesecake I'd brought home from the shop. He sat next to me. "Look, I'm sorry. I thought you knew about my visit to the meeting. Sherry said . . ."

I held up my hand. "I'm so tired of hearing what Sherry said. Look, do me one favor?"

He leaned back in the swing, kicking back his feet in his cowboy boots. He sighed and took a sip of his beer. "You know I'd promise you almost anything."

I curled into him, smelling his cologne and man scents. I was starting to calm down after the meeting from hell. Now I knew what the more artistic members felt every time they drew the short straw to represent. "Now, that's what I like to hear."

I felt his chuckle under me. "Speak your piece, woman, the meat's almost done."

"If you get an invitation to speak at the Business-to-Business meeting from anyone but me, tell me about it. I looked like an idiot." I hated the way Sherry had preened around him after the meeting. Yes, I knew she was dating someone. It still ruffled my feathers even if Greg swore her attention annoyed him.

"You're not good at holding in your feelings, that's for sure. Anyone who saw your face knew you were ready to blow a gasket." He tilted my head toward him so I could see his. "You know that feeds into her ego, right? Sherry always has to be the one in the spotlight, for good or bad reasons."

"Like the over-the-top meeting that was more like a party?" I sank my head back into his chest and ran my fingers up and down his tan arm. "She hired massage technicians, for God's sake."

"And the group loves her for it—for a day or two. Then she's going to expect an outrageous favor and when they say no, she's going to blow up on them. Believe me, Sherry can't be nice for long. Not anymore." Greg kissed the top of my head and stood. "Those steaks are done. Ready to eat?"

As we carried the food into the kitchen and sat down to eat, a thought occurred to me. "If this is out of line, say so, but why in the world did you marry her?"

Greg shrugged, cutting a bite off his steak. "I thought the package was worth the cost. I learned real early I was wrong, but I didn't know how to get out. I took vows. And until she broke them, I felt obligated."

"You're lucky you got out. You're too nice to put up with that kind of person." I pointed at him with my fork. "Hell, you're lucky you got me. I'm a gem. You should treasure me."

He laughed. "You're a pistol, that's for sure. I'm not sure I'd call myself lucky, though."

My lips pursed. "What would you call it then?"

"I'm determined and hardheaded. Two characteristics that work in my favor in our relationship." He took a sip off his longneck, watching me closely. "You sure you want to talk about us?"

Fear of the unknown stopped me. We've been a couple for less than a year now. Maybe *this* conversation was too early. "Not really. You ready for dress rehearsal tomorrow?"

Greg groaned. "Seriously? I thought you recast my character?"

"Not a chance. If I have to act like a twenties flapper, you can be my mob protection." Aunt Jackie had started this whole production with Darla. Now we were having a mystery dinner theatre at South Cove Winery next weekend. The Friday Mystery Reader's group had written the mini play, cast the characters, and were selling tickets. Proceeds supported a local woman's shelter.

Tomorrow was our first run through. Then we'd have a few days before showtime.

"I might have to work tomorrow evening." Greg bent his head down over his plate. "And next Saturday, too."

"Wrong answer, buddy. You'll be next to me on that stage and you're going to act like you are enjoying it." I stood and retrieved the huckleberry cheesecake from the fridge. "Besides, I've already picked up our outfits from the high school. Did you know they did a production of *Chicago* last year?"

"Maybe we should ask the drama club to take over mystery theater?" Greg brightened. "Did you talk to their coach?"

"No, Darla's determined to play the speakeasy madam. I don't think she'd let someone step in now." I held up a piece of the dessert. "You want a slice?"

"It's going to take more than some decadent treat to make me happy." But he took the plate from me.

"Now you know how I felt." I sat back and relaxed. We had a good thing going here, Greg and I. Better than most of my other relationships had been, including my short-lived marriage. I knew more about Greg now than I'd known about my ex-husband in six years. I heard Greg's phone buzz, signaling the arrival of a text. He pulled it out, read the message, then took the last bite of the dessert.

"Sorry, I've got to run." He kissed me quickly. "I'll come by tomorrow about six?"

"That will work." I raised my eyebrows. "Is there a problem in town?"

Greg shrugged. "The bank's alarm keeps going off and the security company has called us down there five times this month. Paine's looking into the problem, but we can't be too safe. Toby was called out to an accident on the highway as backup, so I've got to run."

"Anything to get out of dishes," I joked. I walked him to the front door, where he leaned in for a proper kiss.

"See you tomorrow." He stepped out the door. "And lock up."

I did as he instructed. He meant well. Something you have to accept when you date a person in law enforcement. They tend to be alphas.

I cleaned up the kitchen, poured a glass of wine, and curled up on the couch. Emma, my golden retriever, lay on the floor next to me. I bypassed the remote and grabbed the women's fiction novel I'd started on Sunday.

The best thing about owning a bookstore? The research.

The next morning I'd finished my morning commuters' coffee run by eight. The shop grew quiet. I'd done most of the prep work yesterday during the later shift that had been as dead as this morning was shaping up to be. So I continued my research. I'd finished the book and was sitting in one of the armchairs, thinking about the characters and the world I'd left behind, when the bell rang over the door. A group of women from the small bank branch down the street burst inside, excited chatter filling the shop.

I jumped up and went over to the counter. "Welcome, ladies. I don't typically see you out on a workday."

"The bank's closed until noon. They're working on the security system, and we can't be there." Leslie Talman, a woman I'd met over at The Glass Slipper at my one and only stained-glass class, led the group toward the counter. "So we decided to come here."

"I wanted to go to Diamond Lille's for an early lunch," the tall woman near the back grumbled. Anne, I remembered, her name was Anne.

I threw a clean towel over my shoulder. "Well, I'm glad you decided to stop here first. What can I make you?"

One by one, the women called out their orders, and I started to ring out the group of six. "These will all be separate, I suppose."

Anne pushed toward the front. "I'll get it." She handed me a credit card. When her friends protested, she smiled. "I came into some money, and I'd like to do this. Humor me. It's not like I'm buying you jewelry or a car."

The women settled around a table and I handed Anne a slip and a pen to sign. "That was nice of you." I heated the milk for the lattes as she signed.

"Money's no good sitting in a bank. It needs to be spread around to make a difference in this world." Anne turned away to join her friends.

By the time I'd finished the drinks and cut the last cheesecake to serve, the women were laughing and talking all over themselves. Kent should be the one paying for this little impromptu team-building activity. They'd all go back to work happy and motivated for the rest of the day.

I glanced at the receipt and nearly gasped at the tip. She'd left me almost 50 percent. I took the slip and pen to the table and tapped Anne's shoulder. "I think you made a mistake." I kept my voice quiet, not wanting to embarrass the woman.

Anne glanced down at the paper. "Nope, looks right to me."

"But the tip . . ."

She pushed my hand with the slip away. "I told you, money needs to be spread around." Then she turned back to the table and leaned over. "Did you guys see the boss's girlfriend come in with her panties in a bunch this morning?"

As much as I wanted to hear the gossip about Sherry, I left the table and slipped the charge receipt into the cash register. It was her money. I grabbed the store's handheld and dialed Sadie's number. When I got her answering machine, I left a terse message about bringing in whatever she had done today. Then added "please" and "thank you." I didn't have the strength to be mad at a friend. Not today.

By the time Toby Killian, my midday barista and South Cove's part-time cop, showed up at noon to take his shift, all the tables at the coffee shop were filled and there were people wandering through the bookstore, waiting for places to sit. Toby's eyes widened as he slipped on an apron and started a new pot of the hazelnut coffee I'd just drained. "Tour bus?"

I shook my head. "The alarm company cut a line and everyone's security systems went crazy. So we got the displaced employees." I sighed in relief when Sadie pulled up and parked her PT Cruiser in front of the shop. When her son, Nick, followed her into the store, their arms were filled with Pies on the Fly boxes. "You got my message."

I took a box and unpacked the still warm apple pie, set it in the display case, and went back for another.

"I got all five of your messages. Nick, run out and get the rest." She scanned the crowded shop. "What happened, tour bus break down?"

I filled her in on the cut line. Then added, "Sorry about leaving so many messages, but I was freaking. I was down to my last box of brownies."

"Don't be silly. This was my fault. I shouldn't have taken on Sherry's business without taking care of your order first. I'm still learning how to juggle this small business thing you do so efficiently." Sadie nodded toward the coffeepots. "I'd love a cup to go."

Toby poured her coffee and returned to the cash register, finishing the last customers in the line. Sadie and I packed as many pies and cakes into the front case and then took the overflow to the freezer in the back room.

Nick set the last box on the table and then looked at his phone, quickly reading a text. "Lille's calling me in for an extra shift. I guess she got swamped, too." He gave his mom a kiss on the cheek. "I brought my skateboard. I'll see you at dinner."

Sadie watched him walk through the back door. "He's growing up so fast. Maybe I shouldn't have insisted on the job."

"Nothing wrong with a little elbow grease for the kid. Besides, from the gossip around town, he got into quite a few of those fancy Ivy League schools back East. You're going to need the money."

"His father took care of that. The man loved his life insurance. I'm pretty sure I griped about the premiums early in our marriage." Sadie's eyes had that distant look she always got when she talked about her deceased husband. He'd been killed in an oil rig accident when Nick was a kid. From what I could see, ten years later, my friend still missed him.

"So once Nick's out of the house, are you finally going to think about dating again?" We'd had this conversation several times, but Sadie had always changed the subject. This time, her eyes twinkled.

"Maybe I'm not waiting until fall." She bit her lip, trying not to smile.

I pulled her down into one of the chairs around the table. "Okay, you have my attention. Who are you seeing?"

Sadie shook her head. "It's not like that. We've had coffee after Wednesday night services at the church a couple of times, and he's asked me to go with him to the mystery thing over at the winery."

"Do I have to wait until I'm on stage and see you in the audience to know his name?" I leaned closer. I was so happy for Sadie. She deserved every happiness.

"You're going to laugh." Sadie ducked her head, her checks flaming. "I can't believe we have so much in common, it's freaky."

I held up my hand in some sort of scout symbol. I could never remember if it was two fingers up or three. "I swear I won't laugh."

She glanced around the room to make sure no one was listening. "Dustin Austin."

I stared at her.

"See, I knew you would laugh." She started to stand, but I put my hand on her arm and she settled back into her chair.

"I'm not laughing, I'm shocked. He's so . . ." I reached for a word that wouldn't offend her.

"Granola? I know. He's knows so much about gluten-free baking, it's not even funny. He came to talk to me at church one day wondering if I'd considered adding a gluten-free line to the Pies on the Fly shop."

"Gluten-free pies?" I almost choked. From what I'd seen, Dustin Austin didn't have a shirt that wasn't tie-dyed, and he sported a fine set of dreadlocks for a white dude from Montana. He ran the bike rental shop in town and the annex at the beach in summer.

"He says there's a big market for gluten-free products. Especially if I sell on line. He's working on setting me up a website."

By the time I'd reached home, I was still thinking about Sadie and Austin. People are funny when it comes to love. You never know who Cupid is going to pick as your total soul mate. Sadie seemed happy. Unlocking the door, I heard Emma's bark out the back. She'd been waiting for me. Instead of letting her in, I ran upstairs to change into my running clothes. When I returned to the kitchen, I opened the door. My golden retriever went ballistic when she saw me putting on my shoes. She sat in front of me and made a whining, chuffing noise.

There was no doubting Emma's love for me. Or at least her love of running. We headed down Main Street as it wound out of town and toward Highway One and on the other side, the beach. Our favorite run. The waves crashed against the shore. Soon, my mind cleared and the rhythm of my feet against the sand and the caws of the seagulls were all I knew.

I didn't listen to music when I ran. Not like when I used to run in the city. This was more like having my own noise machine. Calming my nerves and relaxing my muscles, even when my workday had been rough.

Checking the time on my watch, I reluctantly turned back toward the parking lot. I had to get home and cleaned up before Greg arrived for our evening at the winery. I didn't want to give him any reason to back out of the rehearsal. I was sure our relationship was moving into the next stage, the big one that all women dream about. If things kept going this well, next month I was going to ask him to take ballroom classes with me. When I knew he wouldn't say no.

Climbing up the stairs to the parking lot, I was surprised to see two cars. There hadn't been anyone on the beach today. Most days Emma and I had the place to ourselves, no matter what time we ran. I clipped Emma's leash back on her collar and started toward the entrance to the road.

Passing the first car, I saw it was empty but there were two people kissing in the second. I smiled, though the couple looked a little old to be parking. The man had white in his perfectly coiffed hair. The woman's brilliant red hair was pulled into a messy bun at the back of her head. He must have heard Emma and me approaching because he lifted his head and looked right at me.

It was Kent Paine. And Sherry wasn't the woman he was kissing.

CHAPTER 3

I don't think I stopped running until I hit the front porch. Letting Emma wander the house, I ran upstairs to get dressed for rehearsal. The good news was I didn't have to worry about spilling the beans to Sherry about her boyfriend's indiscretions. The woman and I barely talked. The bad news was I knew eventually I'd tell Greg and he'd probably want to tell Sherry. Or maybe not. It wasn't as if I'd caught them naked and doing the ugly. Honestly, what responsibility did I have to say a word to anyone?

My mind was still debating the pros and cons of the question as I finished getting ready for our date. I curled up on the sofa to wait for Greg, trying to read the latest mystery release I'd grabbed from the shop. It was my turn to pick the book for our readers' club and I still hadn't chosen. That was the problem; there were too many good books. As I read, my attention left the troubles of the real world and focused on the antics of two retired sisters who gave cruise tours. *Senior Showdown* was the name of the book, and even though it sounded like something out of a spaghetti Western, the plot had hooked me from the first page.

Loud knocking pulled me off the cruise ship and back into reality. No doubt about it, I was choosing this book for our reading group. Especially now that the woman had befriended a muscular beefcake lifeguard who always seemed to be into trouble. I swung the door open and Greg stood there, a bouquet of flowers in his hand.

"Uh-oh. What did you do now?" I took the flowers and gave him a kiss on the cheek as he walked in.

"Can't a guy bring his best girl flowers without the third degree?" Greg squatted to Emma's level and let the dog give him one of her patented puppy hugs. Of course, being almost full grown, she almost tipped him over.

"Now I know something's up. Don't tell me you have to work tonight." I headed to the kitchen for a vase. As I trimmed the ends and dusted the water with the flower food I kept on hand for the summer's flower bounty, he put his arms around my waist and kissed the back of my neck.

Chills flowed through my body.

He spoke with his lips still lightly brushing my neck. "I thought I might be able to convince you to stay home tonight. We could play hooky from the rehearsal."

I put the mixed bouquet into the vase. "Only if you call Darla."

"Not on your life." Greg stepped back and watched me put the vase on the kitchen table. "I guess it was worth a try."

"Why is it that you have no problem telling me no, but you seem to be scared of most of the women in town?" I lifted on tippy toes and kissed him lightly on the lips. "Especially Darla?"

"I'm not scared. I'm polite. Besides, I have to keep up the strong alpha façade."

I chuckled. "You know façade means fake."

"Are you ready, or do you want to play with your catch for a while longer?" He walked to the door and glanced down at Emma. "You want her in or out?"

"Outside, please. Kevin came by yesterday and sunk that stretch of fence she's been digging at with concrete. She won't escape in that spot." Emma had taken to leaving the yard and sunning herself on Esmeralda's front porch across the road. Our local fortune-teller/police dispatcher didn't mind the visits, but I worried about Emma running out in front of a car. I glanced at the bill sitting on my counter. "He tried to talk me into doing the entire backyard that way, but I'm hoping she'll grow out of this stage."

"Hope springs eternal." Greg opened the door and Emma trotted out. He threw her a chewy bone. "Be good."

"Like that's going to happen." I grabbed my purse and swung the long strap over my head.

As we walked into town, we fell into an easy silence. There'd be plenty of time to catch up on our day's activities later on. Now I wanted to enjoy the moment, being with him.

Most of the cast had already gathered by the time we arrived. Matt Randall, the winery's new manager, and Darla's new boyfriend, greeted us with two red Solo cups filled with beer. I studied the contents of the cup, then raised my eyebrows. "Beer?"

Matt grinned. "Not just beer. Coastal Spring Ale. The winery's first addition of on-site brewed micro beers to our product line. I think you'll like it."

I sipped the smooth clear ale. The light brew tasted of summer and a little tang of strawberry. I took another sip. "It's good."

Matt's smile widened. "I wanted something that would appeal to the non-beer drinker since most of our clientele are die-hard wine drinkers. Maybe we'll get a following, maybe not, but it's been a lot of fun."

"Let me know when you need a taster for the next creation. I'll be glad to be a guinea pig." Greg slapped Matt on the arm. The two men hadn't spent a lot of time together as Matt was a recent addition to our South Cove community. He still lived in Bakerstown, the closest big town north on the highway, but he spent most of his days at the winery with Darla. I wondered if I should arrange a couples' night over at the house. We could invite Matt and Darla, Amy and Justin, and—I paused. I'd probably have to invite Aunt Jackie and Josh. And maybe Toby and Elisa, if they were still dating. After the holidays Toby had been pretty quiet about his social life. Maybe she'd thrown down the gauntlet, asking our bachelor barista to make a relationship commitment.

"You're lost in thought." Greg took my cup out of my hand and set it at our table. Then he helped me slip out of my light jacket.

"Sorry, I was planning." I slipped into a chair, glancing around for Darla, who was our director as well as being the Chicago bordello madam where the mystery had been set.

Greg chuckled. "Lord help us, what are you plotting now? Should I guess or do you want to spring it on me later?"

"I'm not that bad. Besides, you'll have fun."

Greg mumbled something as Darla and Matt walked up to the microphone at the front of the room.

I leaned closer and whispered, "I didn't hear you."

"I said, that's what you said about tonight's activities. And I'm definitely not having fun." Greg pulled me close into a hug. "Okay, well, maybe a little."

I leaned against him while Darla walked us through the evening's lists of events. We'd get into costume first, then line up on the stage, where any changes that needed to be made would be noted by the cast's self-appointed costume designer and seamstress, Esmeralda. She'd declined an acting part claiming she never knew when the "sight" would come on and she didn't want to mess up the play. After that, we'd have a full-run dress rehearsal. "I plan on wrapping up the rehearsal no later than nine," Darla announced. "So be quick about your costume changes. Girls have the Breakwater room, and guys, you're in my office. Your costumes are waiting in the room."

Matt leaned into the microphone. "Fellows, follow me. The office has been prestocked with pitchers of ale to keep your throat from getting dry."

Greg and the other men in the room cheered as they stood to join Matt.

As I walked toward the Breakwater room, Amy Newman slipped in step next to me. Amy was South Cove's city planner, City Hall receptionist, and secretary to Mayor Baylor. She was also my best friend. Her short blond pixie cut bobbed with each step, showing her enthusiasm for the night's activities. "Justin would follow Matt anywhere if he thought free beer was involved."

"Him and every other man in the room. What's up with that?" I teased. "Darla better have some alcohol ready in our dressing room, too."

Darla didn't disappoint us. In the Breakwater room, a table had been set with bottles of wine on ice, glasses, and chocolate-covered strawberries. The women gathered around the table, filling glasses before they found their costumes. Amy and I found our bags labeled with our names together near the end of the room.

"I haven't changed in front of this many women since high school P.E.," Amy grumbled.

The woman changing next to us eyed my thin friend. "And you still look like you did back then. Slender and gorgeous. I don't know what you're complaining about." She patted her stomach. "You're about to see what happens to real women as they age."

"You look fine," I assured her. Although I'd been thinking the same thing. I guess it's human nature to question the state of your body, especially undressed in front of a group. "I do have this nightmare every once in a while."

"Standing in front of Mr. Higgins's sophomore English class

doing a book report in your underwear?" She grinned. "Rotating nightmare number 434."

Amy laughed. "It's Algebra II for me. Although for some reason, the entire football team is in the class. Which I know isn't true since they took Consumer Math."

Darla called time and we hurried out to the stage to stand in order of our appearance in the play. Henry Montgomery checked us off against his list of cast members, then Esmeralda and Darla ran through the costume check. When she reached Greg and me, she paused.

"These are perfect. You did good, Jill." Esmeralda touched the red fringe that layered my short dress. "Even the shoes are perfect for the time period."

I'd gotten lucky and found a pair of ankle-strapped heels at a thrift store in Bakerstown last Monday when I'd gone shopping. I was about to tell her where I'd found them when she spoke again.

"You must take caution this time. You can either be the key or the clue." Esmeralda had frozen in front of me.

I looked into her face and saw the blank stare. She'd gone all vision-glassy-eyed, right in the middle of the rehearsal. Although I didn't really believe she could talk to the dead, I had seen her fall into this trance state more than once. And her predictions, although strangely worded at times, made complete sense later. I shivered and stepped closer to Greg.

He slipped his arm around me while trying to get Esmeralda's attention. "What did you say?"

Her eyes cleared and she smiled. "Jill did very well with both of your costumes. Now, don't try to tell me you dressed yourself, Greg King." She nodded to Darla, who checked off our names before moving on to the next person in line. Darla's eyes were wide and she looked like I felt—scared to talk about what had just happened.

I sighed, letting my shoulders sag a little bit. "I hate it when she singles me out like that. It's never a good sign."

Greg squeezed me and walked me back to our table, where we'd wait for our turn on stage. "She has to keep her image up even with the town folk. I'll talk to her tomorrow and ask her to stop playing with you if it freaks you out."

"It's no big deal." I tried to shrug it off, but the fortune-teller's words kept ringing in my head. Quickly, the costume check was over and it was time to start the rehearsal. Greg and I didn't come on until the second act, so I settled in to watch the fun.

"Act One, Amy and Justin, enter stage left," Darla called out. As the curtain opened, I saw Amy, but she wasn't in the middle of the stage. Justin was there, leaning over the body. I frowned. "Someone got their directions mixed up. We don't have a body until scene two."

I watched Justin stand and scan the room. His gaze stopped at Greg, who was already moving toward the stage.

"It's Kent Paine," Justin stammered. "He's really dead."

CHAPTER 4

By the time Greg had secured the scene and talked to the entire cast and crew of *Dying for Trouble*, a name that had seemed cute when we made the playbills, it was long after midnight. After changing out of my costume, I rode home with Amy and a still visibly shaken Justin.

"I've never seen a dead body before, much less touched one," he murmured under his breath. Darla had opened the bar in the back of the winery, and after Greg questioned each person, they were directed there to wait until he let everyone leave. Justin had taken full advantage of his waiting time, and now, he was drunk off his butt.

"He gets weepy when he's drunk?" I turned and stared at the crumpled man in the backseat.

Amy glanced up at the rearview mirror. "Never before. I think seeing Kent threw him over the edge."

Justin moaned and laid his head back. "There's no going back from dead."

"Now he's a philosopher?" I smiled at Amy. "You going to be able to get him up the stairs to your apartment?"

"Austin will help if I can't." Amy shrugged. "If he's not home, I'll leave Justin in the car until tomorrow when he sobers up."

Dustin Austin owned Amy's apartment building. Austin, as he liked to be called, lived in the apartment on the third floor. On the ground floor, he ran the only bike rental shop in town. During the summer he set up a trailer on the beach so he could work on his tan in his downtime. Austin had been a hippie from the time he dropped out of an Ivy League college back East. The man reeked of the sixties, wearing his tie-dyed T-shirts and cargo shorts, a pair of Birkenstocks always on his large feet. I'd yet to get him to attend one of the Business-to-

Business meetings, or what he called the Gathering of the Establishment. He tolerated me as a pawn of The Man, but he adored Amy.

Amy pulled Justin's Grand Cherokee into my driveway. I gave her a quick hug before opening the door. "Thanks for the ride."

"No way would I let you walk home." Amy looked back at the now sleeping Justin. "I can't believe Kent's dead. He seemed like such a nice guy."

"Not from what I've been hearing. I think he and Sherry were meant for each other. They both only cared about themselves." I thought about seeing Kent with the woman at the beach yesterday. I probably should tell Greg before I started gossiping to Amy, but I was torn.

A groan from the backseat stopped my internal debate. Amy rolled her eyes. "I guess I'd better get my traumatized boyfriend home and tucked in bed."

Amy didn't pull the car out of the driveway until I'd found my keys, unlocked my door, and turned on the living room lights. I waved and Amy responded with a quick beep of the horn. After I let Emma out for a quick backyard break, I grabbed a bottle of water out of the fridge. I considered tea, but I felt beat. Watching out the window and waiting for Emma to return, I realized what Amy had said in the car. *Boyfriend.* She'd moved past the Hank the Jerk phase, finally.

A smile teased at my lips as I let my dog in and locked the house up for the night. Amy and Justin were official.

No smile rested on my face the next morning when the alarm blared way too early. I dragged myself out of bed and sat at the table for a few minutes power-drinking the coffee I'd set on delayed brew last night. Emma ran around the backyard looking for an unwise rabbit and I wanted to return to bed. Maybe I could invent a coffee patch that filled you with caffeine on mornings like this. I discarded the thought. Part of the experience was the feel of the brew warming your body up like a fine race car.

I left Emma outside while I got ready for my morning shift. After a shower and pulling on my favorite capris and floral tank, I felt almost human. I checked her food and water, gave my dog a hug, and got a wet slurp of a kiss in return.

"We'll run when I get home," I promised. The last few weeks had been busy with getting ready for the now-postponed mystery dinner theater. Coffee, Books, and More was a major sponsor, along with

South Cove Winery and South Cove Bed-and-Breakfast. Jackie had designed the marketing promos, including getting a free announcement on the local radio and television stations. Now she had to rework all of the promotions with a new date. I didn't even want to see my aunt today. She'd be grumpy as a bear.

When I arrived at the store, Sasha Smith, our newest employee, sat at one of the patio tables, reading. She looked up at me as I unlocked the door, her coffee-colored skin almost glowing in the soft early morning light. She held up the book she'd been absorbed in, an advanced reading copy of a new adult series. Sasha had taken on the role of our young adult and new adult expert. She had blown through all the publishers' advanced readers copies I'd set aside, hoping for some time to read.

"Hey, boss." Her honey Southern tone made the address almost tender. "I love, love, love this author. I think she'll be the first read in our teen book club. The kids will adore this book, just enough angst. I'm so glad you let me spin the older kids off into their own group. It opens up a whole new batch of books and subject matter."

"I'm so glad you agreed to take on another club. Sorry if I kept you waiting." I flipped on the lights as we entered the store, the smell of books and coffee filling my senses.

"I don't mind waiting, it gives me time to get a few pages done. Olivia hasn't been sleeping well this week, so I'm reading a lot of Dr. Seuss and Shel Silverstein until she finally drops off." Sasha laid the book on the counter and tucked her purse into my office on a shelf. After washing her hands, she started a pot of coffee. "The teachers at the center think it's a stage."

"If you need some time off to take her to the doctor or something . . ." I hesitated. I didn't know if poor sleep habits were something a kid needed to see a doctor for or not. Heck, what I knew about kids mostly focused on what books they'd read and at what age level.

"She's fine. Healthy as a horse. She gets checkups over at the clinic on a regular basis. I think she is just realizing Mommy's not around as much anymore." Sasha smiled. "Single parenting has its drawbacks."

"Well, if you need something, all you have to do is ask." I opened up the dessert case and pulled out two pieces of vanilla bean cheesecake. "Like breakfast. You want one of these? I'm going to cut open a fresh cheesecake for the display later this morning."

"Don't have to twist my arm. Let me finish the opening list, and I'll sit down with you until the commuters hit." Typically, on a Thursday, the morning shift was slow. I'd added Sasha to the schedule full-time at the first of the year. Next month, I'd let her work several shifts alone, but for now, she always had a backup—and no one's hours were affected. When she did start working by herself, I'd give her some of Jackie's shifts or mine so I didn't short Toby. We worked on the opening, and then I opened my laptop to my bookseller's website and started making a list for next week's order.

Sasha joined me, bringing over two cups of coffee and the cheesecake. "So you're okay with the after-school club? Jackie thinks it's a good idea."

"I think it's a great idea. Ever since we installed free Wi-Fi, the teens have been hanging here after school anyway. Why not get them excited about books?" I pulled up the book she'd been reading that morning. "This one's not out until July. But the book is part of a series. You want to start with book one?"

We made plans, ordered twenty copies to start with, and framed out a timeline. Jackie could take over the promotional part tomorrow night when she worked with Sasha. Fridays were my day off with Toby opening, then Sasha joining him midmorning and staying to help out Jackie. All in all, I had to admit, Coffee, Books, and More was running like a well-oiled machine.

Which made me worry. Nothing came easy, but not seeing a shoe dropping at the present, I pushed aside my unease.

I'd settled into reading a contemporary romance, putting aside the murder mystery I'd been devouring. It seemed wrong to be reading about a murder when we had found a dead body the night before. Of course, Doc Ames, the county coroner in Bakerstown, could have ruled Kent's death due to natural causes by now, but you never knew.

Especially in South Cove.

The bell over the door rang and Darla Taylor burst in. She'd taken to running the mile from the winery to town three to four times a week. I'd even seen her out on the beach some days when I ran with Emma. She'd been diligent, and the effects were starting to show. She glanced at Sasha, then found me over on the couch and beelined directly for me. Sasha brought her a large glass of water.

"Thanks, doll." Darla sucked down half of the water, pausing to breathe. She pointed to the menu board. "Get me a skinny latte, too."

As Sasha disappeared to make the coffee, Darla finished the last of the water and wiped her mouth with her hand. She sank into the easy chair next to the couch. "I swear, getting in shape is going to kill me."

I used a bookmark to keep my place and set the book on the coffee table. This wouldn't be a quick conversation. "You look amazing."

A small smile creeped onto her lips. "Let's just say I look better. I've got a long way to go."

"A journey starts with a few first steps," I quoted a Facebook post I'd seen the other day. "Or something like that."

Darla waved her hand. "Enough about me, what have you found out about Kent? Does Greg know who killed him yet?"

"Darla, the body was only found last night. I'm sure Greg doesn't even know if it was murder." I'd known Darla would be looking for insider information. She wrote for the *South Cove Examiner* part-time and had a nose for gossip, if not news.

"That's not what I've heard." She pulled out a small notebook she'd stuffed in a fanny pack she'd clipped around her waist, along with a five-dollar bill that she handed to Sasha as she dropped off Darla's coffee. "Thanks, keep the change."

Sasha disappeared behind the counter and I noticed her book disappeared, too. I'd gone and hired another book addict. Smiling, I turned back to Darla and her notepad. "You might as well just put that away. Apparently you know more than I do about the case. Why do you think it was murder?"

"I was cleaning up the stage when Doc Ames and Greg were talking about Kent." She flushed at my look. "I wasn't eavesdropping, if that's what you're thinking. I can't help it if they were talking loud enough for me to hear."

I couldn't help myself; I leaned forward. "So what did they say?"

Darla glanced around, checking the empty shop for listening ears, then whispered, "They found cocaine in a Baggie in his pocket."

"No." I thought about the always cheery banker. "Kent Paine did drugs?"

Darla shrugged. "At least they thought it was cocaine. Greg said he would send it to the lab today."

"Couldn't that have killed him? You hear about people dying from drug overdoses all the time. Why do you think it was murder?" Darla wasn't telling me the whole story, I could tell.

She pressed her lips together, then blurted, "What, you think a healthy man just dies?"

I thought about Darla's statements and shook my head. "I think you are writing fiction instead of your normal, factual news articles. You don't even know if it was drugs they found."

"I guess you're right. Ever since we had that problem at The Castle, I've been seeing ducks." Darla leaned back again and sipped her coffee.

"Ducks?" Sometimes I had a hard time following her logic.

Darla waved her hand in the air. "You know, if it looks like a duck, and quacks like a duck, it's a duck? I'm saying it's weird for a guy to just die. So, it looks like a duck."

"I think you're reading too much into this. Kent died. Until Greg says different, I'm going to go with unfortunate incident rather than murder." I sipped the last of my now cold coffee and stood to get a refill.

"Just wait, you'll find out I'm right." Darla quacked a few times for emphasis, then finished off her coffee. When I walked to the counter, she followed, stuffing her notebook back into her fanny pack and zipping the leather case closed. "I'll be back when you have something to tell me."

As Sasha and I watched Darla leave the shop, I wondered if her radar for gossip was spot-on. Greg hadn't called yet. Maybe it was time to see if my boyfriend wanted to buy me lunch or if he was too busy trying to solve the latest murder.

The oversized clock on the wall showed eleven. Sasha had the shop under control, Toby would be here in thirty minutes—I could take a break to call Greg. I excused myself to the back office and hit speed dial on my cell. While I waited for him to answer, I stood at the back door and watched birds wander through the small parking lot behind the shops. Mayor Baylor had proposed making all the back lots into a public parking lot, but so far, the shop owners had resisted, each side of the street making strong arguments why it should be on the other side of Main. Besides, with the beach parking and the available street parking, we were okay for all but the largest of our festivals, when people parked on the side of the entry road and walked into town. Like I did each morning.

The phone rang into voice mail and I heard Greg's deep voice booming out a request to leave a message. Thoughts of Lille's fish and chips ran through my mind, so after leaving a message about lunch and a quick, "thinking about you," I dialed Amy's work line.

This time a real human picked up. Or what passed for a human. "South Cove City Hall," Mayor Baylor barked into the phone. "What do you want?"

"Good morning, Mayor." I pulled out the sweet, charm soaked voice I used, well, never. "I take it Amy is out on a break?"

"The girl is probably surfing, since she called in *sick*. I don't know why I keep her on." I could hear paper being shuffled loudly on the desk. "You'll have to call back tomorrow, I can't find anything to write a message on."

I was about to tell him to look in Amy's left-hand drawer in her desk, but he hadn't waited for an answer. The line was dead.

Now I was oh-for-two on lunch buddies. I heard Toby's voice in the front and made a strategic decision. I grabbed my purse and the book I'd been reading. Heading out to the front, I watched as Toby pulled on an apron and organized his counter. Sasha had commented on the stupidity of each of us reorganizing the cups and utensils at the beginning of each shift, but I noticed the mornings she worked with me, she set up the counter with her own method, too. I guess we all knew our way was the *right* way.

"Hey, Toby, you hear from Greg this morning?" I leaned over the counter, checking the status of the dessert case, trying to appear nonchalant.

"Don't even start. You know Greg gets testy when I tell you anything about open investigations. I'm not getting another lecture about leaking sensitive police information." Toby sipped his coffee. "Man, this hits the spot. I'm used to my evening shifts being pretty quiet. Instead, I spent the shift interviewing all those pretend actors for your play."

"They're called amateurs for a reason, Toby. Besides, I thought you were going to audition for a part?"

"No time. Between working here and for your boyfriend, and trying to see Elisa at least once a week, I'm booked. I barely get six hours of sleep most nights." He grinned. "No wonder I ran through chicks like bottled water. They need a lot of attention."

"But she's worth it, right?" I liked the fact Toby was finally in a real relationship. We'd even double-dated a couple of times, taking in a show in the city or a late dinner when Tim took over the on-call for a night. Greg had been hinting that we should sneak away alone for a weekend trip while the tourist season was a little slow, but finding Kent's body would put a wrench in that plan, especially if Darla was correct and it was murder.

Dating a cop was hard. No way around it.

Toby cocked his head, watching my thoughts flash across my face. "There's not trouble between you and the boss, is there?"

"We were talking about you and Elisa, not my love life."

He shrugged. "So? I hear things."

Now he had me hooked. "Like what things?"

He glanced around the still empty shop, looking like he was praying for a busload of tourists to flood into the store. "Okay, he told me you were ticked off about his report to the Business-to-Business meeting. That's all, I swear."

"Men are such gossips." I smiled. "I was mad. But we talked about the issue and he promised never, ever to talk to Sherry again."

"Boss—" he started, then stopped.

"What?" I laughed. "I know, it's a stupid rule, but I needed some reassurance, especially since Sherry opened a business down the street. We'll be running into her day and night now. I guess I need to get over myself, but she can be so, well, pushy. At least when it comes to Greg."

Toby ran his hand over his face. "Look, you didn't hear it from me, right?"

I stared at the man across from me. "I didn't hear what?"

"I mean, it could be nothing," Toby started.

Sasha came up next to him behind the counter. "You better spit it out, boy. Jill looks like she's going to climb over the counter and shake it out of you."

Toby cleared his throat. "As I came into town a few minutes ago, I saw Greg going into Vintage Duds."

CHAPTER 5

My cell rang as I bit into the first of the onion rings I'd ordered as an appetizer to my fish and chips lunch. Add in the vanilla milk shake I'd sucked down half of already, and my total calorie count would feed ten women on a low calorie diet for a day. I glanced at the display. Greg.

"What?" I answered, not hiding my frustration.

Greg laughed. "I guess I'm too late. The gossip mill has already told you I paid a visit to Sherry today."

"Why would you say that?" I had to give him props, he wasn't hiding the fact.

He paused. "Where are you? Lille's?"

"It *is* lunchtime." Okay, so I was still being a brat. He probably had a perfectly good reason to have visited his ex-wife and turned off his cell phone.

"Order me the meat loaf plate, I'll be right there." He clicked off the phone.

I thought about ignoring his request, but then I thought about his baby blue eyes and how his chin stubble tickled my ear when he whispered totally inappropriate but funny lines while we were watching movies. I waved Carrie down.

By the time he arrived, his food was sitting on the other side of the booth, waiting. He quickly kissed me, then sat and drank down half his iced tea. He snagged an onion ring off my plate. "I'm starving. I've been going since I sent you home with Amy last night. How is Justin doing? The man was freaking when I interviewed him."

"I don't know. I tried to call Amy earlier, but she took the day off. Maybe Justin needed some TLC from the hangover he probably has this morning. He was pretty hammered last night." I leaned back and watched him devour half of the meat loaf. "So you were at Sherry's to talk about Kent?"

He nodded, but didn't say anything, digging his fork into the pile of mashed potatoes. He held up a bite. "These are so good."

I watched him eat and nibbled at my French fries. I tried another tactic. "So Darla's saying Kent was murdered."

"Ah, shit." Greg dropped his fork and I leaned back. "I wish she'd stop spreading rumors so we'd have a least a day to investigate."

"Was it murder?" Now I was intrigued, my fried-to-perfection fish forgotten. "Who would want to kill Kent?"

He finished his iced tea and set the glass near the end of the table, waving to catch Carrie's attention. Then he picked his fork back up and dug into the mashed potatoes again. Before he took the bite, he shrugged. "Not a clue."

"You're mean." I dipped a fry into ketchup and bit into the crunchy slice of salty heaven.

He scraped the last bite of gravy off his plate. Greg was a member of the clean plate club. At least when he was hungry and liked the food in front of him. Once when I made a creamy shrimp over potato gnocchi, he picked out all the shrimp and left the gnocchi. But at least he tried it. The man could be a picky eater. When Carrie picked up his plate and refilled his glass, she paused.

"You want some apple pie? Fresh this morning from Sadie's bakery." She glanced at me. "Looks like you still have a ways to go before you need dessert."

"Thanks. Bring over a piece with a scoop of ice cream on the top." Greg grabbed one of my fish fillets and consumed it in two bites.

"So why did you visit Vintage Duds?" I grabbed the last piece of fish before it disappeared like the other one.

"I'm a cop. I investigate. Until Doc Ames tells me Kent's time on this world was up naturally, I question people." Greg settled for a few more of my fries. "You're not going to let this go, are you? Sherry was at the winery just before our practice started. The tapes show her sitting in her car for ten minutes, then storming into the tasting room. Twenty minutes later, she gets back in her car."

"Do you think Sherry might have killed him?" Part of me was cheering Greg's calm demeanor, especially since his ex-wife might be a murderer. Another part knew it was probably awkward if not impossible for him to stay totally impartial.

"We don't know if anyone killed him. Seriously, Jill, you need to stay out of this. I'm the investigator in the relationship. If I need help, I'll work with Doug over in Bakerstown PD." He shrugged as Carrie set the pie in front of him. "I can tell you this, all I know is she was there and now, I know her side of the story. She claims she got an anonymous text saying Kent was meeting another woman for drinks. When she got there, all she found was Darla and Matt getting ready for the rehearsal."

"Now, was that so hard to say? Sometimes you take all the fun out of my day." I broke off a bit of the flaky crust before he could move the plate out of my reach.

"Yeah, like when I try to keep you safe?" He cut a large bite and popped the treat into his mouth.

I leaned back, ignoring the cinnamon smell that was making my mouth water. Usually, one bite satisfied my craving. And I'd had freaking cheesecake for breakfast. Now, all it had done was whet my appetite. Kind of like Greg's denials about Kent's death status.

Greg cleared off the last bite of the pie and pointed his full fork at me. "I'm serious, Jill. You deal with your business, I'll deal with mine."

I watched the fork as he waved it in the air in front of me, thinking of grabbing the utensil and ignoring his clear directions.

A smile crossed Greg's lips, right before he devoured the last bit of pie. "I know you can hear me." He pushed the plate aside. "Look, sorry I broke our agreement about Sherry, but my visit was part of my job. That's the last I'm going to say about it."

"So should Sherry get a lawyer?" I smiled at my own joke. Before he could answer, his phone buzzed with a text.

He thumbed to the message, then put the phone in his pocket. When he stood, putting cash on the table for the meal, I wasn't surprised. This was life dating a cop; plans got changed with a phone call. He kissed the top of my head. "I have a lot on my mind. I'll call you later."

I watched him stride out of the diner, wondering when I'd see him again. Dinner, if Kent had been called up naturally by Saint Peter's list. Next month, if someone had moved him up the list intentionally. No matter what Greg said, when murder happened on his watch, my life was always involved, even when I tried to stay out of it.

* * *

After running with Emma to counteract at least a few of the lovely fat-filled calories I'd consumed that day, it was time to throw a load of laundry into the washer and make a list of the things I wanted to do on my first day off of the week. Usually, I read most of the day, ran with Emma, and did the few house chores needing done. Living alone with my dog as company, the house didn't get extremely dirty. So I didn't worry about extreme cleaning. The situation worked for both of us.

Don't get me wrong, I loved my little house. Especially now that the downstairs had been painted and filled with keepsakes from my life instead of the prior owner's, Miss Emily. The woman loved her crosswords. I was still finding piles of ripped pages from the local paper with half-completed puzzles upstairs as I tried to clean out the other two bedrooms. I glanced upstairs, weighing the thought of digging into cleaning one of the bedrooms versus reading the few final chapters in the contemporary romance. Love won out.

It always does.

As I curled up on the porch swing, I threw a blanket over my legs. After a few chapters, I promptly fell asleep.

In my dream I was chasing kittens, trying to keep them safe and out of harm's way. They weren't cooperating. I'd wrangle one back into the paper box and another would take off, running with scissors. Finally, exhausted, I'd lain by the box, and the kittens had come to sleep by me. I could still feel the purrs vibrating on my legs as I woke from the dream.

When I looked down at my legs, still covered by my wandering quilt, I found the source of the vibration. A black cat opened her yellow eyes, blinked twice, then laid her head on my leg and fell back to sleep.

"Who are you?" I reached down to stroke the cat's soft fur. She purred her response, but I felt a collar and a tag. I adjusted on the swing, bringing her closer so I could read the tag. "Maggie?" I read further down to see the address.

Pulling her into my arms, I stood and walked around the house, Emma following at my heels. "Some watchdog you are," I chided as I locked her into the front yard. "Allowing another animal to come and cuddle with me while I slept."

Maggie meowed and Emma let out a short bark, like, *Where are you taking my new friend?*

Crossing the empty road, I made my way to Esmeralda's front door via her winding stone path. I had to admit, the woman knew how to set a stage. As the town's resident fortune-teller, Esmeralda's home was her office. At least when she wasn't working her second job as a dispatcher for the police department. Small towns, everyone is related or works with someone you know. I liked my neighbor. She kept to herself. Her business didn't attract a lot of traffic on the street, and she had started working on the outside of the house. When I first inherited the house from Miss Emily, Esmeralda's had been in worse shape than mine—a fact that the city council overlooked due to her relationship with our Honorable Mayor Baylor. I was getting tear-down notices; she was giving fortunes with positive outcomes in her private sessions at City Hall.

Not that I held a grudge.

I pushed the doorbell and a cascade of wind chime music tinkled behind the door. No response. I looked down at the kitten, not willing to trust that if I put it down in the yard, it wouldn't cross the road again, this time with not as favorable results. I pushed the bell again, thinking that maybe Esmeralda was on the phones at her other job. I snuck a peek toward town. I didn't think Greg would take kindly to me dropping the kitten off at the police station. I could take her inside the house and wait. I returned my gaze to the sleepy kitten in my arms. "What do you think, Maggie?"

She blinked twice at me. Then I heard the door creak open.

"Jill. So nice of you to stop by." Esmeralda was dressed in full costume, a scarf tied over her long black hair, a white peasant blouse with a neckline that showed more cleavage than most of the beach babes who frequented the store on summer days. Layers of skirts rustled with her slightest movement.

Maggie meowed and shifted in my arms.

"I had a visitor this afternoon." I held the cat toward her.

She shook her head, holding up her sparkling red nails. "Can you bring her inside? I finished my touch-ups for tonight's reading. My hands are so important to the presentation, I'm always refreshing my mani."

Then she disappeared into the hallway, clearly expecting me to follow. Hesitantly, I stepped into the cool, dark house. I'd never been inside the house before. The smell of lavender and jasmine filled my senses, taking me back to days when I visited my grandmother in South Dakota. Her bedroom had held the scent of fresh sheets that she dried outside on the line, making them crinkle and feel hard.

"Do you want me to sit her down?" I called to the empty hallway.

Her voice echoed from another room. "Close the door and bring her into the reading room. She has a bed in here so she can learn to draw in the spirits. I'm teaching her to be a familiar."

I shut the door and looked down at Maggie. "So you're going to have a career in the fortune-telling business," I whispered to the now purring cat. I swear she smiled in response to my words. I walked through the hallway, with the large pictures of people who were obviously long gone based on the frames and the photo quality. I felt their eyes on us as we walked through the hall to the first door on the right that was open. I stepped into the room and knew I was in the right place. The walls were covered with velvet fabric, and a single table sat in the middle of the room, a real, swear to heaven, crystal ball placed in the middle of the table.

Esmeralda was moving a blanket over a small couch on the side of the room. "Put her down here. I can't believe she got out again. I think I should have named her Houdini, not Maggie."

The kitten gave a tiny meow in protest as I set her on the couch. "Emma must like her. I thought she would keep her out of the yard. Instead, I woke up to her sleeping beside me out on the porch."

Esmeralda studied my face. "She's drawn to you. I should have seen it before."

I held up my hands, blocking the idea. "I do not need another pet. Emma and I do quite well together."

"No, I don't mean that." She gestured to the table. "Why don't we sit for a few minutes? I believe we need to talk."

Inside my head, I groaned. I didn't need a trip to crazyland today. Esmeralda was always bringing me messages from beyond, like she was my personal answering machine. I couldn't believe I'd let myself be sucked into her reality again. "I really need to get back." I grasped for a good excuse. "Laundry. You know how it stacks up."

Her gaze drilled into me and I knew I'd chosen the wrong excuse. "Surely you can spare a few moments to talk to your closest neighbor."

Crap. Instead of running out the door, which is what every cell of my body was screaming for me to do, I settled into a chair. Glancing around the room, I asked the only question I could think of, "So, you have a reading tonight? I thought you only did the fortune-teller thing on weekends?"

She chuckled. "Normally, I only have appointments on the weekend, but a good client asked for a favor. She's out of town with her family this weekend and needed some guidance before she left." Esmeralda's face contorted in a look that appeared to be worry. "I feel like she's gotten herself into a mess. One I warned her against."

"Sometimes people don't listen."

She focused back on me. "Out of the mouths of babes."

Okay, this was getting creepy. I tried to change the subject. "You busy at the office these days?"

"The current case is very interesting." Esmeralda tapped her apparently now dry fingertips on the table. "I believe your Greg is going to have some hard choices to make in the near future. Are you willing to support him?"

"Look, I really don't like to talk about my relationship with Greg. Some things are private, you know?"

She nodded. "I understand your reluctance. Let me do a quick reading with you. I've never looked at your future before." She held out her palm. "Give me your left hand."

"I really can't stay."

Her hand grabbed mine in a tight grip. "Let me thank you for bringing back my Maggie. Please?"

I blew out air a little too hard but sat back in my chair. "Go ahead."

"You give up too easily." Esmeralda's grip loosened. She stared into the crystal ball and the thing started to cloud.

This can't be real. I stared into the mist, certain I could see the telltale signs of trickery. "I'd say I pick my battles carefully."

She chuckled. "You let things boil up, then you blow."

With my free hand, I pointed at the ball. "You can see that in there?"

"Jill, we live in a small town. There isn't anything about your daily life, or your history for that matter, that doesn't come up in gossip somewhere." She nodded back to the glowing orb on the table. "Now, be quiet so the spirits can reach me."

"Sorry." I wished I could take back the word as soon as I saw her grin. Crap, she had me nailed on that personality trait. I'd always been the one to get along. My mom said I'd follow a crowd off the cliff if it meant I could be part of the group.

She waved her free left hand over the ball in the center of the small table. "Oh, spirits, please answer our pleas. Show us what we need to see. Show us the future to keep us safe. Honor your living children here on this plain."

The table shook under my hands. When I looked up at Esmeralda to see if she'd felt the mini-earthquake, her eyes were cloudy, like the ball. "Are you okay?"

"You'll need to see past your pain in order to save the ones you love." Her voice cracked and had dropped a couple of octaves. "Things aren't what they seem."

I pressed my lips together, holding back a wisecrack. Typical fortune-teller speak. No real surprises here.

"Some are silver, the other gold," Esmeralda whispered and her head dropped. Our session was over.

CHAPTER 6

As Emma and I ran the next morning, I thought about my "reading." Or at least the things Esmeralda had said before she went into her trance and started chanting camp songs. I'd been challenged by the partners at the law firm that I wasn't strong enough. I'd had coworkers take my prime cases in the guise of helping out, then when the partners praised them in our weekly meetings, realized that somehow they'd become first chair on a case I'd brought to the firm. After the last incident I'd stormed into my mentor's office and listed out all the inequities I'd had to face during my tenure. The woman smiled and nodded during my tirade.

"I wondered when you'd see what was happening." Her words stung. Had I been blind or naïve, allowing my peers to step over me and expecting someone else to stand up for my interests? She poured me another cup of coffee. "The only one who is looking out for you in this world is you. The other associates understand that. The partners want what's best for the firm. You need to stand for what's best for you."

Thinking back over the last few years, I realized I'd changed my pattern, along with the rest of my life. Today I wouldn't roll like a well-worn tire. I'd do what I wanted, when I wanted. Now, all I had to do was figure out what it was I wanted. Crap, I sounded like a case study for all those self-help books I stocked. After the local history and tourist books, the "charm books" I called them, I sold more self-help tomes than any other specific category. How to find your Zen. How to raise a normal teenager. How to get that next promotion. Everyone wanted the easy answer. Bless the midday talk shows.

Maybe there was one that addressed my problems. Like *How to Grow a Backbone*.

By the time we'd returned home and I'd showered, my mood was less than cheerful. Typically my run cleared my mind of all the doubts I carried around. Today, it had added to them.

I let Emma out to the yard, checked on her food and water, then power-walked into the shop, determined to seek out a book that could help me find my inner goddess.

Toby looked up as I entered the shop. He'd been reading the newspaper and the shop was empty, a typical early morning shift. "You know you're off today, right?"

I stepped over to the counter. "Can't a girl get a coffee without getting the third degree?"

"A girl, sure. You, on the other hand, must have a reason to leave your cozy house before noon." He started a skinny mocha for me. "Everything okay?"

When Toby's gaze didn't meet my eyes, I started doubting my impulse. I should have waited until tomorrow, and no one would have been the wiser.

After pulling off the two psychobabble books on the shelf that dealt with displaying confidence in relationships and finding your Zen, I glanced at my watch. Too early to call Amy for lunch, but I could stop by on my way home and visit for a few minutes. Besides, Greg hadn't called last night, so I was beginning to think that Darla's nose for news had been spot-on with Kent's murder.

"You want this to go?" Toby glanced at the books under my arm. "You doing some light reading today?"

I shrugged, feeling uncomfortable with his scrutiny. "Let's just say, I've been told I roll too fast when challenged. I figure learning some new tricks might not be a bad idea."

"Jackie been giving you trouble again?" He poured my mocha in a travel mug and handed it to me. "I think you're perfect just the way you are. And I know one more person who'd say the same thing."

"I love that author." Leslie from the bank tapped the top book titled *Be a Tiger, Not a Kitty Cat,* or what I would subtitle, "How to Be a Predatory Animal in the Office." "We had the author come in for a bank conference I went to last summer. She's a pistol. Doesn't take crap from anyone."

The lady standing next to her nodded. "She told her manager to get his stuff together or she was reporting him to the corporate office.

She got fired and sued the company. Then she wrote the book. I think she speaks all over the nation."

Great, I'd run into a true believer. I smiled. "Thanks for the reference. I'm sure I'll love it."

The other woman shook her head. "I hated the book. I guess I'm just not that type of person. I'm not someone who would get in anyone's face."

"Anne, you're too nice. You should have sued Kent last summer when he started hitting on you." Leslie leaned closer to the table. "He was a pig. I hate to speak ill of the dead, but I swear to God, the man should have been shot years ago."

"Leslie." Anne's face scrunched together, and I could see she was fighting tears. The woman's blond hair was cut in a cute pixie. Not the redhead I'd seen Kent sucking face with in the car at the beach. The man *was* a pig, Leslie had gotten that part right.

"Two large coffees and two slices of that black forest cheesecake." Leslie put her hand on her friend's arm. "I'll get Anne settled at a table and be right back to pay."

Toby watched the two walk away. "I wonder if Greg knows about her. Man, that guy made me look like a choirboy."

"I take it you didn't know about his multiple friends." I kept my voice low and watched as Leslie and Anne argued quietly at the far table. "She doesn't look like Kent's type."

"I think she looks exactly like his type. Female. The man was a horndog, plain and simple. Sherry's better off without him, even though from what Greg says, she's pretty broken up about the whole thing."

I wanted to ask more about what they'd talked about, but the good side of me told me to trust my boyfriend. Greg hadn't called last night because he was busy with the case, that was all. Still, I stalled. "So what's going on with the case? I didn't hear from your boss last night."

Toby held his hands up in mock surrender. "No way. You're not getting me to tell you anything. Last time, Greg sat me down and explained confidentiality to me. For an hour. If you want gossip, you're going to have to go directly to the source."

"Who said I wanted gossip?" I tried to sound casual, but Toby just laughed. "What?"

"You don't have an innocent look. Except for when you're clueless about something. You want to know if Kent died of natural causes? You call Greg."

"Like he's going to tell me anything," I muttered under my breath. I glanced over at the table where Leslie and Anne were still arguing. "Seems like something struck a nerve there."

"Best Friend Bulldog Syndrome. They always have that one friend who will try to show them that the guy they're dating is the devil." He grinned. "And typically, they're right, especially in this case."

"I take it you've run into this syndrome a time or two."

He shrugged. "A few times. I can't say they were wrong, either. I was a pretty free spirit, but some of the chicks I dated, they thought the fun was going to end with a ring on their finger. I just knew the fun was going to end."

"Pig." I smiled to soften the word.

He held up three fingers in a Boy Scout salute. "Reformed pig. Elisa has me tied around her little finger."

A noise drew my attention. Leslie stood behind me, her usually friendly face a mask. "Those coffees ready yet? We only have a short break."

Toby handed her the two coffees and nodded to the tray he'd placed the plates with the cheesecake on while we were talking. "I can carry this out for you."

Leslie flushed and set the coffees on the tray. "I can do it myself."

The bell over the door rang, and three of Toby's regulars from the cosmetology school entered the shop giggling and heading straight to the counter.

"Looks like you're going to be busy. I'll see you tomorrow." I tucked the books under my arm and nodded to the women who were heading to the counter. "Good morning."

My greeting was lost as the three dashed to Toby. I opened the door onto the sunny spring day and headed down to talk to my own BFF. If she'd gotten to work today.

As I passed Antiques by Thomas, Kyle Nabors greeted me as he swept the sidewalk. Kyle had been the intern Josh had reluctantly taken on over Christmas for the Work Today program in Bakerstown. Like Sasha, Kyle had been offered a real job because of this placement. I noticed Kyle had dressed in jeans and a button-down shirt today, a far cry from the leather and studs he'd shown up with last December.

"Hey, Miss Gardner." Kyle put his hand on the top of the broomstick and paused. "I didn't think you worked on Fridays."

Did I mention South Cove was a small town? Seriously, where else would I be questioned about being out and about before noon on my day off? I held up the books. "Just stopped by for a bit of light reading."

He laughed. "Light reading is my stack of comic books. That looks more like you're taking a class over at the university."

"I read fast. It's a side benefit from owning a bookstore." I nodded toward the store. "How are things going with Josh? You two getting along?"

"Mr. Thomas is amazing. You wouldn't believe all the stuff he knows about antiques and shit." Kyle reddened. "I mean stuff. Don't tell Mr. Thomas I swore. He's been on my case about my language lately. He says I need to learn to be polite in any situation in order to be a good salesman."

I bit my lip. Josh Thomas was the very opposite of polite. Cold, demeaning, rude even at times, Kyle's boss was teaching his student something Josh needed to learn, as well. "No worries." I waved my hand to brush the words away. "He won't hear it from me."

Kyle beamed. "Thanks. I love working here. Josh says on Monday I get to go with him to an estate auction up the coast. He's scoped the offerings and says we'll make a killing if we get the lot."

Now, that sounded more like the Josh Thomas I knew. "I'll let you get back to your work then."

"I'm supposed to sweep the sidewalk three times a day when I'm working. I can't believe how fast the trash builds up. Have you seen the pictures Mr. Thomas took with the piles of trash?"

I looked down and saw a Coffee, Books, and More logo on a disposable cup in the gutter. "I guess my store isn't helping." I grabbed the cup and put it in the trash bag next to Kyle.

"Not your fault the customers are slobs." He grinned, then lowered his voice. "No matter what Mr. Thomas says."

I said my good-byes and made a mental note to fill the agenda for the next Business-to-Business meeting with anything but Josh's agenda items. He had gotten his five minutes under Sherry's agenda. I'd make sure he wouldn't get the chance again.

You're being childish. I swept the good angel off my shoulder. I hadn't even opened the self-help books, and I was already making better decisions. Look out, South Cove, Jill Gardner was on a roll.

Amy glanced at the clock when I stopped in front of her desk. "What are you doing out this early?"

Seriously, I needed to mix up my schedule more. I shrugged. "Wanted to see how Justin was today."

"I haven't heard from him since he left the apartment about noon yesterday. He doesn't drink more than a couple of glasses of wine or a beer or two usually. I don't think the boy has had a hangover since college." She snuck a peek at the closed door of the mayor's office. "Man, Marvin was hot this morning when I came in. I guess he had to answer the phone all day yesterday because Esmeralda told him the calls coming in to his office weren't part of her job duties."

"I bet that went over well." I kept my voice low, not wanting the mayor to hear us talking. I didn't need a dose of Mayor Baylor today.

"He's got me putting an amendment to the police dispatcher's job description into the city council agenda next week. Of course, Greg is going to fight it. He says Esmeralda can't be expected to juggle everyday calls and emergencies at the same time. And right now, the council loves your boyfriend." Amy looked at the clock again and sighed. "So, no lunch at Lille's today?"

I thought about my plans to do laundry and drive into Bakerstown for groceries. And clean the bathroom. When I reached that item on my to-do list, I made a quick decision. "I'll meet you in our regular booth at eleven o'clock."

"Not feeling the housework list?" Amy guessed.

"Exactly." I nodded to the hallway leading to the police department. "Is Greg in yet?"

Amy frowned. "I haven't seen him. Esmeralda said he was heading over to Bakerstown to see Doc Ames this morning."

Interesting. "Did she say why? Is this about Kent?"

Amy scanned the still-empty waiting room, lowering her voice. "I don't know. What have you heard?"

I sighed. "Nothing. Darla thinks it's murder, but you know Darla. She's always looking for a juicy story for the *Examiner.*"

"Well, I haven't heard anything, but I was out yesterday. According to Esmeralda, Greg wasn't around much yesterday at all." Amy cocked her head. "What did he say at dinner?"

"I didn't see him last night." My Spidey senses started to tingle.

Amy's eyebrows raised, just a bit. "I thought you guys always ate together, at least dinner."

"Not when he's on a case." *Or avoiding me*, I added in my inside voice.

Crap. There I went again, thinking the worst. I squared my shoulders and put on a smile I didn't feel. "I'm sure he's just busy."

Amy opened her mouth, then the buzzer on her phone interrupted.

"Did the mail come yet?" Mayor Baylor's voice echoed through the empty room.

After rolling her eyes, she pushed a button. "You know it doesn't arrive until after ten. Jillian doesn't even open the post office until nine."

"I told her we needed to be the first stop. I've got important things to do. I can't be waiting on a postal carrier strolling around town gawking at the sites." The intercom button went dark.

"I'd better get on the phone and see what's holding up the mayor's mail." Amy laughed. "See you at Lille's."

I left City Hall wondering what the mayor could be expecting. Most of my snail mail now was junk or bills. I got most of my correspondence from friends through e-mail. Although the historical commission always sent their semiannual "we're working on your application" letter through the mail. Still, the only news they would provide was a generic status that wasn't worth the cost of the stamp.

I stepped out into the bright sunlight and almost ran smack into Mary Sullivan, the heart and soul behind South Cove Bed-and-Breakfast. I'd always thought Bill was the business guy of the couple, but after seeing Mary's analysis of the Christmas festival, I had begun to wonder. Mary's blond hair, usually neatly combed into a short pageboy, was off center. And she looked like she'd been on a five-mile run. "Hey, are you okay?"

She blinked at me, like she was trying to remember my name. Which made me even more concerned. Mary and Bill were older, maybe not as old as Jackie, but definitely considered retirement age. Was this what a stroke looked like? Should I call an ambulance?

Questions floated through my head as Mary settled in front of me and finally smiled.

"Jill, what are you doing here?" She glanced around the street, like she wasn't sure what she was doing here, either. She peeked behind me. "Is Jackie with you?"

"Like she could hide behind me?" I stole a look at my capris and tank top. "I don't think I'm big enough to hide a fully grown woman."

Mary's eyebrows furrowed. "Of course not, why would you even say that?"

I was about to point out she'd just looked around me for my aunt when she waved my words away.

"Of course she's not with you. Today's your day off, right? Jackie will be at the shop." Mary took a step away from me and toward Coffee, Books, and More. She stopped, realizing she'd been impolite. "Sorry, I'm just in a hurry to talk to your aunt."

I put my hand on Mary's elbow and walked her to the park bench in front of City Hall under the large pine. Her hand shook as she moved her purse onto her lap. "Hold on a second. Take a breath. Are you feeling okay?"

Mary's eyes lost that distant look and she focused on my face. No, that wasn't right. Her gaze bored into my soul like she could read my thoughts. "Why? What have you heard?"

I put my hands up, trying to calm her. "All I know is you look like crap. I don't want to walk away from you and find out you collapsed in the middle of Main Street after we parted ways. Do you want some water?"

She shook her head. "Sorry, I've been a little frazzled lately, but I'm fine, really."

I watched as she ran her fingers through her hair, moving the do into a respectable shape. She took another deep breath and pasted on a smile so fake it could have been synthetically designed.

"You can tell me anything. I won't blab." My gaze dropped to the two-carat diamond ring on Mary's left hand. "You and Bill okay?"

She waved away my question. "We've been married fifty years, of course we're okay. I've just been"—she paused, seeking a word—"distracted for a few weeks. Our anniversary is coming up, and I want everything to be perfect."

I weighed her words. They rang true. Except I could feel that there was more to what was going on besides a celebration of their nuptials. "If there's anything I can do to help..." I trailed off as Mary's cell rang. She dug in her purse, not looking at me.

Answering the phone, she stepped away and absently waved at me as she focused on the phone call. "I'm so glad you called me. I've been worried. I left several messages."

I couldn't hear the other side of the conversation, as Mary almost ran down the sidewalk to get away from me. I put call Aunt Jackie on my mental to-do list, along with maybe a call to Bill, strictly about the next Business-to-Business meeting. If he was acting as weird as his wife, then I'd know something was up with the two of them.

Trouble in paradise. Seriously, Bill and Mary were the last married couple I'd have pegged for having problems. If they couldn't make it, what did that say about the rest of us?

CHAPTER 7

Aunt Jackie hadn't answered her cell. I'd gotten the machine when I called Bill. And now Amy was late for lunch. For a Friday, it wasn't living up to my expectations. I thumbed through the ton of e-books I'd bought and downloaded onto my phone with the expectation I'd read them when I found a spare minute of time. Like now.

Instead, I thumbed through the covers, wondering which one I wanted to start. Scrolling through my phone was like walking through the bookstore; I had too many choices.

I heard Amy slide into the booth across from me. I closed out the program and set my phone aside; I'd figure out a book to read the next time I had a few minutes alone. Then I looked up. Amy wasn't the person sitting across from me.

"Hear me out." Pat Williams held up a perfectly manicured hand.

I shook my head. "I really don't think we have anything to talk about." Pat was Sherry's best friend. If the two women stood side by side you'd swear they were sisters. They both had that trophy wife look, all polished and professional. Although, I guess, to run a shop where you charged the kind of prices they did for used clothes, looking professional was part of the package. Sherry and Pat just took their "work uniform" to a 24/7 level of commitment.

"You have to help her. Greg will listen to you." Pat grabbed my hand and squeezed. "You have power over him."

I swear she almost tripped over what she didn't say at the end of that sentence, something like *even though I have no idea how*. But I couldn't fault her for words not spoken. "Look, Sherry's just going to have to get over the fact that Greg and I are dating. She had her shot with him, now that's over."

"You don't understand—" Pat started, then looked up at Amy standing by the table, glowering at the interloper.

"You're in my seat." Amy's words were chilly cold.

Pat looked from me to Amy, then let out a dramatic sigh any high school theater coach would be proud of. She slipped out of the booth but stood while Amy sat. She tapped her manicured nail on the table. "You have to help her. Sherry's my best friend."

Then she turned and walked out of Diamond Lille's, her designer stiletto heels clicking all the way to the door.

Amy pushed her purse into the corner of the booth. "What was all that about? I know I should have been more charitable, but I've never liked that woman. Besides, the fact that the mayor adores both her and Sherry makes me dubious of her personal worth."

"I didn't know Mayor Baylor knew Pat, too. I thought the connection to Sherry was through Greg." I stared at the menu like I hadn't read it two or three times a week for the last five—no, make that six—years.

Amy picked up her own menu. "For some reason, Pat showed up at City Hall this morning. The mayor was still obsessing over the fact that our mail was an hour late. He kept her cooling on the couch in the waiting room for at least an hour."

"What did she come in to talk about?" I set aside the menu. It was Friday and that meant homemade clam chowder and fish and chips. I'd run that morning; I deserved the treat.

Carrie showed up at the table before Amy could answer. "Hey, girls." Carrie snapped her gum. "What can I get for you, the usual?"

Amy shook her head. "What exactly is the usual?"

"Oh, you nonbeliever. No worries, we can play it your way." Carrie looked at me, then she listed off my order, down to the vanilla milk shake. Pointing at Amy, she said, "You will have a double-stack cheeseburger, curly fries, and onion rings, because you had a light breakfast, and a chocolate shake."

Amy pushed the menu toward Carrie. "Ha, you're wrong. I want a cookies-and-cream milk shake."

"Whatever," Carrie mumbled and picked up the menus. "I'll have your drinks out soon."

When Carrie was out of earshot, Amy leaned close, taking a look around the crowded diner before she spoke. "I think she had a business situation to talk to him about. I kept hearing Sherry's name come up in the discussion. Did you know that Pat has forty percent ownership in Vintage Duds?"

"Seriously? I thought Sherry had gotten the start-up money from her folks. At least that's what Greg said." I thought about Pat's words. Were they meant as a plea for me to step aside so Sherry and Greg could live happily ever after again? Kids held a torch for their parents' relationship longer than either of the married couple. Maybe Pat felt Sherry and Greg were her parental relationship. As sick as that sounded.

Our shakes arrived, and I sipped on the pure, cold vanilla and smiled. Sweet, icy goodness. What else was there to say about an ice cream treat on a hot day? I realized Amy had started talking again and tuned in to her words.

"That was what Sherry told everyone. But the real story, according to what I could hear from Mayor Baylor's office, was that her parents refused her the money, thinking the idea was another one of her get-rich-quick schemes." Amy shrugged. "I guess Pat got a good settlement in her last divorce, so she helped her friend out."

"They must be really close." I picked up a fry from the basket Carrie had popped on the table with Amy's meal without even stopping to talk. I guess we'd insulted her waitress mojo by questioning her knowledge of our *usual* order. I wasn't worried; Carrie couldn't stay mad long. Her boss, on the other hand, could hold a grudge for years. Lille still gave me the stink eye for keeping time with her last loser boyfriend, even though I hadn't been interested in Ray, not at all.

Amy broke an onion ring in half. "So you wouldn't bankroll me in a new storefront? Maybe a surfing shop?" Her eyebrows raised. "That's not a bad idea at all. South Cove could use a board store, and I could give lessons, and . . ."

I held up a hand. "Not going to happen. I've got my hands full owning Coffee, Books, and More, even if Aunt Jackie treats me like a silent partner. No way would I start another business."

Her smile widened. "Who said I wanted your help with the store? In my daydream, you're the perfect Daddy Warbucks and it's a silent movie track."

"You're crazy." It wasn't like I couldn't have used the Miss Emily fund, as I'd come to call the money I'd inherited from my friend, but I was superstitious. You never needed money until you didn't have any. And with the age of both my house and the building where the shop sat, I figured we were just holding off the inevitable. I bit into the fish. Heaven. Crunchy, with a solid filet inside and seasoned to perfection. I could eat fish every day and twice on Sunday.

"I'd probably get bored anyway. I never was much of a salesman. Even when I had to sell cookies for the troop, my mom bought most of my allotment because I didn't want to go door to door." Amy picked up her cheeseburger and started devouring the sandwich. We ate in silence.

"You know I'd do anything for you, including bankrolling your business, but it feels wrong somehow." I paused, not knowing what else to say. I realized I'd also broken Rule Number Fourteen in the self-help book I'd glanced through that morning: *Never be the first to talk after an uncomfortable silence. It makes you appear weak and vulnerable.* I remembered it because my reaction had been summed up in two words: *Bull crap.* Now I wondered if I'd been hasty in my assessment.

Amy held out her hand, stopping me from talking. "Earth to Jill. I was kidding. No way I'd be an official beach bum like Dustin Austin. Sometimes it's too easy to tease you. Hey, I've got a great idea. Let's do a girls' night tonight."

"Tonight? You and me?" We hadn't been out together without the guys forever. This was sounding like an amazing idea.

"You, me, Sadie, Pat, Sherry, I'd invite Darla, but she won't leave the winery. But we could meet there and she could join the group for a while. Maybe even invite Esmeralda." Amy's eyes shined bright as she formalized the plan in her head.

"No way will Sherry and Pat join us. You know Sherry hates me." I grabbed the last onion ring from Amy's plate. "Sadie might come, depends on what Nick's doing. Esmeralda has readings scheduled."

"We'll invite her anyway, can't hurt. Besides, the more people, the easier it will be to talk to Sherry about her relationship to Kent. And what she wants with Greg. If Pat's right, it might be good to keep an eye on the woman." Amy started texting. "I'm sending out the invite right now."

I wasn't sure Amy's plan was to anyone's benefit, but the old saying about keeping your enemies close kept ringing in my head. And who knows, with a couple of beers, I might just find something the woman and I had in common, besides Greg.

* * *

Walking home after lunch, I thought about Amy's words. I did get too involved in others' problems, especially those of people I cared about. Often, it got me in trouble. Especially with Greg. I'd had my life threatened more than once because I'd kept pushing for answers when really, it wasn't my business.

"I swear I'll never try to solve a problem that isn't mine again." I held my hand up as I used the other to open the gate. Now to read that book and figure out a way to keep my pledge.

A noise came from the side yard and I froze.

"Nice to hear your promise, but honestly, honey, do you really think you can make a tiger have spots?" Greg stood at the corner of the house, a wet tennis ball in his hand and a panting Emma staring at him with eyes filled with doggy love.

Smiling, I walked toward him and reached up on tiptoe to give him a kiss. "You weren't supposed to hear that." I glanced toward the driveway. "Where's your truck?"

"Back at City Hall. I needed a break, so I walked out here to play with my favorite girl." He waved the ball at Emma. Throwing it into the backyard, he called, "Get it!"

The dog took off like a rocket.

We ambled up to the back porch and slid into the swing, his hand taking mine. "I missed you last night."

He leaned back and put an arm around my shoulders, pulling me close. "This Kent thing has been a disaster."

"Really?" I turned toward him. "What's happening? Was he murdered?"

I saw the grin on Greg's face before I realized what I'd done.

"And I'm trying to solve someone else's problem again." I sank back into the swing, watching my dog throw her ball up in the air, then catch it herself. "Why do I do this to myself?"

"You're hardwired to think this way. I swear, you'd have been a good cop if you'd gone that way instead of law school." He ruffled my hair. "I love you just the way you are. As long as you're not messing with my investigations. Go figure out who took one of Austin's bikes last weekend. Then he'll stop calling the office three times a day to see if I've apprehended the suspect."

"He should take the rider's photo ID before letting just anyone rent one of his bikes. We've talked about his lax business practices before." I sighed. "The guy wants to think everyone is as honest as he is."

"Well, to his defense, the bike disappeared from his locked storage sometime between Sunday night and Wednesday morning when he opened the shop. He didn't just rent it out to the wrong guy."

"My bad. With Austin, you never know. Maybe I should stop by with some of the city's safety pamphlets and cookies. I could invite him to the next Business-to-Business meeting. At least then we wouldn't need to talk about Josh's trash obsession." I sat up. "You want some iced tea?"

Greg nodded, apparently lost in thought again. "Sure. I'd forgotten about Josh's pictures. I need to . . ." He stopped as he noticed me watching. "And I'm setting you off again. Maybe you need a boyfriend who has a safe job."

"Like banking?" I stood up and opened the back door, pausing to add, "Look what that got Sherry. A dead boyfriend."

Greg didn't laugh.

"Wait, am I missing something here?" I leaned against the doorway. "You've been MIA for a few days dealing with Kent's death, Darla's running all over town telling people he was murdered, and Toby tells me you've been talking to Sherry. You don't think . . ."

I didn't get the rest of the sentence out before he kissed me. "I do think that you need to stay out of this investigation. I don't know if Kent died naturally or if it was murder, but I do know you need to stop poking around in things. I worry about you when you go off and sleuth."

I led him into the kitchen and handed him the self-help book Leslie and Anne had raved about. "Not to worry, my cure is forthcoming."

He paged through the book as I poured two glasses of tea over ice. "Not your usual reading choice. This is about how to be more confident. What's that got to do with staying out of my investigations?"

I pondered his question, sipping down almost half of the tea. I'd been thirsty from the walk. Then I shrugged. "I couldn't find a book about learning to mind your own business in thirty days or less. I guess this will have to do."

His laugh echoed through the kitchen. He set the book down on the table and leaned against the cabinet watching me. "You are something else, you know it?"

"A good something else?"

He nodded and pulled me into a long kiss. "A great something else."

"You'll be glad to know that Amy and I are doing a girls' night tonight, no talking about investigations or murders allowed. Just girly drinks and talk about men, and beauty products."

"Sounds like fun. I'm glad you're taking a break. Just don't be driving," Greg teased.

I held a hand up in a pledge. "No way will I give Toby the satisfaction of hauling me in."

Over our second glass of tea, I brought up the mystery dinner. "Darla was wondering when we could schedule another dress rehearsal. We need to send out a new date for the performance. The women's shelter was kind of hoping for the boost this quarter. I guess their state funding has been a little unreliable this year."

Greg shook his head. "I don't know when this investigation will be complete. I'm waiting on a call from Doc Ames with the autopsy results, but you know it takes a couple of weeks for the tox reports from the lab. Even if Doc thinks it's natural, he won't issue a final determination until he sees those."

"Darla says it's drugs." I gave him the rumor since he would hear about it sooner or later.

He sighed. "I told her to keep her mouth shut. I guess that was a little hopeful."

"Maybe she only told me?" I tried to put a positive spin on the situation.

"More likely she's already submitted her article for Saturday's edition. That woman burns me sometimes." Greg finished his second glass of tea and opened the screen door. He took the wet, slobbery ball from Emma and threw it. Emma bounded off the porch. He grabbed a kitchen towel from the counter and wiped his hands.

"She is a reporter. What did you expect?" I stood and got the pitcher from the refrigerator. "You want a refill?"

Greg's phone buzzed and he put up a hand. "Hold on." He read the text and then returned his phone to his pocket. He put his glass into the sink. "Sorry, I've got to run to Bakerstown again."

"The autopsy's done?" I filled my own glass and returned the pitcher to the fridge.

He nodded. "And from what Doc Ames said, you can tell Darla that we need to postpone the dinner for a while."

I put my hand on his arm. "Kent was murdered?"

Greg leaned down and kissed me good-bye. "Official wording is suspicious."

CHAPTER 8

Ispent the rest of Friday before meeting Amy doing laundry and reading. I pulled out a notebook and made a list of all the rules from *Be a Tiger*. I had to admit, the woman had lived an interesting life, although some of the things she did, I could never pull off. When I worked at the law firm, I worked many long hours mostly because the other associates knew I wouldn't say no when they asked for help. What they hadn't known was that I liked working long hours because it kept me away from home and my ex-husband. Not one of my proudest memories, but true. This woman would have kicked the jerk out, told the other associates no, and probably still made partner two years sooner than anyone else had before.

The author was a pistol. Or this self-help book was completely fictional. Which was what I was starting to believe. However, there were some good takeaways, which I wrote down in my notebook.

Before I had to get ready, the book was finished and I read over my notes, then turned to a blank page.

I wrote *Kent Paine* at the top and started writing down everything I knew about what I assumed was his murder since Greg hadn't returned for our usual Friday pizza and a movie date.

I felt a bit guilty doing that after my conversation with Greg this morning, but it wasn't like I was going to really investigate. I just wanted to keep my thoughts clear in case Greg asked me something. Like about when I saw Kent kissing that redhead, since I still hadn't mentioned that to him.

The winery was buzzing by the time I arrived, walking from the house. Being on foot limited my choice of footwear, so I decided to wear my black cowboy boots, tucked in skinny jeans, and a sparkly silver shirt I'd bought online. With my hair loose, I felt pretty.

Or I did until I walked into the tasting room and saw Sherry and Pat already seated with Amy. My friend looked like me, wearing jeans and a pretty shirt. The other women looked like they were attending a play in the city, or as my mom would say, all dressed up with nowhere to go. Amy waved me over.

"Hey, glad to see you. Sadie couldn't make it. Esmeralda never answered, and Darla's swamped, so it's just the four of us." She held out a bottle of my favorite beer. "I ordered you one, but you're already behind so drink up."

I sat on a chair, nodding to the still silent Pat and Sherry. "Thanks for coming. I think it's time we got to know each other."

Sherry sniffed. Pat shot her a look and then held up her glass of wine for a toast. "Here's to new friends."

We clinked glasses and bottles, waiting a full moment before Sherry moved her glass to the others. Amy grinned. "So that wasn't so hard." She looked at Sherry. "I wanted to give you my condolences about Kent. I know you two were close."

Sherry made a big show of pulling a lace-trimmed linen handkerchief out of her black Coach clutch and dabbing at her eyes. "Thank you. Kent was a dear man, and we were so happy. I'll be lost without him."

Pat squeezed Sherry's hand. "I know you will."

The table was quiet for a while and I found Sherry staring at me. "Oh, I wanted to express my condolences, too." I took a sip of the beer.

Sherry's face didn't react. "A little late, don't you think?"

Again Pat shook her head and an unspoken warning flowed between the two women.

"Thank you." Sherry mumbled.

Amy jumped up, "Who's ready for another round?"

"My turn to buy, I'll come with you." Pat stood and the two walked away, leaving Sherry and me at the table alone.

I took another pull from the bottle. By the time this "relaxing" night was over, I'd be drunk off my butt if I kept this up. I set my nearly empty bottle on the table. "So how's the shop doing?"

Sherry shrugged. "Tomorrow we have an exclusive on an estate. Everyone loves a good deal, especially when the clothes are designer and from a celebrity owner."

"I guess that's true." The silence grew between us.

Finally Sherry sighed. "I need you to tell Greg I didn't kill Kent."
Her statement shocked me. "Greg thinks you killed him?"

Sherry waved away my question. "There's the unfortunate fact I
was at the winery around the time he died. I was there to see if he was
cheating. You understand, right? Trust but verify."

"You got a text about him seeing someone else." I thought about
what Greg had told me earlier. "Were you having problems?"

Sherry glanced around the room to make sure no one was listening,
then leaned closer. "He cheated on me. Seriously, can you imagine?"

I pressed my lips together, knowing why Sherry was worried about
Greg's impression. She sounded like she could have killed Kent just
for straying. "I don't understand what some men are thinking."

"Exactly. He had me. What did he need anyone else for?" Sherry
bit her bottom lip. "I always trusted Greg when we were married. I
guess I made a mistake when I left."

"I don't think you being at the winery is really enough to convict
you of murder. You know Greg, he's just tying up all the loose ends."
I sipped on my beer, wondering why the woman was confiding in me.

Sherry nodded. "I just need you to convince him." She considered
me for a second. "I'm not sure why, but he seems to like you. Even
trust you."

"I hope so." I felt my lips curve into a slight smile.

"So you'll help me. I told Pat you'd help." Sherry smiled and
sipped her wine. "All you have to do is ask nicely and things happen
your way."

I wondered about Sherry's philosophy on life. Was it really that
easy? Ask and you shall be given? Finally I saw Pat and Amy walking
back. "Oh, here comes the next round." I lifted my bottle to finish off
my beer.

Sherry leaned forward. "Thanks for helping me."

Pat slipped into the chair between me and Sherry. "So what are
you two talking about?"

Sherry took the new glass of wine from her friend, smiling, and
lied, "The trunk sale. I was telling Jill all about tomorrow's sale.
She's really excited."

I didn't challenge her. For the rest of the two hours, Sherry led the
discussion about everything and nothing. I was still processing her
request when Pat called it a night and the two left.

Amy leaned back in her chair, eyeing me. "Well, that was interesting. You were quiet."

"That woman just never gives up." I stood and pulled my friend to her feet. "Come on, I'll walk you home."

Saturday morning, even after the beer I'd consumed, I was up earlier than normal. Emma and I ran before I got ready for work, and the crashing waves on the beach helped clear my mind. The Tiger Lady, which was what I'd started calling the self-help author, encouraged physical activity to keep your body tuned and your mind clear. This step in the thirty-day detox she recommended would be easy for me to reach. I'd already run most days when it wasn't raining. When it was, I had the treadmill in the upstairs bedroom I'd planned to turn into a home gym. Soon.

Tiger Lady also suggested cutting out caffeine. I ignored that advice. Maybe I could cut down, but out? Who was I kidding? My blood was half coffee and half whatever blood was made of. Besides, the author didn't own a coffee shop. I had to try the new blends to stay up on the options for my customers. When I looked at it that way, my level of coffee intake really was a job responsibility. I filled my travel mug and screwed on the cap before I began my walk to work.

A line filled the sidewalk when I reached Vintage Duds. Women chatted excitedly as I crossed into the street to go around the crowd.

"Jill, over here!" Aunt Jackie called me over to where she stood in heels, a pencil skirt, and what looked like real pearls.

I muscled through the line, getting a few dirty looks for my apparent cutting, but no one said anything. To my face. I heard more than one mutter about who I thought I was. When I reached my aunt, she reached up and fixed my shirt collar. "What are you doing here?" I waved my hand at the closed front door. "What's happening to cause this commotion?"

"You really should read the *Examiner*. They interviewed Sherry and Pat last week about the estate sale they'd bought out." Aunt Jackie lowered her voice. "Rumor is the clothing is from one of the old film stars. I'm guessing Rita Hayworth."

I'd forgotten about last night, Sherry telling me about the sale. I shook my head, pushing aside memories of the tense girls' night. "Didn't she die about thirty years ago? Who would still have her clothes for an estate sale?"

Jackie frowned at me. "You always know how to kill a party. So it's not Rita. The paper still said shoppers would be pleasantly surprised. So I'm waiting to be wowed."

"You know Sherry's a pathological liar, right? This is probably the estate sale from some local nursing home or something." That comment got me a dirty look, not only from my aunt but from the woman standing in front of her. The words had slipped out of my mouth before I could stop them. This being on Sherry's side was going to be harder than I thought.

"You need to get over this issue you have with Sherry." Aunt Jackie sniffed. "The council's liaison can't hold grudges against any of the town's business owners."

"This isn't personal," I argued.

Aunt Jackie raised her perfectly tweezed eyebrows. "Really?"

I shrugged. "Okay, so it's totally personal. I just don't get what people see in her. She's 100 percent fake."

"You can say that again." A dark-haired woman standing close to Aunt Jackie muttered. She started when she realized we'd heard her. Her lips curled into an embarrassed smile. "Sorry, I guess I'm a total hypocrite. I can't stand the woman, yet I'm here, waiting for the circus to open. What does that tell you about me?"

"You like a good sale?" I smiled and held out my hand. "Jill Gardner. I own Coffee, Books, and More, just down the street. After you get done here, stop in and I'll buy you a drink. I like honesty."

She reached out a slender hand to shake mine. "Claire LaRue. My husband and I just bought a house out on the highway. I've been meaning to stop into your shop, but the move has kept us busy."

"Speaking of the shop"—Aunt Jackie pointed to her watch—"don't you think you should be opening soon?"

"Yes, ma'am." I nodded to Claire. "I'm serious about that coffee. I think we'd have a lot in common if we started talking."

"Gossiping, you mean," my aunt grumbled.

"Fun is fun." I waved at Claire as I pushed my way out of the throng. Of course, this time, since I was leaving, people were more than willing to let me pass. *Never stand in between a girl and her sale.*

As I hurried to unlock the door and let a few waiting regulars into the shop, I wondered how Claire knew Sherry. More importantly, I wanted to know why she wasn't a fan. Aunt Jackie might call my interest gossip, but I called it intelligence gathering. Keep your friends close and your enemies closer. If I had any enemies in South Cove, besides Mayor Baylor and his wife, Tina, it was Sherry.

After the crowd thinned from my Saturday morning regulars, I had a few minutes of quiet, which I took advantage of by making a mocha and curling up with a mystery I'd stuck in my purse that morning. I could only take so much nonfiction reading, especially when I was reading the self-help diatribe of the Tiger Lady. I'd just reached the part in the mystery where they'd found the body when the bell over the door rang.

"Figured I'd find you goofing off. You know the monthly reports need reviewing. Or you could work on the supply order." Aunt Jackie picked up several cups off the far table. "Or even just clean up the mess from the morning rush."

"I was getting to that." I held up the book. "And I am working. It's called research."

She threw the cups in the trash and poured herself a black coffee into one of the travel mugs. "Whatever you need to tell yourself. I'm heading upstairs to relax before my shift."

"Hey, what was on sale?" I put the book down and went to the counter. "Or should I say, who was on sale?"

"Some low-level actress I'd never even heard of. And her clothes were dreadful. Tacky colors, skintight, not a quality piece in the lot." She shook her head. "Total shame what some people will spend money on."

"Sorry it was a bust for you." I cleaned a spot on the countertop with the bar towel I kept on my shoulder. "Did Sherry sell anything?"

"People are idiots. She sold out the lot and they were clamoring for more. Claire and I left about the same time. At least that girl has some fashion sense." Aunt Jackie stepped toward the door that led to the back office and a stairway to her apartment. "Oh, I'm supposed to tell you that Claire can't make coffee today. She'll come by next week. Something about her husband."

"Oh." I felt a tad bit disappointed, even though I'd just met the woman. Sometimes you can just tell about people. Claire seemed like someone I might like. And not just because she was another member of the I Hate Sherry Club. Or at least I thought that wasn't the only reason. "I'll see you later."

As I stepped back to the couch and my book, my aunt called out,

"You'd better have those books closed out by Tuesday morning. I'm taking everything to the accountant then."

"I hear you." I didn't even turn around. I could feel Aunt Jackie's eyes boring into my back. A few more chapters wouldn't hurt. Besides, until Greg got Kent's situation all tied up, who knew when I'd see him again. Definitely not this weekend, so I'd have lots of time to finish up the accounting chores.

By the time Sasha and Toby showed up at eleven, the story was finished and I'd grudgingly started reviewing the reports. The store had been slow for a Saturday. A couple of moms had come in for a coffee date, their chatter about their kids and local gossip filling the shop. I loved the sound of customers talking, not that I'd eavesdrop, but the sound of happy conversation made me smile.

Walking out the door, a brand-new novel in one hand and a bottle of water in the other, I took a deep breath, enjoying the clean salt air breeze. If Greg wasn't sitting on the porch waiting for me when I returned home, I planned to take a blanket and a thermos of iced tea down to the beach. Emma could run in the waves chasing seagulls and I could lose myself in the second book of the new mystery series I'd found this week. One of the members of Aunt Jackie's mystery group had ordered the whole series last week, so I'd ordered a second copy for my research. Referrals from that group were gold. They knew how to pick a story.

As I passed by Antiques by Thomas, a child's school desk in the window display caught my eye. Polished walnut and about three feet high, the desk had to have been in one of the old schoolhouses. When Josh Thomas pulled open the wooden door, the top bell clanging, he stopped short.

"Can I help you with something, Miss Gardner?" Josh's words were friendly, but the tone he delivered them with could freeze butter.

I decided to ignore his bad humor. I pointed to the desk. "Where did you get that?"

He labored closer to the window and peered into the crowded display. "Which *that* are you referring to? There are several items on display."

"The desk. The one for kids?" I tapped the glass with my finger.

Josh pulled out a handkerchief and polished the area where my finger had touched the glass. "If you must know, I came across that particular desk at an estate sale north of here. The former owner claimed the desk was from the first schoolhouse in Idaho. Somewhere in the Lewiston area, I believe."

My heart sank. If the desk really was historic, no way would Josh let me buy it for a few dollars. He'd be reaching out to the historical commissions and museums that dealt with that type of find. "I guess you want a lot for it, huh?" Then my evil side kicked in without me even batting an eye. "Aunt Jackie had her heart set on putting it in the children's book section of the store. You know, so they could pretend to be in school, reading a book?"

"Oh, Jackie wants the desk?" Josh shrugged, an action that made his belly jiggle even through the black mortician's suit he always wore. I didn't remember ever seeing him in anything but a suit. Maybe he even slept in the thing. "I said the previous owner claimed the desk was authentic. My research has put it more in the range of desks used in the nineteen-sixties."

I was going to hell for using the offer of my aunt's affections to barter a cheaper price. Yet I pushed harder. "So it's reasonable? I'd sure like to make Aunt Jackie happy. You know how she gets when she doesn't get her way." I held up my hands. "Not that I would blame you in any way for the desk being too expensive. A man's got to make a profit. Aunt Jackie just doesn't understand business."

"You really shouldn't talk that way about her. Jackie is an amazing woman." He stopped, his face beet red. "I could let it go for three hundred dollars."

"Two-fifty?" I hated to spend money on an impulse buy, but the desk would look so cute in the shop.

"Miss Gardner, this isn't an auction." Josh glared at me. I let my shoulders drop and heaved a sigh worthy of an Oscar for Best Supporting Actress. His eyes flickered to the apartment over the shop. A perfect place for him to play Romeo to Aunt Jackie's Juliet, except she was more of a modern theater girl.

I stepped around him and he grabbed my arm. "Fine, you're killing me, but if I don't take any profit, I could let it go for two-seventy-five. That's my bottom. Take it or leave it."

Smiling, I nodded to the desk. "Slap a sold sign on that puppy. I'll bring over a check on Tuesday as soon as Toby starts his shift."

"We have a deal?" Josh peered at me through his half-closed eyelids.

"Do I need to sign something? I'll uphold my half of the bargain; you just don't sell the desk out from under me."

He nodded. "I'll trust you."

I thought about Josh's ending words all the way home. Was our bond becoming more than the annoying shopkeeper next door? Was his and Jackie's relationship turning more serious than I knew? I mentally added *call Jackie* to my to-do list. I didn't want to be blind-sided if Josh Thomas was soon to be Uncle Josh. The thought made me shiver.

When I reached the house, Greg's truck was in my driveway. He sat on the top step of the front porch, reading the *Examiner*. My dog slept at his feet. Smiling, he folded the paper when I walked up. "I would have picked you up at the shop, but when I called, Toby said you'd left ten minutes ago. Take the long way home?"

I kissed him and sat down beside him. "Shopping."

He frowned and looked closer at the only thing I had carried from the shop, my purse. "You shop light."

"Actually, I shop heavy." I went on to tell him about the new addition to the kids' area for the shop. "I think the kids will love it."

Greg nodded. "You could paint that short wall under the windows with chalkboard paint and the kids could draw, too."

"I hadn't thought of that." I thought about the corner of the shop where the kids hung out, reading books. It was small, but it might just work. "And we could advertise sales on the board."

"I guess so." He chuckled. "You're always thinking like a business owner."

"And what, you think like a dad?" The words were out of my mouth before I could stop them. We hadn't even talked about marriage, let alone kids.

"It's possible." He stood up before I could say anything else. "Come have lunch with me in Bakerstown. I have to pick up some supplies for the station and I'm tired of staring at a whiteboard that's not giving me answers, just more questions."

"So," I started but Greg stopped me, holding up his hand.

"I'll buy you lunch at that seafood place you love on one condition. No talk about the case. No questions, no comments, nothing. We're just a couple having lunch."

"Anything I want on the menu?" I raised my eyebrows.

He reached down and gave Emma a rub under her chin. "Anything. I need some time away from this to try to get clarity from all the white noise."

"What if I slip and ask you a question, like, was Kent murdered?"

Greg didn't look up. "Then you get a hamburger off the value menu at my choice of fast-food joints."

The man knew my weakness. Ply me with food, especially seafood, and you could have anything. I pretended to consider the offer, pushing out my bottom lip.

"Get in the truck. You know you want to." He pulled me into his arms, then leaned down and lightly bit my lip. When I complained, he laughed. "I've missed you."

As we drove toward the highway, I stared at Esmeralda's house. Her driveway was filled with cars, and there were several parked on the street. "She's having a reading today?"

Greg glanced at the house as we passed. "Some guy's family is here for his birthday. She says they need to help the guy cross over because he's stuck here." Greg finally noticed now that I was staring at him, not the fortune-teller's house. He blushed. "Sue me, I get bored at the station sometimes and overhear my staff's phone conversations. It's not like she was being quiet about the whole thing."

I pressed my lips together, trying not to laugh. For all his lectures to me about confidentiality, my boyfriend was one of the biggest gossips in town. If it didn't deal with official police business. "Hey, did I tell you she did a reading on me last week when I dropped off Maggie?"

"Who's Maggie?" Greg turned the car north onto the highway.

"Esmeralda's new cat. She showed up when I was napping the other day." I pulled my hair into a ponytail and rolled down the window, enjoying the wind.

"Oh. So what is up next for you? A fortune awaits you? Travel is in your future? It better not be a new love. I'd hate to have to fire her." He took my hand in his and squeezed.

"Nope." I put a waver in my voice. "Things aren't what they seem. And the old favorite, some are silver and the others gold."

"Why does that sound familiar?"

"It's an old Girl Scouts camp song." I stared out Greg's window, watching the waves in the distance. Living by the ocean never got old. I felt sorry for the people who lived in land-locked states. What did they do to revive themselves?

Greg drove in silence for a while. Then he muttered, "Things aren't what they seem, that describes this case to a tee. I wonder if I'm not the only one listening in on others' conversations."

I turned my attention from the flock of seagulls back to him. "What are you saying?"

He tossed the paper over to me. "Someone's been talking to the press about confidential police matters."

I only had to read the headline before I knew what had Greg upset. Darla's byline was under the two-inch headline I read aloud. "Killer Leaves No Clues—Police Stumped."

CHAPTER 9

The cab of the truck was silent as I read Darla's exposé on the investigation into Kent's murder. She had included several quotes from an undisclosed member of the police department. When I finished, I folded the paper and set it between the two of us.

"You don't have anything to say?" Greg slowed the truck to make the turn onto the road that would take us to Bakerstown and away from the ocean.

"I really want a bowl of that clam chowder. It's been months." I tapped the paper with my unpolished fingernail. "I don't break deals."

Greg barked out a short laugh. "Since when?" He ran a hand through his sandy hair. "Fine, we can talk about Kent. Who do you thing is spilling to Darla?"

"Doesn't seem like Esmeralda's style." I thought about Toby and Tim, the only other official employees of the department. "Toby won't even talk to me about what's going on. No way would he talk to Darla. So that leaves you or Tim."

"And it's not me." Greg sighed. "Tim's my guess, too."

I thought about the tall, lanky man who wasn't much more than a kid, straight out of college and a criminal justice major. Honestly, it didn't seem like his style, either. The kid was too into the rules to break them just for some press time. Something Esmeralda said the other day nagged at me. Then I remembered. "What if Darla's just observing the obvious?"

"What do you mean?" Greg pulled into the parking lot of the seafood restaurant, the site of our first date. Of course, I hadn't realized it was a date back then.

I slipped out of the truck before I answered. "Esmeralda said living in a small town, you start knowing people. Maybe Darla just knows how you'll react when a murder happens versus when someone dies by accident. Maybe your actions, like driving in to meet Doc Ames or spending more time at the station, tells her a story."

"Plausible, but I'm still going to talk to Tim. Just in case." He held the door of the restaurant open and smiled. "After you."

"You're such a gentleman."

"I just don't want to be trampled when you smell the bread." Greg nodded to the hostess. "Two for lunch."

Walking to the table, Greg's phone buzzed. He took it off the holder and checked the display. He shrugged as the woman seated us and set our menus on the table.

"What's up, Tim?" His gaze met mine and he held up one finger as he listened to the dispatcher.

"Can I bring you something to drink?" The chipper hostess paused at the table, looking at me.

I raised my eyebrows, silently asking Greg if we'd actually be having lunch and he nodded. I guess our nonverbal communication as a couple was spot-on. I ordered two large glasses of iced tea and opened the menu, trying not to listen to Greg's conversation and hoping we wouldn't be taking our lunch in to-go boxes.

"I'll be back by three. I've got to stop to talk to Doc Ames. Jill and I are having lunch now." I could hear Tim's frantic response. "Seriously, if they want to talk to me, they can wait around until I get back. Send them over to Coffee, Books, and More to relax."

When Greg put his phone back into the holder, he picked up his menu. "So, what looks good?"

I peeked over the menu and caught his gaze. "Thanks for lunch."

He shrugged. "It's just the bank auditors. They can cool their jets for a few hours. They've been on a tear about this alarm system issue for the last week. Of course, before Kent died, we couldn't even get the security service to return our calls. Now everyone's covering their butts."

"You think Kent's murder has something to do with the faulty alarm?" I set the menu down. "He wasn't even at work when he died."

Greg held up his hand. "Not your circus, not your monkey."

"No fair, you brought up the subject," I reminded him.

"Jill, repeat after me: Not my circus, not my monkey." He studied the menu, avoiding my stare.

The waitress returned with our drinks. "My granny always said that when I'd get all worked up about something she didn't think was my problem. Like when my friends were having troubles with teachers at school. I'd come home all vigilante, and she'd respond with that old saying." The waitress smiled at the memory. "It used to tick me off. Anyway, what can I bring you?"

Greg listed off enough food for three people and then turned to me. "What are you having?"

She turned to me, obviously surprised at the size of his order.

"I'm having the scallops, with a side salad, garlic mashed potatoes, and add a cup of clam chowder." I closed the menu and handed it to her. "Oh, and bring me that crab dip appetizer, with two plates. I'll share."

After the waitress walked away, Greg laughed. "I bet she thinks we're being joined by friends."

"Hey, I ran this morning." I took a sip of the tea. "Besides, it sounds like you're going into cop mode as soon as we get back into town. So this is date night, and I'll take the leftovers home and watch movies."

"Sounds like a perfect night." Greg sounded thoughtful.

I put my hand on his. "It would be if you were cuddled up on the couch next to me."

"Even if I insisted on the new Mark Wahlberg movie?" Greg squeezed my hand. Even though we watched a lot of movies together, we were still getting used to each other's tastes in humor and entertainment.

"I'm planning a Disney princess marathon," I teased.

As the appetizer arrived, he leaned back, spreading a napkin in his lap. "Then I'm glad I'm working."

I tore off a piece of the fresh bread loaf, still warm from the oven, and dipped it into the crab mixture. "Is there any way Kent's death wasn't murder?"

He raised his eyebrows as he mirrored my actions with the dip. Then he sighed. "I guess I started this." He took a sip of tea before he continued. "That's why I'm going to see Doc Ames. The tox screens are coming back wonky. I mean, we know the good banker was a cokehead. But there's something else in his system."

"So he could have overdosed?" I shrugged. "I don't know a lot about the whole drug thing, but people are always dying because of drugs."

"Not the high-class drug addicts." Greg ripped a bigger piece of bread off the loaf. "People like Paine tend to use cocaine as a supplement to their lifestyle. They can work longer and harder because they never sleep. And, apparently, it's good for the libido."

"You make it sound like an herbal supplement." I shook my head. "I can't believe they wouldn't drug-test him at the job. Doesn't Rotary Bank have a drug-testing program?"

He polished off the dip before he answered. "Apparently only when you apply for a job. He missed the mandatory testing that's now in place for bank managers when they promote. The man was a smart player. Probably why he stayed at the smaller bank instead of trying to advance. He didn't want to risk being tested now."

I thought about what Greg had told me as our chowders arrived. After taking my first spoonful, I asked, "So he took it to have better sex?"

Greg's grin widened. "I wondered if you caught that. Sherry was all about the wild sex she and Kent were having. She let a few tidbits slip out the last time we talked."

Sherry. It always came back to her. "Trying to make you jealous?"

He shrugged. "I guess so. I told her you used to be a gymnast."

That made me laugh. "You didn't."

He held his hand up in the air. "Swear to God, I did." Greg chuckled. "She suddenly had to be somewhere else."

"You are so bad." The closest thing I'd ever done that remotely resembled gymnastics was a section in ninth grade P.E. And I was pretty sure I only passed the test because the teacher knew I was trying. My mother used to call me Grace, not because it was my middle name, but because I was klutzy.

"She deserved it." Greg dug in to his dinner. "I get tired of her dogging on you all the time. Just because you and her are night and day, doesn't mean she's the better choice."

My lips curved into a smile, and I mentally blessed Greg for standing up for me. Then his words echoed in my head. "Wait, she dogs me? What, does she think she's all that?"

He patted my hand. "I knew that would get you riled up. Sherry just doesn't understand why anyone, especially me, would choose you instead of her." He pulled my hand to his lips. "But she doesn't have to understand. I love you and that's the only important thing you need to remember."

"You can be smooth, Mr. King." I paused, considering telling him about Kent and his kissing partner. In the end, I decided I didn't want to make him think about the case. That bit of information could wait. The rest of the meal we talked about our upcoming trip to Napa Valley. The weekend at the end of April would be our first getaway together as a couple. Justin and Amy had raved about the bed-and-breakfast they'd stayed at last fall, showing us the hundreds of pictures they'd taken as they explored the wine country. Topping their experience would be hard, but Greg and I were willing to give it the college try.

After dinner, he drove us over to Bakerstown Funeral Home, where the county coroner, Doc Ames, had his office so he could keep an eye on his business even while he performed the random autopsies required in our quiet area. When we pulled into the parking lot, two women stood at the front door, a harried Doc Ames standing in the middle. I could hear the shouting through the closed windows and over Toby Keith on the stereo.

Greg leaned forward as he parked the truck and turned off the engine. "What the hell?"

"Is that Sherry?" I couldn't believe the woman was even intruding on our minidate. What would she be doing at the funeral home? Unless she was there about Kent. But who was she yelling at?

I watched Sherry poke the other woman with a long red fingernail. The woman grabbed her hand and twisted. I felt rather than saw Greg jump out of the truck. A rush of wind as Superhero King ran to save his ex-wife. *That's not fair*, I chided myself. He was a police officer and this was a disturbance. Besides, Doc Ames looked terrified. I could see his mouth moving as he tried to calm the two down. He had a very soothing manner, but I guess Sherry and the other woman didn't want to be soothed. I unbuckled my seat belt and followed Greg to the circus.

By the time I got there, Greg had Sherry with her arms trapped behind her. Doc Ames held the other woman by one arm, and they had increased the distance between the two to avoid accidental physical contact. Or well-placed kick. I couldn't help it. I pulled out my cell and snapped a picture. Darla would love this.

"Jill, stop it." Greg's voice was firm.

I slipped the phone back into my pocket. "Sorry, too good to pass up."

Sherry's burning gaze moved from her original target to me. "If you even consider showing that to anyone, I'll sue you."

"I'm scared," I muttered. I wanted to pull out my cell, snap a photo of the crazed look on the woman's face, and post it to the Business-to-Business webpage. I could title the post, "See our newest shop owner in her customer service finest." I pushed the demon inside me away, but I was sure it wasn't gone.

"Jill? Do you want to wait in the truck?" Greg gave me the look, the one that asked, *Why are you stooping to her level?*

Sherry smirked and relaxed her body into Greg's, just so I could see her wielding her physical prowess. I wanted to smack her and my hands weren't being held back by either of the two men. I took a deep breath and called on my better side to stop me. I wasn't sure it would work, but I knew I didn't want to be banished to the truck.

"That woman has no right to be here. She wasn't married to Kent," the unnamed woman shrieked at Doc Ames. "This is a family matter."

Sherry's eyes widened and I saw her jolt forward, forgetting that Greg was holding her back. "You weren't married to him anymore. He never even talked about you."

"Idiot. He told me all about you and the game he was playing on you. Have you checked your business account lately? Or do you really think your investments are doing that well, just because Kent said so?" The woman's voice was ice-cold. Which made me shiver, her words taking on a seriousness that made me worry about Sherry, just a bit. Then she opened her mouth again.

"Kent wouldn't do that. He loved me," Sherry screeched. She turned her head and pleaded to Greg, "Make her go away. She shouldn't be here."

"Sherry, you need to go home. Let me figure this out with Doc Ames and I'll call you when we're done," Greg said in his calming cop tone.

"You won't tell her anything," the other woman said. "This is my business, not hers."

"Now Mrs. Paine, please calm down and come inside with me. We'll talk about Mr. Paine's wishes and see if we can work out some sort of compromise." Doc Ames gently pulled the woman closer to the front door and away from Sherry.

"I know his wishes," Sherry yelled. "You should be talking to me, not her."

As Doc Ames and the woman, now identified as at least a sometime Mrs. Paine, disappeared into the home, Sherry actually snorted.

Greg released her arms and pointed to the pink Mercedes sports car sitting in the parking lot. "I'm serious, Sherry, go home."

Sherry straightened her Chanel suit and glared at me. "I don't know what you're doing here. You always seem to be where you're not wanted."

"Sherry," Greg warned.

She fluffed her long blond hair and actually purred at Greg. "I'll be waiting for your call." Then, as she passed by me, she whispered, "Don't think you're going to keep him. He'll always come home."

My eyes widened, and I glanced at Greg, who just shook his head.

He came and stood by me as we watched her drive away. "Typical Sherry, can't just leave, has to leave a wake of destruction in her path. You okay?"

"I'm fine. She doesn't get to me," I lied. I still wanted to slap the chick silly, but at least Greg had stood up for me. Now I was more curious about the woman inside. I nodded to the building. "Did you know Kent was married?"

"Divorced. But I haven't been able to reach her for questioning." He looked thoughtfully at the door. "I guess this afternoon is as good of a time as any."

"I'll come in with you. After that, I could use a cold drink." I held the door open for Greg, who stood watching me. "What, did you really think that I was going to go wait in the truck? Sherry might listen to you, but I'm my own woman."

He chuckled. "Even when it gets you in trouble." He didn't even form it into a question, just motioned me into the cool building. "But you aren't coming in the office. You don't need to be part of the investigation."

Shrugging, I pulled a book out of my purse. "I came prepared. I never know where our excursions will wind up. So I brought reading material." I'd actually been excited to read this last long-awaited installment in a popular paranormal series. My pre-orders for the book had been unbelievable. I'd tried to get an advance reading copy, but my sales rep hadn't been able to hold one for me.

Even with all that built-up excitement to start reading, it took a while for me to settle into one of the plush couches in the Bakerstown Funeral Home's front parlor. Especially since the opulent waiting area was right outside Doc Ames's office. And surprisingly, the walls were pretty thin. I could hear Greg's voice as he asked the woman questions, but most of the words were garbled. I did find out her first name was Cheryl. The name rang a distant bell. Had she visited the shop? I made an effort to call customers by their first name if I saw a driver's license or a credit card, just to add that personal touch. But I didn't remember seeing the woman before. So that couldn't be it.

Finally I gave up trying to decipher the noise into any human language. I opened the cover of the book, put my feet up, and within pages, was returned to the world the author had built for me in the last installment. It felt like coming home. Or revisiting a favorite travel destination.

I didn't notice the woman standing in front of me until she spoke.

"That woman's trouble. She thinks she can wrap a man around her finger and use him for anything she wants. For a while, she wanted Kent, and now it looks like she's out to get your man back in her claws. Don't let her kill him, too." Tears flowed down Cheryl Paine's cheeks as she stared at me.

"You think Sherry killed Kent?" Cheryl's words had surprised me, not because I liked Sherry, but because I didn't think she'd stoop that low just to control the male of the species. Besides, what would be in it for her?

"I know she did. The woman thought she'd be named in Kent's will, but he never removed me. I'm still the beneficiary, and there's nothing she can do about it."

With that declaration, Cheryl Paine marched out of the building, letting the door slam behind her.

"Sounds like motive to me." Greg watched the door thoughtfully.

I tucked my book back in my bag, reluctant to leave the author's world. I stepped toward Greg, "Yeah, but for which one? Cheryl or Sherry?"

He put his hand on my back and led me through the door and out into the sunshine. Time to return to South Cove. "Both."

CHAPTER 10

Greg leaned on my porch railing, watching me unlock the front door. "I can get into the house all by myself." I dug in another section of my purse for my key ring. "I've been doing it for years now."

"How many times have I come over to unlock your door after a run this spring?" His voice was warm, comforting, and hearing him, I could just see the self-satisfied smirk flowing over his features. We rarely fought, not true smack down, hurt your feelings fights. But when we did, it was usually because one or more of us thought ours was the only way. Or we insisted on some sort of crazy superiority over something, like who was the better keeper of the keys. A contest Greg would always win. The man was a security fanatic.

I felt the teddy bear fob that was part of the key chain and pulled the mass of metal out of the bottom of my purse. I held it up for him to see. "I told you I would be fine."

"Maybe I like to spend time with you?" His lips curved into a crooked smile, drawing me toward him. Then his phone rang and killed the moment.

Greg glanced at the display before answering the call. "Yes, Tim?"

I watched him as cop mode took over and he listened carefully to the deputy's voice. I turned the key in the lock and left the door open so he could come in after he'd finished the call. Emma sniffed at my feet in greeting, then ran to the back door, ready to run the yard. As I passed through the living room, I glanced over at my sofa and saw the couch cushions were still intact. I poured a glass of iced tea and sat down at the table, my to-do notebook in hand. Time to plan the rest of my weekend. Jackie had my shift at the coffee shop tomorrow, so I had two whole days with nothing to do. I made a quick grocery list and was just finishing up when Greg appeared in the kitchen doorway. "You want steaks tomorrow evening, or should we order Chinese?"

He shook his head. "Let's not plan anything definite. I'm not sure where this investigation with Kent's going." He held up the phone. "I've got to go meet with the bank auditors. They're camped out in my office and won't leave, according to Tim. I guess now is as good of time as any."

"Do you know what they want to discuss?" I tapped my pen on the notebook. "Maybe someone from the bank killed Kent and they know why?"

Greg laughed. "Seriously, who do you think at the bank could be a murderer? John, the janitor? I guess he's a possibility, he carries Mace, but he's over seventy."

"You don't have to be so sarcastic. There's a chance it was someone at the bank, okay, maybe not John, but one of the clerks. Kent was a horndog, maybe he scorned the wrong woman." I chewed on my bottom lip. This was a most excellent train of thought. "Maybe the redhead killed him."

His phone beeped with an incoming text, and as he read the message, I could see his attention shift. "Crap, I've got to get downtown." He walked over and kissed me on the top of the head. "I'll see you soon."

"Tomorrow?" I squeezed his hand and then let it fall to his side. "If you're coming for dinner, I'll walk into town and get Sadie's Chocolate Temptation Pie for dessert."

"You are pure evil." He waved, turning toward the driveway. I heard the truck start up and Emma whined at the door.

"I miss him, too, girl." I let my dog in, and she settled near my feet while I finished my list of projects. That done, I made plans for a light dinner and refilled my glass of iced tea. Then I took the paperback out of my purse and Emma and I went out to the back porch to relax.

Later, I started working down my list of chores, feeling just a bit sorry for myself. It wasn't like we always spent Saturdays together, but sometimes, I just wanted a little more. I'd just put a load in the washer when a knock sounded at the door. Maybe his meeting with the bank examiners had been shorter than expected. Of course, he'd only been gone an hour. The only way that was Greg at the door was if the meeting had been postponed and the auditors were already out of town. My luck didn't run that good.

I pulled the door open without looking out the window to see who it was, a habit that drove Greg crazy. I kept explaining we lived in a small town. He kept saying I lived on the edge next to the heavily traveled Highway One. Anyone could be at the door. He had a point. One that I just ignored.

Emma whined at the visitor, Aunt Jackie. She and my dog had a love/hate relationship. Emma loved my aunt, my aunt claimed to hate my dog. Yet at times, I'd see her stroking Emma's head.

Aunt Jackie was dressed in a coral pantsuit, pearls at the neck and sensible but cute walking shoes. She thrust a box from the shop into my hands. "White chocolate macadamia nut cookies. Sadie's been experimenting."

I opened the box, the smell of fresh baked cookies filling my senses. "Yum, did we buy some for the shop?"

"I told her to leave me a sample and I'd let her know next week." Jackie smiled. "We have three dozen, which should sell nicely tomorrow."

"Seriously, you have got to stop playing hardball with Sadie. She's our primary dessert supplier. I'd hate to have to go into Bakerstown more often." I followed my aunt into my kitchen, where she'd already started a pot of coffee. "Besides, she's a friend."

"Can't let friendship affect business. Sadie knows what she's doing. She'd be a fool to stop trying new things." Jackie sat at the table, Emma lying quickly at her feet, her nose inches away from my aunt's shoes.

I decided I'd talk to Sadie next week and make sure she charged us for the "sample" when she did her weekly order. Changing the subject, I joined my aunt at the table, opening the box of cookies and offering her one. "So, what's up?"

She waved away the box and watched as I took a cookie and set the box down in the middle of the table, within reaching distance. I thought I saw regret in her eyes as she eyed the box. "Just checking in. Rumor mill says that Kent was still married and that's why Sherry killed him. Is that what Greg thinks?"

I brushed the cookie crumbs off my lips before I spoke. South Cove's small-town rumor mill was where I got my best intel. Especially since my aunt was plugged in to the main source. I wondered not for the first time where she found out her gossip. Maybe Mary? More likely Josh; that man would do anything for my aunt, including asking the inappropriate questions.

"You know, there are two subjects that are taboo between Greg and me. One of them is open investigations. And the other is Sherry." I polished off the cookie and thought about a second one, but got up to pour a couple of cups of coffee from the just-brewed pot instead. "I did meet the former Mrs. Paine this afternoon at the funeral home. She and Sherry were ready to kill each other, and would have if they'd had real weapons. I'm just glad neither one of them had guns."

Aunt Jackie took the coffee and leaned forward. Her eyes sparkled. "What were they fighting about?"

I shuddered a bit. "Kent's funeral arrangements." I took a sip of the dark brew. "Can you imagine anyone wanting that chore?"

She stared at me hard. "It's an honor, not a chore. You wouldn't have let some stranger handle Miss Emily's requests, would you?"

My friend had died less than a year ago, but for the first few days after her death, I'd hoped for someone, anyone, to take over the planning. I hadn't wanted to make a mistake. Luckily, Sadie Michaels had stepped in, and with Doc Ames's help, my friend had been sent off to her final resting place without a hitch. As long as you didn't talk about the unfortunate will-reading incident. Or the fact that her relatives tried to kill me. Shaking those memories away, I put on a customer service smile. "I guess you're right. But who does get the honor? Current girlfriend or ex-wife? Seems like a dilemma."

"Wife trumps girlfriend any time." Aunt Jackie shook her head. "I would have thought you'd know that by now. Weren't you a divorce lawyer?"

"Family law," I corrected. "I was talking social etiquette, not legal regulations."

"Same thing." Aunt Jackie looked at me, pausing at my hair, tied back into a loose bun with a clip. She sighed, but instead of the lecture I'd expected over the mess, she asked, "Can you take my shift tomorrow? I know I told you I'd work, but I've got a few things I have to do in the city. Mary and I are leaving tonight after I close the shop."

"Sure, Greg's tied up with the Kent thing so I don't have real plans except laundry. I forgot to mention that Mary was looking for you the other day. What's going on?" I eyed another cookie, wondering if I could wait for my aunt to leave and therefore skip the lecture about eating too much sugar. Except she'd brought the box, so she must expect me to eat a few. My hand reached toward the cookie box, but my aunt snapped the lid shut and stood.

"We're just doing a girl trip, why would you ask?" My aunt dug in her purse, avoiding eye contact.

I studied her, wondering what she wasn't telling me. Before I could push the issue, a knock sounded at the door. "Hold on. I've got some questions."

I followed Emma to the front of the house and pulled open the door. This time, I should have looked first. Someday I'd learn and avoid awkward conversations like the one that was just about to occur.

Pat Williams stood at my door. Her brunette hair was twisted into a French braid, and her casual uniform of designer silk dress, gold chains, and what I liked to call hooker shoes topped off the ensemble. Between Pat's outfit and my aunt's, I looked like one of the homeless on the city streets dressed in jeans. Pat's lips curved into a smile that would have had a football team of males running to help her pick up a dropped napkin. The action had no power over me, however; I knew when someone wanted something. And this favor was going to be a doozy.

"Jill, I can't believe I've never visited your lovely house." Pat glanced around the porch. "So quant and homey. This place was quite a wreck when that nasty old lady owned it. What was her name again?"

I leaned against the doorway, and Emma softly growled at my feet. "Her name was Emily and she was my friend." I let my words sink in, and as I saw her smile dim, I went in for the kill. "Get to the point, Pat. What do you want? You didn't come to visit."

Pat sighed, then reached into her Coach bag and pulled out a tissue. She dabbed at her dry eyes. "I've come to ask for your help. You are the only one who can save her. Greg's trying to send Sherry to prison."

I shook my head. "Greg's not vindictive. Besides, they've been divorced for years. The only way Sherry will be arrested and sent to prison is if she killed someone." Dawning realization filled my mind. "You think she killed Kent, don't you?"

Pat shook her head, but her smile disappeared. "No. There's no way." But something in her eyes made me wonder if even Sherry's best friend had doubts.

"Look, I still don't know why you're here. You know Greg. If the investigation proves it's Sherry, then that's what will happen. He doesn't make things up. He finds the truth." I put my hand on the door.

"Ha. You don't know how ugly it got between those two. I thought for a while he was going to kill Sherry, he was that mad when she left." Pat seemed to consider something, then kept talking. "I want you to prove Sherry didn't kill Kent."

"Are you freaking nuts?" I'd died and gone to crazytown. "Why should I?"

Pat stared at me hard. "Because if you do, I'll make Sherry back off Greg. She's been pushing hard for a reconciliation. I can make that stop."

By the time Pat left, I'd found out all about the dozen or so women whom Kent had been dating in the last few years in addition to Sherry and now, his ex-wife, Cheryl. When I returned to the kitchen, Aunt Jackie pushed a pad toward me.

"I wrote down every name she said." She tapped her pen on the list. "Looks like you have a few people to check out on Monday."

I took a bottle of light beer out of the fridge and slipped into a chair, staring at the list. "You think I should? I mean, there's no way Greg would even consider going back with her."

Aunt Jackie tucked her purse under her arm and kissed me on the cheek. "I know you. It doesn't matter why you get involved in an investigation; you just like to solve problems. Don't let Sherry mess with your head. Besides, if she gives Greg a break for something you would have done anyway, you both win."

I followed my aunt to the door, where we found Maggie sitting on the porch rail, sunning herself. I closed the door, blocking Emma in the house, and went over and picked up the warm cat. She started purring as soon as I touched her.

"I didn't know you adopted a cat." Jackie reached out and scratched Maggie between her ears. "Why didn't you tell me?"

"Not my cat. She belongs to Esmeralda, but she keeps escaping." I glanced over at my neighbor's house. "I worry she's going to get run over one of these times. You know people fly through here too fast."

"That's why Toby sets up just down from your house to pick up speeders. You know that boy has made so much money for the city with his stops the mayor is thinking about hiring him on full-time."

Aunt Jackie kissed me on the cheek. "I hope that doesn't happen soon. He's good for our business, too."

I watched her get into her car and drive toward town; the entire trip would take less than two minutes, even if she had to stop at the entrance to my driveway to wait for a tourist driving into town. Of course, it was Aunt Jackie. She never walked anywhere except in the city. But out in the sticks—her words, not mine—she lived up to her California heritage and took the car everywhere.

As my aunt turned the car out of the driveway and onto the road, I crossed over with Maggie in my arms toward Esmeralda's. She really needed to keep a better eye on her cat.

Maggie meowed, like she was agreeing with me. I rang the doorbell and listened to the round of church bells echoing through the house. Esmeralda must have finished playing fortune-teller since there wasn't a car in the driveway. I hoped I wasn't interrupting a reading or a visit to the other world for someone. I didn't believe in my neighbor's ability, but I respected the allure her so-called profession or talent had for bringing tourists to our small town. Including my shop.

The door flew open and there she stood in her full costume, a beaded scarf tied around her head, the beads and small bells mixing in her long dark hair. "Jill, I didn't expect you today." She looked down at the cat in my arms. "Oh, Maggie brought you."

"Actually, I brought her. She was on my porch again. You really need . . ." My words trailed off as I watched Esmeralda walk away and sit at her reading table.

"Come sit, we'll find out what Maggie thinks you should know." She patted the chair next to her and Maggie meowed again.

Seriously? *The cat* thought I needed to know something? I needed to know how to keep my nose out of the cat's business, that's what I needed. I should have sent her with Aunt Jackie. "I've got stuff to do." I turned toward the door.

"Please, Jill, it will only take a second. Maggie won't give up, and I'd hate to see her hurt while trying to get you to listen." Her voice was calm, but an image of a speeding car flying toward town came to me.

I closed the door, then put Maggie down on the hardwood floor. Immediately, she ran to the open chair, then jumped onto the table and sat. Her eyes bored into me.

This was stupid. "I really don't have a lot of time," I grumbled as I walked toward the chair.

"Laundry can wait."

I eyed Esmeralda. Maybe the woman had a bug set up in my house, listening to me. Now I was being paranoid. Greg thought he had a leak in the department; maybe I'd be able to find out if his dispatcher was the source of Darla's information or just a good guesser. "Fine."

I sat in the chair and Esmeralda grabbed both of my hands, pulling them to the table. "Relax, and let your mind wander. I'll do the heavy lifting."

I started to giggle, but her harsh look quieted me. I closed my eyes and wandered through the list of names Pat had given me. Kent had been busy his last few months on the earth. I felt sorry for Sherry; no one deserved that type of betrayal.

"You're on the right path, but the reasons will be different than what appears at first." Esmeralda's trance voice broke my thoughts and my eyelids flew open. Her gaze was focused on the crystal ball in the middle of the table.

The ball had been clear when I sat, but now a gray mist floated in the middle. *Cheap parlor trick.* Then I noticed Maggie watching the ball, as well. *This better keep the kitten off my porch and out of harm's way.*

The cat looked up from the swirling mist and meowed.

"A woman scorned. Some are silver and the others gold." Esmeralda repeated the line she'd given me the last time she'd read for me. Apparently she believed in friendships. Maybe that was the point; the woman wanted a friend. Maybe I'd ask her to go with me and Amy on our next girls' night out. I glanced at the gypsy outfit. Or maybe shopping in town would be a better start.

The grip on my hands loosened, and I felt the fortune-teller lean back into her chair.

"Sorry about that, I guess I was wrong. Sometimes the spirits don't want to talk when we want to listen. Do you want to come back tomorrow and we can try again?" Esmeralda picked up Maggie, rubbing her under her chin.

"But you d—" I broke off my statement. It could be like sleepwalking; you were never supposed to wake the guy up unless he was about to walk off the window ledge. "Sure. I'll talk to you later then."

I walked the few steps home and wondered if Esmeralda was just messing with me. Had she not heard herself talk? I decided to do some research on the practice. Maybe she did have a gift. She'd been right before, but I'd chalked that up to hindsight. The old camp song echoed in my head . . . *Make new friends but keep the old* . . .

Friends like Pat and Sherry. Or Aunt Jackie and Mary. Or me and Amy. What would you do for a friend? Pat's visit seemed to be a prime example of a way to be stupid for a friend.

After grabbing a bag of chips and my beer, I pulled out my laptop and looked up the list of names on Facebook. Not Investigation 101, but a good place to start. On the third name, I hit pay dirt. The photo was a group shot with what appeared to be a husband and a cute three-year-old. The woman had been the model who'd slipped out of the Business-to-Business meeting. And according to her last Facebook post, she and her spouse were celebrating their tenth wedding anniversary next week.

She'd have reason to keep the affair secret. And reason to kill Kent.

CHAPTER 11

"Since you can't make our weekly breakfast date, I brought the food to you." Amy slapped a bag from Diamond Lille's on the front counter of the shop. "You can thank me by making me a large mocha with an extra shot before you sit down to eat."

The smell of gooey omelets and salty hash browns made my stomach growl. I quickly made Amy her drink, then glanced at the door to make sure I didn't have an incoming customer. Aunt Jackie had mentioned that the Sunday early shift was slow, but this was glacial. I made a mental note to discuss changing hours for the day until the summer tourist season started. "Thanks for the grub. I figured you'd be checking out surfing spots with Justin this morning."

Amy shrugged and looked down at her cup.

"Whoa. Is there a problem with you and Justin?" I slipped onto a stool and pulled out the Styrofoam cartons that held our breakfasts. Three-egg Denver omelet for Amy and a mushroom and Swiss for me. Both had a generous side of hash browns tucked in next to the eggs. Steam rose when I opened the lid. I guess after being friends for over five years, the girl could order for me as easily as herself. I dug my fork into the cheesy delight and almost groaned when the flavors hit my tongue.

Amy picked a lone piece of ham off the top of her omelet and stared at it like she couldn't recognize the type of meat she held. Finally she shook her head and popped the cube into her mouth. "He's been a little jumpy lately since he found Kent's body. I think he's staying home this weekend and cleaning his apartment."

That got my attention. According to Amy, Justin's apartment looked like the typical campus bachelor pad, filled with pizza boxes and half-consumed sodas. Justin had said life was too short to worry about cleaning a place where he slept and showered. "I'm sure he'll get over it. It's not every day you find a dead body."

She picked up her fork. "I guess. It's just this isn't the Justin I knew. I thought he was beginning to think about something more between us. I mean, he took me to meet his parents for Christmas. Now I can barely get him to answer a text."

I'd remembered the holiday incident. I'd thought Amy was going to have a nervous breakdown when she thought Justin was even thinking of them as a couple. Now she was worried that the relationship was over. I had to get her thinking of something else. Then a plan came to me. "What are you doing this afternoon?"

"Washing my hair, arranging my closet, maybe reading a book, if I can get my mind to focus. Why?" Amy picked at her hash browns, discarding a bite as too burnt when really it was only crunchy and delicious.

I filled her in on Pat's visit yesterday and the mystery model's Facebook page I'd found. When I finished, I realized I'd also finished the omelet, so I took the last bite of potatoes and cleaned up my spot. "So, come talk to her with me."

"How do you expect to find her? People don't leave their home address on their Facebook pages. Or at least if they're smart they don't." Amy closed up her own container with the omelet half-eaten and threw the rest into the trash.

I smiled. "I didn't need her to leave her address. I have a phone book." I held the local phone book up for her to see. "And they still list addresses in the white pages. How stupid is that?"

I opened the book and found the name on the page. Baker, Thomas and Evelyn. "They live in Bakerstown. Want to come with me on a short road trip?"

Amy eyed me suspiciously. "What does Greg say about this?"

Now it was my turn to avoid eye contact. I went back behind the counter and started restocking the cup supply.

"Jill?" Amy's voice was hard. "You *have* told Greg what Pat said, right?"

I threw the empty cup box into the trash. "Which part? The part where she says Sherry's trying to get him back? Or about Kent's other girlfriends?"

"Greg's not going anywhere, you know that." Amy put her hand on mine. "You do know he's crazy about you, right?"

"Aunt Jackie said it yesterday, ex-wife trumps new girlfriend." I pushed back the tears I'd been carrying around all morning. I'd woken up from a bad dream early that morning, and not even a fast-paced run with Emma on our favorite stretch of beach had calmed my nerves.

"In death, not in real life." Amy fell silent for a minute. "Okay, I'll go with you."

"Thanks." I wiped the back of my hand over my eyes, feeling stupid for letting my fear show.

"Hold on. I'm not done." Amy swung her purse over her shoulder. "I'll go with you, if you tell Greg everything before we leave. I don't care if it's by voice mail or snail-mail letter. I'd feel better if someone knew where we were going before we disappeared."

"Aunt Jackie knows the story."

"And she's somewhere in the city having fun with Mary." Amy shook her head. "If this is Kent's murderer and she gets upset while we're talking to her, I want to know someone has our backs."

"Fine, I'll tell Greg." I swung a towel over my shoulder. "If you stop freaking about Justin."

"That's different." Amy walked toward the door. When she reached for the handle, I heard her say, "But I'll try."

I watched her walking toward the bike rental shop and her apartment wondering when Amy had started feeling this way about Justin. And what the guy was thinking, hurting my friend.

Don't get involved in others' problems. It only limits your own potential. The advice from the Tiger Lady's book echoed in my head. But wasn't that what friendship was about? Caring for others when they didn't have the strength to carry themselves? I'd read halfway through the book a few nights ago and had to put it away. The author was self-absorbed and teaching others how to be the same way. Sherry, however, could give this woman lessons. I glanced over at the small self-help section of the bookstore and wondered if there was anything about not letting people walk all over you and not turning into a complete jerk. After wasting all that time reading, I realized my life didn't have as many problems as I'd thought when I started the book. Maybe being hooked on investigating murders and solving puzzles was one of my strengths rather than a weakness.

The bell on the door kept me from walking over to the shelf and the steady stream of customers kept me busy until Toby arrived at one to take over the rest of the day.

"Hey, boss, you look stressed." He glanced around the shop; all the tables were filled with tourists. "You should have called me in early. I was just hanging around the house with the girls."

Toby's new girlfriend kept him busy with repairs to the small cottage she'd bought the last year. That and playing with Isabell, her daughter. The guy had a full life, especially since he worked two jobs.

"If it got worse, I would have called for help." I put the back of my hand on my forehead and batted my eyelashes. "You know a woman can't handle much more."

"Fine, I get it. You're a grown woman and I'm just a jerk trying to help." Toby put on his Wired Up apron and started setting up the coffee bar for his shift. "But my mama raised me to be polite and offer, so I guess you're just stuck with me."

"I'm teasing." I thought about the self-help books. Maybe Toby would have a suggestion. "Hey, do you know of any books about being assertive without turning into a complete . . ."

"Tiger?" When he looked into my face, he laughed. "I saw the book in your purse. Listen, you're just fine the way you are. Sure, you care about what people in your life think. But everyone does, except people like that author, who probably doesn't have a family or friends who will still talk to her."

I shrugged. "I don't know. I keep hearing I should be more confident."

"Why don't you sit down? I'll get you a piece of cheesecake, and you can tell Father Toby all about your problem." Toby swung a towel over his shoulder and leaned over the counter, resting on his forearms.

"I prefer the anonymity of a good shrink book, thank you anyway." I laughed and took my own apron off. "Besides, I'm meeting Amy this afternoon to run into Bakerstown."

I left off the part about stopping by the model's house to see if she'd killed Kent. If things went right, I'd have Greg's investigation solved and we'd be able to spend Monday at the beach. Or Greg would be mad and not talking to me for a week or more. I paused and thought about my promise to Amy.

Toby hadn't moved from his spot, where he still watched me. When I turned back, he shook his head and backed away, dumping out an almost-empty pot of coffee to make more. "I know that look. You're going to get me in trouble."

"I'm just leaving an address with you, just in case." I quickly wrote the information on the back of a take-out menu card Aunt Jackie had printed up last month.

Toby stared at the paper like it might bite him. "In case of what?"

"If you don't hear from me this evening, give this to Greg and tell him Amy and I went to visit with this woman." I tried for an innocent look. "No big deal, Amy just wants someone to know where we are. The whole Kent thing has her spooked."

I could see Toby's mind whirling as he tested the idea, and then he nodded, letting me off the hook for additional questions. "I know Justin's kind of a mess right now. The guy called me last night and we talked for over an hour about life and death. I didn't think we were friends, but I felt bad for the guy."

And now I felt bad for lying to Toby. But instead of backing up, I kept going. "Amy's worried about him. It will do her good to get out of town for a few hours today."

He picked up the menu card and tapped it on the counter. "What time should I send in reinforcements if you don't call?"

I calculated the drive time and a few stops in town, like maybe a mani-pedi appointment. "I'll call you before nine. Does that work? Or do you have plans tonight?"

"Nine's fine. I'm heading back to the apartment tonight to do some laundry and grocery shopping for the week. You know, bachelor stuff."

A woman who'd just entered the store approached the counter. I recognized her as one of Toby's cosmetology school regulars. "You know you don't have to be a bachelor, Toby darling. I'm sure I'm not the only woman who'd be glad to do your laundry for a few concessions on your part."

Toby started making the woman's drink. "Now, Debbie, you know I'm dating someone right now. I can't be playing the field if I'm going to get anyone to take me seriously."

"Who says it has to be serious?" The woman winked at me. "I'd settle for a few one-night stands."

I decided it was time for me to leave. "I'll call you later. Have a good shift."

As I walked out the door, I heard Debbie laughing at Toby's response. Toby had a way of making every woman who walked into the shop feel special. Even if he was off the dating market.

I walked home and got ready for our secret agent outing. I took the laptop and printed off a copy of the Facebook page, writing down the Bakerses' information from the local phone book. I grabbed a few bottles of water, put them and an ice pack into a minicooler, and grabbed Emma's leash. She could at least lick the attacker to death if we were put into a difficult position.

I packed it all up in my Jeep, put Emma in the backseat, and headed back into town. I parked on the street in front of the bike rental shop where Amy rented the top floor apartment, right behind Sadie's Pies on the Fly tiny car. The PT Cruiser was hard to miss with the dark purple color and the big slice of pie logo applied to each door, including the hatchback in the rear. I rolled down the windows for Emma, told my dog I'd be a few minutes, and headed toward Amy's door.

Sadie left the bike rental shop at the same time, her face turning a bright pink as soon as she saw me. "Oh, Jill, I didn't expect to see you here. Isn't today your day off?"

I felt my lips curl upward into a large grin. "I bet you didn't. And yes, typically, this is the start of my weekend, but Aunt Jackie took the day off. What are you doing? Planning a bike trip?"

Sadie slapped me on the arm. She looked around and, lowering her voice, she muttered, "You know what I'm doing here. I just don't want the whole town or Darla to find out."

"You're right about that. If Darla knew you were dating Dustin Austin, it would be front-page news." I gave her a quick hug. "Don't worry, your sex life isn't the most interesting thing going on in South Cove these days."

Sadie's face turned a brighter shade of red. "Don't say 'sex life.' It's trashy. I don't want to be seen as a wanton woman."

Honest to God, I broke out into giggles. When I could catch my breath, I wiped my eyes and focused on the now-frowning Sadie. "There is no one in town who would ever call you wanton. You're the most churchgoing, friendly, helpful, caring, and utterly awesome woman in town."

Sadie inched toward her car. "Well, that being said, I still don't want to be a subject of gossip. I'll see you Tuesday morning with your shop order."

And with that, she put the car into gear and almost burned rubber getting away from me. I turned and found Amy standing next to me, watching Sadie leave.

"What's got into her? She's been acting weird lately." Amy went over to the car and gave Emma a pat on the head, before ordering her to return to the backseat. She waited for my dog to settle on the backseat before opening the passenger door. Emma liked Amy and listened to her. Not like me. Sometimes I can talk till I'm blue in the face, and my dog will still ignore my commands.

I climbed into the driver's seat and wondered what I should say. Amy was my best friend. But I considered Sadie a friend, too. Finally, I went with a shrug. "Beats me."

Fortunately Amy had already moved on to the next topic: Justin and his issues. As I drove, Amy listed off all the positive and negative qualities of the man. As we pulled into Bakerstown, I realized she was doing a pros and cons list. "Are you thinking about breaking up with him over this Kent thing?"

It was Amy's turn to shrug. "I don't know. But it's weird, isn't it? You've found a dead body before and you didn't go all hermit on me."

She was right. I had found a couple of dead bodies in the last year. First Miss Emily, who appeared to have died in her sleep. Then last fall, I'd been the one to notice that Ted Hendricks had taken a bullet to the brain in his precious Mustang. I keyed the address into my GPS and waited for it to load. "You're wrong about one thing. Finding someone dead does leave a mark. Even on me. I guess I just handled it differently than Justin is. Cut the guy some slack."

Amy stared out the window as the GPS told us where to go. "Now you think I'm a bad person."

"I do not think you're a bad person. You're jumping to conclusions because you're scared, that's all." I thought about the fear I'd seen in my friend's face when she'd told me Justin wanted to take her home for Christmas. "He's a good guy. Let him work it out."

The GPS lady told me to take the next left and we'd be at our destination. I turned down the wide residential street and slowed to check out the minimansions on what appeared to be acre lots. "I sure hope Pat was wrong about this woman. Seems like dating Kent would be a downgrade in status."

Amy was focused on the large houses, too. "I don't know. I hear Kent had a few bucks stashed. He was always flashing money like he made it at the bank. With a printing press or something, I mean."

Something Amy said was making my internal radar go crazy. Kent and the bank and his apparent wealth. Made sense that Sherry would go for that type. He had the money to keep her in the style that she preferred, if not deserved. I was trying to focus on the niggle when Amy pointed to the left. "That's the house."

I pulled the Jeep to the side of the road and watched as a woman dressed in a sleek tracksuit, opened the door to the house leading a large wolfhound. I heard Emma's whine from the backseat. "And that's her. Stay here with Emma."

I quickly clambered out of the Jeep and sprinted over to meet the woman before she started her run. She glanced up and put a hand on her dog, who immediately sat by her side. A great trick and one I wished Emma could learn. "Evelyn Baker?" I called as I walked toward her. "We need to talk about Kent Paine."

CHAPTER 12

The woman's face went from a bright welcoming smile to a look of fear, her long black hair making her tanned skin seem twice as pale. She glanced toward the house, then nodded. "Can we walk?"

I fell into step beside her. "So you knew him." I let the statement hang, wondering how she would play this.

We'd reached the end of the first block when she nodded. "I knew him. And if you're here asking questions, you know I had an indiscretion with him."

"I've heard rumors." I looked both ways before we crossed the street, but the neighborhood was oddly quiet for a Sunday afternoon. Too many people out of town or just enjoying a weekend afternoon out on their back deck.

"His girlfriend confronted me at the modeling gig. I thought it was funny he wanted me to take the job, but he said he knew the owner and it would be a big favor to him." She shook her head. "I think he wanted to break it off without him doing the heavy lifting."

"So you stopped seeing him?" I thought back on the Business-to-Business meeting from hell and the gleam in Sherry's eyes as she talked to Kent.

"That woman told me if I didn't, she would e-mail my husband. And she said she had pictures." She quickly added, "I don't know whether that's true. I mean, we never took shots while we were together, but you never know what type of games people play. I never would have started something with him if I'd thought he was with someone."

The irony of her morality around sleeping with an attached man didn't escape me. "It was okay for you to cheat, but not him?"

She sighed and pulled the dog away from a flower bed he was attempting to flatten. "You may not believe me, but I respect marriage. My husband and I have an open arrangement. Mostly on his side. He likes to experiment. I guess I was feeling lonely and Kent just kind of was there."

Not my type of relationship, but who was I to judge? "You wouldn't mind if your husband found out? So why did you stop seeing Kent?"

"Because I minded that he was cheating." She put her hand on my arm and turned me to look at her. "Believe me, I have no interest in messing with anyone's relationship. He told me he was single."

We started walking again, and I thought about Evelyn's reasoning. It made sense in a twisted way.

"And before you ask, I was at a play with my husband in the city on Wednesday. We drove up Tuesday night and came back Thursday. I didn't kill Kent." There was intensity to her words and I believed her.

"Date night?" I didn't like the snark in my voice, but there it was anyway.

"Look, we're trying. He's agreed to stop sleeping around and I told him about Kent. I think he just needed to know I'd play the game, too, if he didn't stop." Evelyn let the dog's leash extend as she continued. "Kent was my financial advisor. I have a little money my grandmother left me, so he was helping me invest. I don't know much about the stock market, so he was teaching me what to buy and what to stay away from."

"And one night it went too far?" I guessed.

A strained smile crossed her face. "One night we were celebrating the stock split of an investment. We bought wine for dinner. Thomas was out of town, and, well, you know the rest."

"I need to ask: Would your husband kill Kent because of your relationship?" I studied the woman and knew she'd had the same thought.

We were at the end of a cul de sac and turned back toward the house before she spoke. "I don't think so. Honestly, I don't think he cares that much what I do."

I said my good-byes and wished Evelyn Baker well. Watching her walk up the steps toward her beautiful home, I hoped she could find some peace within the stone walls. Having worked family law, I knew women sometimes stayed in relationships longer than they should for all the wrong reasons—including big houses.

I climbed into the car and got a wet doggy kiss from Emma. Amy put her phone into her purse, watching me expectantly. When I didn't answer before I started the Jeep and pulled a U-turn toward the highway, she prompted, "Well?"

"I don't think she killed Kent." I hit the speed-dial for the shop and Toby answered.

"Coffee, Books, and More, what can I prepare for you today?" His low voice filled the cab of the Jeep and Emma let out a short, friendly bark. "Oh, hey, Emma. Who's a good girl?"

Emma wiggled in her seat and smiled in her doggy way. I took my eyes off the rearview mirror and my happy pet and focused back on the road. "Oh, she is. I guess you have this effect on all types of females, huh?"

"Now, boss, don't go dogging on my special talent. It brings in the business." Toby laughed and I heard him welcome a customer into the store. "I take it you're fine and on your way home?"

"Definitely. Just wanted to check in. See you on Tuesday." I clicked off the phone and snuck a glance at Amy.

"You told Toby, not Greg?"

"You said someone needed to know where we were going. There was no reason to get Greg all upset before we knew something." I sped up and merged into the highway traffic.

"And now?" Amy prodded.

I sighed and turned up the music. One of my favorite dance tunes from the eighties was talking about the abundance of men. I hoped it was true since my boyfriend just might dump me after this stunt. "Now I have something to tell him."

I dropped Amy off at her apartment, waving at Dustin Austin as he sat in the sun, dressed in a Hawaiian shirt and khaki shorts, looking more like a tourist than a local business owner. The only thing that identified him as a professional was the laptop he had powered up on the table. As I watched, he turned the screen down as Amy walked by. Typical, he was probably surfing porn.

When I got home, I let Emma out the back, filled a Crock-Pot with a couple of frozen chicken breasts and a jar of salsa, and sat on the back porch with my phone in my hand. I took a sip of the iced tea I'd poured and speed-dialed Greg's cell.

"Hey, you." His voice came over the line warm and deep, and for a second, I regretted I'd ever made the trip into town. But you can't change the past.

"Hey, yourself. Can you stop by the house for a few minutes? We need to talk." My heartbeat raised as I waited for his answer.

"You ditching me for a younger man? Maybe someone who has bankers' hours and weekends off?" He chuckled.

"Not funny. I just need to tell you something." I threw the ball Emma had dropped on my feet out to the yard.

"I'll be over in a couple of minutes. I need to take a break or I'll blind myself on all this paperwork anyway." He paused. "You aren't in trouble, are you?"

"No. Just come over." I felt the distance between us growing as the call extended. No way was he going to just take the information I had and run with it. It was time to pay the piper and 'fess up that I'd been playing amateur detective again. "Please."

"Give me five minutes." Then he hung up. No "love you," no "see you soon," only a dial tone. Yep, I was in for a lecture. Or worse.

I was still outside when his truck pulled into the driveway. When I heard the knock, I called out, "On the porch."

He came around the corner and my heart rate sped up. With long dark Wrangler jeans, boots, a pressed sheriff's shirt, and his black Stetson, he looked like a hero out of one of the romance novels I had shelved at the store. He leaned against the porch rail and folded his arms. "What have you done now?"

"That obvious?" I pulled my legs up under me and settled in for the ride.

"Honey, I can read you like one of those books you sell." He leaned down to pet Emma, then tossed her ball out to the backyard. "So spill."

"I'm trying to figure out where to start." I took a sip of tea. "You remember the woman who followed Kent out of the store the day we had the Business-to-Business meeting at Vintage Duds? The model?"

"Vaguely." Greg's eyebrows raised. "Who was she?"

"Long dark hair, skinny, her name's Evelyn Baker. Pat told me that she was having an affair with Kent." This time, I threw the ball for Emma.

He pressed his lips together. "Pat told you? When did you start hanging around with her?"

"Amy and I had drinks with Sherry and Pat a few days ago, but I'm not her friend. She came over yesterday out of the blue. You can ask Aunt Jackie, she was here when Pat showed up." I shook my head. "Anyway, Pat said Sherry thinks you're convinced she killed Kent, so Pat wanted me to know there were other suspects."

"Typical. You should have sent her right to me rather than listening to her stories. You know she'll say and do anything for Sherry. When we were married, Pat lied to me countless times on where my wife was and who she was with." Greg's eyes darkened. "Can't you just stay out of things?"

"I got curious, so sue me. Aunt Jackie wrote down the list of names Pat gave me, and I started looking them up."

"How are you looking people up? If Esmeralda gave you passwords to the office servers, I'm going to fire her." He frowned. "Or was it Toby?"

I held my hand up. "Stop. I looked the names up on Facebook."

Greg laughed. He kept laughing. Then he threw Emma's ball again and wiped the moisture from his eyes. "Okay, super sleuth. What did Facebook tell you?"

Okay, so maybe Facebook wasn't a high-tech search engine, but I had found something. "I went through the list of names and found that Evelyn Baker is married to Thomas Baker and maybe had something to hide from her husband."

"Like an affair with Kent."

I nodded. "So Amy and I drove to Bakerstown to talk to her today."

"Are you kidding me? You just drove off to her house and accused her of killing Kent?" He leaned closer. "How'd that turn out? I didn't get a call from the Bakerstown police that you'd been thrown in jail."

"I was more tactful than that." I thought about my approach and decided I didn't have to tell Greg everything. "Anyway, she claims to have an open marriage and she was in the city the night Kent was killed. With her husband."

"So neither one could have killed him?" Greg pulled a notepad out of his pants pocket. "Give me their names and address again. I'll check them out, just in case. Sherry is throwing anyone and everyone under the bus to keep her own butt out of jail."

I listed off the names and then gave up the other thing I hadn't told Greg. "The afternoon of the dress rehearsal, I saw Kent making out at the beach with some girl."

He tapped the notebook. "This woman?"

It was my turn to shrug. "Unless she was wearing a red wig, someone else was kissing Kent's face off in the car."

"I've got to get back to the office and see if we can pull footage from the beach cameras. You should have mentioned this before."

I had tried to tell him, but he'd brushed me off. "Look, I've been trying to tell you about her, but . . ."

Greg's phone rang. He scowled at the display, then took the call. "I'll be back at the desk in ten minutes tops. Can't this wait?"

I heard a man's voice on the other end. Tim took dispatch calls on the weekends when Esmeralda had readings. Greg's gaze caught mine as he returned the phone to his side holster.

"What's wrong?"

He walked over to me and sat next to me on the bench. "Jill, it's your aunt."

My stomach rolled at his words, and I couldn't hear from the blood rushing in my ears. I repeated my question, not sure I wanted an answer. "What's going on?"

"She's been arrested."

CHAPTER 13

Mary Sullivan met Amy and me on the courthouse steps. We'd driven not to the city, where my aunt had claimed to be taking a girls' night, but instead, the short distance to Bakerstown for the second time that day. Greg had offered to come, but I knew he wanted to work the Kent case. Besides, with Amy riding along, at least we'd talked during the drive.

Greg had called as we pulled into Bakerstown, letting us know he'd gotten my aunt released to his custody. Moreover, he wanted us to stop at the station so he could have a chat with her. I had a feeling neither of us were going to be on Greg's good list for a while.

Mary pulled me into a hug. "I'm so glad you're here. Jackie told me not to call anyone, that she'd talk her way out of it, but then she didn't come out. I waited in the car forever, but I was getting nervous."

"You should have called anyway," I chided, sounding more like a mom picking wayward teens up from their night of street racing than the two older women.

When Mary's face crumpled into tears and she leaned against my shoulder, I knew I was preaching to the wrong party. "I know," she sobbed into my T-shirt.

I passed her over to Amy. "Why don't you wait here and I'll go get Aunt Jackie. Amy can drive her car home and the two of you can ride with me." *Where I can keep an eye out on you* was what I didn't add.

I pulled the big doors open and stopped to drop my purse and clean out my pockets for the metal detector. Security had heightened even in little counties like ours. Although the last time someone had brought a gun into the courthouse, it had more to do with a cheating wife than terrorism. The guard nodded me through and I retrieved my items.

Greg had told me Aunt Jackie would be waiting for me at the county sheriff's office. I checked the building directory and headed up to the second floor. When I reached the top of the stairs, the waiting room was crowded with women and children. Confused, I walked up to the desk. The officer sitting there must have been in her twenties, her dark hair pulled back into a severe bun. She looked up from her computer. "Sign the log and we'll be starting visitation in ten minutes. You're cutting it pretty close. I'm closing out the group right now. Did you bring your license?"

"I'm not here for visiting hours." No wonder the room was filled. "I came to pick up my aunt? Jackie Ekroth. Greg King from South Cove talked to someone about her release?"

The woman focused on her computer. "Hold on. I've got to finish the visitation group, then I'll get your aunt. I think she's in the drunk tank." The officer nodded to the rows of benches near the wall. "Have a seat. It will be a few minutes."

I turned around and viewed the room. Finally, I spied a spot next to a young woman with a three-year-old at her feet and a crying baby on her lap. No wonder no one wanted to sit next to her.

When she looked at me, I nodded a greeting and smiled. "The baby is pretty." Although really, all I could see was the red face scrunched up in an Amazonian yell.

The girl laughed. "She is, just not right now. I don't understand why she always gets so upset when we visit Thom. It's like she knows her daddy did a bad thing and she's upset about it."

"Daddy is in jail," the little boy repeated. "He did a bad, bad thing."

I pressed my lips together, trying not to smile. "I'm sorry to hear that."

The girl held out her hand. "I'm Mary Beth. This is my little boy, Jax, and the princess, Lizzie."

"Nice to meet you. I'm Jill." I guessed first-name anonymity at jail visitation was the protocol. "You have a beautiful family."

"Thanks. I'm trying. As soon as Thom gets out, we're going to move to Oregon and live on a farm. My uncle has already found us a place to live and Thom a job. I think getting him out of the area will help."

"Sounds like you have a plan." I smiled at the baby, who had stopped crying and was now staring at me, waving a chubby pink hand.

"It's a new start." She pushed her son's hair out of his eyes and then asked, "What's your man in for?"

"Oh, I'm not here to visit." I wondered how much information this woman I'd just met would share with a total stranger. "I'm picking up."

The girl looked at me, nodding. "You didn't look like one of us."

"Line up against the right wall for visitation," a male guard called out and everyone stood, grabbing their children's hands and stepping toward the line.

Mary Beth rose and took Jax's hand. "Good luck with everything." She smiled and then disappeared into the crowd.

When the room cleared, the woman at the desk waved me toward her. "She's coming out now. You can meet her over at the left door."

I stepped toward the steel door and waited. When it opened, Aunt Jackie emerged. She was dressed in black cashmere pants and a black sweater. Her normally poufed hair had been pulled back and she pulled a beanie out of her bag, covering her hair quickly. She was without makeup, and when she saw me, her face paled. "Jill, I didn't expect you to be here. Where's Mary?"

"She's in the car with Amy. Give me your keys, you're riding home with me so we can talk. Amy can drive your car back to South Cove." My voice held a hint of displeasure. For the second time in less than a few minutes, I wondered why I was taking the parental role and how long it would be before it happened more often. My aunt was getting older, and I was her only relative. Could this be the start of some type of dementia?

As we walked out of the courthouse, Aunt Jackie dug in her purse for her sunglasses. "Hold up, can't have the paparazzi recognizing me."

Holding the door open, I groaned. "Seriously? You spend a night in jail and that's all you got?"

Aunt Jackie strode past me. "I didn't spend a night in jail. You need to get your facts straight. I've only been in the big house for"—she looked down to check her watch—"five hours. It would have been less if they would have let Mary bail me out."

I herded her toward my car. "Why were you arrested anyway? What about your girls' night out with Mary?"

We'd reached Mary and Amy by then, and Mary flew out of the car to hug my aunt. "I was so worried. I can't believe you did all of this for me. You're an amazing friend."

"Wait, what did she do for you?" My Spidey sense was tickling.

Aunt Jackie shrugged and handed Amy her keys. "I'll tell you on the way home. I seriously need a shower and a change of clothes after sitting on that awful cot for so long. And a bathroom. Did you know they have metal toilets in your cell? With absolutely no privacy? No way was I going to give the guards a peep show." She stopped Mary. "Do you still have the notebook?"

Mary nodded and took a brown leather-covered notebook out of her purse and handed it to Aunt Jackie.

"This is going to fix everything, you'll see." Aunt Jackie hugged Mary and sent her off with Amy in the direction of her car.

When we got into the Jeep, I turned down the stereo. "You want to tell me what's going on now?"

"Of course. We had to get evidence that Mary was swindled, and it's all right here. That travel agency takes money up front, then refuses to book the trips without additional funds. More than a trip to the moon would cost." She tapped the book. "The proof's all right here."

"Wait, you broke into a travel agency and stole their records?" I glanced in horror at the book in my aunt's hands. The verification that could land her in jail for her breaking-and-entering charge. "Throw that out the window."

"Now, Jill, don't be silly. They aren't going to charge me with B&E, because if they do, I'm going to prove they are crooks. This book"—she held it up for emphasis—"proves that they were scamming a lot more people than just poor Mary."

"Why didn't she use their regular agent? I don't understand why she went with someone like this." I kept my eyes on the narrow highway, wanting to stop at the beach and run some negative energy off, but I drove past the parking entrance and toward South Cove.

"Mary was trying to surprise Bill for their anniversary. Nice sentiment, but poor execution. She really does have a good heart." Aunt Jackie turned and stared out the window. "Your uncle Ted gave me a cruise for our tenth anniversary, then one for every five years after. He called it our marital checkup time."

"You still miss him." I hadn't really known Uncle Ted. He worked a lot of hours and wasn't home the times I visited.

"Every day." Aunt Jackie patted my leg. "Thanks for coming to save me. I suspect your boyfriend is a little miffed at me."

"You and me both today." I turned the Jeep onto Main Street and drove past my house. I'd turned a light on before I left, and the house glowed a friendly welcome. "He wants to talk to you before you head back to the apartment."

"I figured. You don't have to wait, my dear. I'll have Amy leave my car at the station and I can drive it back to the apartment. Thanks for covering for me today."

I should have walked her inside, but a part of me felt relief when she refused my company. "This is one conversation I need to have alone with our local detective."

Waving to Amy, I drove back to the house, parked my Jeep, and unlocked my door. Emma was outside the back door, waiting for me. I let her in and went to the sink to get a glass of water.

My aunt had put herself in danger to help a friend. Was my playing investigator making her reckless, as well? Was I being reckless? I sat and stared at my list of suspects for Kent's murder. I crossed off Evelyn Baker. After talking to her that morning, I knew she couldn't hurt a fly. Maybe I should leave this investigation to Greg. He was a detective, after all.

I finished the water, locked up the house, and took a book upstairs with me to read myself to sleep. But sleep came late, long after I'd turned off the lamp near my bed.

The next morning, sunshine streamed into my bedroom window, waking me and letting me know I'd slept way too long. I needed to talk to Aunt Jackie. I needed to call Greg and let him know I wouldn't be doing anything stupid ever again. I'd been on the other side of finding out someone you loved was taking risks with their life. I needed to go cold turkey from now on.

Emma raced me to the kitchen, where I let her out and made a pot of coffee. I'd just had time to brush my teeth and pull my hair into a ponytail when I heard the knock on the door. Greg stood on the porch, petting Emma when I peeked out the side window, another resolution I'd made in the wee hours of morning.

"What are you doing out so early?" I swung open the door and he stepped into the living room, pulling me into a tight hug and covering my mouth with his own.

When he pulled back, I saw the smile on his face. "Good morning, beautiful."

A buzzing sound filled my ears, and all of a sudden, I was back in bed. Emma put her cold nose on my cheek, and my alarm was blaring. Greg's kiss still felt warm on my lips. I needed to talk to him today. I dragged myself out of bed, the sunshine not warming my face as brightly as it had in my dream, and went to let Emma out, for what seemed to be the second time that morning.

I sat with my cup of coffee and made up a to-do list. I had to make a third trip into Bakerstown in the last two days, this time for groceries. My cupboard and Emma's bag of dog food was down to crumbs. The only things I had in my fridge were the leftover cheesecakes I'd brought home from the store on Sunday and a bag of caramel-flavored coffee beans. I could make it another day or two, but Emma would be hunting down small animals in the yard. Which might just include Esmeralda's cat, Maggie, if she pulled her Houdini act again today.

I planned for two weeks of healthy dinners, adding in a few necessities, like a bag of kettle-cooked chips and a few bags of fun-size candy bars. The only thing fun about the bags was how long it took you to unwrap the things. But I liked having one or two after a run, just to keep my blood sugar up.

Oh, the lies I told myself. I went through the kitchen, laundry room, and bathroom, to make sure I didn't need any other supplies, and when I was done, I had a complete list.

I glanced at the clock. If I threw a load of laundry into the washer, I'd have time for a run with Emma to clear my head. Then I could stop by the police station, and with a bit of luck, Greg would be at his desk and we could talk.

The beach was empty, mostly due to the hour and the fact that the tourists this time of year tended to be weekenders. They were all back in their cubicles by now, making money for their next trip, while I got to enjoy the sound of the gulls and splashing waves any day of the week. After a few minutes, I let Emma off the leash and we ran side by side to the large rock. The cliffs started a few steps more and I sat on the beach, getting my breath back and watching Emma explore the water. The gulls kept flying over her, wondering what this dog was doing on their turf and probably hoping she'd find something they could eat after we left.

Sitting there, I thought about my dream that morning. I'd been convinced I needed to keep away from investigating, not only for my own sake, but for the people I loved. Greg would be happier, I knew that. And what kind of example was I setting for Aunt Jackie, who just got arrested for her own detective work? But I realized it didn't matter. My natural curiosity was part of me. And probably something I'd inherited from my aunt. I knew what I was going to say to Greg this morning, and for once, I felt confident about the discussion.

Looking back on the Tiger book, its ideas had been out of my comfort zone, because they weren't me. I wasn't aggressive, or in your face. I was me. And that was enough. Curious, determined, headstrong, and caring. I stood up and brushed the sand off my running shorts. Maybe I had just found the secret to happiness: being true to yourself.

As Emma and I ran back to the parking lot and the rest of my day, I thought about what I enjoyed and hoped that Greg would see my epiphany as a good thing, rather than the straw that broke the camel's back. Either way, we needed to talk.

Showered and changed into jeans and a peasant blouse, I started the Jeep and took a right to go into South Cove. At the police station, Esmeralda sat at the desk reading a biography of a recent First Lady. The woman had become a good customer, even if I had to order in most of her choices. There wasn't much of a market for the books she enjoyed, but that was the good thing about reading. You didn't have to follow the trends. You could read anything you wanted. And the dispatcher/fortune-teller did. The one thing I never ordered for her was what I'd expected, the magical arts books.

"How's the story?" I nodded toward the book. I'd been interested in how anyone could have stood by her man in such a public way, but not enough to actually read the biography.

She smiled and put a bookmark into the book, laying it on the counter. "I never knew how much she'd struggled, even before becoming First Lady. That's one job I'd never want. Too many people up in your business."

"Kind of like living in a small town, right?" I joked.

Esmeralda cocked her head. "I wasn't going to ask how your aunt was, but since you brought it up. What the heck was she thinking?"

"If I knew that, I could rule the world. You know Aunt Jackie works on a different set of rules for herself." I nodded toward Greg's closed door. "My guy in yet?"

She nodded. "Something came up this morning and he's been locked in there with Doc Ames for a good hour now."

"On Kent's murder?" The question came out of my mouth before I could stop it. So much for good intentions.

Esmeralda shrugged. "Greg doesn't talk to me much lately. I get the feeling he's trying to keep the investigation under wraps." She laughed. "Like I'd tell anyone. You wouldn't believe the secrets people tell me during readings. I need to write a book someday, but it would be going against the professional code of ethics."

"Fortune-tellers have a code of ethics?" I'd never considered that they might be like lawyers or doctors.

"Maybe not all of them, but I do. That's why you have to make sure your psychic consultant is trustworthy. Many of the people in the business are trying to get rich, no matter what the method." She picked up the phone. "Let me tell him you're here."

I pressed my lips together, trying not to smile at the image of a convention full of fortune-tellers dressed in their gypsy finest, sitting in a ballroom, listening to speakers. Maybe they had topics like *Ten Ways to Reach the Departed Quickly*, or *Reaching Out to the Historical Dead, Things to Consider*, or even *Fashion Tips to Upsell Your Predictions*.

"He says to go on in." Esmeralda broke into my daydream, her look amused.

Maybe she could read minds, but I knew she could read body language better than anyone I'd met, and my face heated as I thanked her and quickly turned toward Greg's office.

Doc Ames stood as I entered the small office. "Hey, Jill, nice to see you."

"At least you're not trying to break up a catfight this time." I extended my hand to the coroner and smiled. "I thought those women were going to plow right through you."

"Emotions around a loved one's death can be extreme." He looked at Greg. "I'm heading back to Bakerstown. Did you need anything else?"

Greg shook his head. "Thanks for driving out this early. I could have come to you."

Doc Ames waved off the comment. "Does me good to get out of the office. I enjoy driving the coastal highway; it clears my head."

I thought about all the work the man did with the dead and the families of the dead and wondered if a short drive would be enough to bring him back to the world of the living. Every time I saw Doc, he was cheerful and kind to everyone he met. That would be a hard act to keep up day in and day out. Maybe he went home and punched the wall—or maybe he was just a caring man.

"Well, I appreciate your time. Let me walk you out." Greg smiled at me. Not quite the smile he had during my dream, but not the scowl I'd expected after yesterday. "I'll be right back, honey."

I settled into the chair that Doc had left and pulled out my shopping list. I needed flea treatment for Emma and I'd forgotten to write it down. I dug in my purse for a pen, but came up empty. So I reached over onto Greg's desk and promptly knocked a few loose sheets of paper onto the floor. Sighing, I set down the notebook and gathered up the pages. It was the tox screen for Kent. Two words stood out, written in Greg's neat block style. *Cocaine use* and *poison*—epibatidine. I wrote the unfamiliar name down on my shopping list and had just sat back down when Greg came back into the room.

He kissed me on the cheek as he passed by. "Hey, you, I'd hoped I'd see you today. I planned on stopping by this morning, but I got a call from Doc that he needed to see me."

Funny, my dream had been almost on target, yet the day had turned out differently. I shook the coincidence away. "I know I shouldn't ask, but was it something on Kent's murder?"

Greg sat in the chair behind his desk, gathered up the loose papers, and put them into a manila folder. "Yep. Seems like the rumors of his drug use were true. But there's more that we can't figure out."

"Like?" I pushed.

"Good try." He leaned back and put his hands behind his head. "Have you talked to your aunt today?"

I shook my head. "Not yet. Did she tell you why she was in that office?"

Greg pulled out a different folder and read aloud. "The man is a scammer and needs to be put in jail." He closed the file. "Direct quote."

"She seems to be on some kind of a mission. Mary was taken by this guy, and Aunt Jackie believes she can fix the problem." I leaned forward. "Tell me the truth, is she going to serve time for this?"

Greg rubbed his face. "Hell, I can't even confirm that she's going to be charged. I guess the district attorney is on some type of Caribbean vacation, and no one else wants to make the decision."

"Jailing an old lady on a mission may not look good in an election year." I thought about our county DA. He'd made no secret of his plans for the governor's seat in the future.

He laughed. "I believe you understand this game. That's the one reason I'm not looking to hold an elected office. Even though the mayor keeps putting my name up for the county positions."

"Mayor Baylor is promoting you? Isn't that a good thing?" This was the first I'd heard about our mayor giving Greg props to anyone.

Greg cocked his head. "And if I got elected, who would be at my door wanting more favors than he already asks for? Now I can hold him off since the city council is the one who decides if I'm going to keep my job or not. Luckily, most of them like me."

"I hadn't thought about it that way." Thinking of my own appointment to the council as the business liaison, I'd thought the mayor had kept me on because no one else wanted the job. Maybe he didn't have the power to get rid of me. I'd have to talk to Bill Sullivan about the details one of these days. Bill was the head of the council and knew everything. And he liked me. Or at least he did before Aunt Jackie almost got his wife arrested.

"Anyway, can we plan dinner tonight? I'd take you out, but with this case, I think we need to grill. I'll do the cooking, though. What do you have on hand?" Greg leaned forward, looking at my shopping list.

I quickly pulled it toward me with the borrowed pen. "On hand? Cheesecake and coffee. I'm heading to Bakerstown to shop. What do you want me to pick up?"

We batted around a menu between surf or turf or both, and finally settled on kabobs. I'd marinate the meats and get the veggies chopped, and then Greg could grill when he arrived. He came around the desk as I stuffed the notebook into my purse.

"I'm sorry I was gruff yesterday." He kissed me. "I'll make it up tonight."

I pushed his hair out of his eyes. "You need a haircut."

"I thought you liked it long." He slapped me on the butt. "Get out of here, woman, you're a distraction."

"I bet you say that to all the women visiting your office," I teased but headed to the door. "See you tonight."

I didn't even feel bad about using my phone to Google the name of the unfamiliar poison when I got back to my car.

CHAPTER 14

First stop in Bakerstown was Pampered Pet Palace. The place was a gold mine for all things pet related. They had a vet on staff, grooming facilities, and of course, all the food, toys, or bones Emma could dream about. They allowed leashed pets to visit with their owners, but I'd left Emma home today because, although she could go into Pampered Pet, she'd have to stay in the car while I shopped for groceries. The back porch was cooler in the heat of the day.

As I wandered through the store, I passed through the fish and snake display. There, in a glass case, was the brightest-colored frog I'd ever seen. I waved over a clerk and pointed. "That's not a poison tree frog, is it?"

The young man smiled. "You know your frogs. That happens to be our newest addition. We've been carrying them for about a month, and they're selling like hotcakes."

"People buy them as pets? What about the poison?" The frog was strikingly beautiful, but I wouldn't want one. What if Emma decided to eat her new playmate?

The guy opened the top of the cage and pulled out the frog with his bare hands. I took an involuntary step backward. "Hold on, these guys are harmless. The poison comes from what they eat, and since these were domestically raised, they only have a trace of the stuff in their systems." He pointed to a little bump by the frog's ear. Or what should be the ear. "In the wild, the frog stores poison in this pouch, then uses it to hunt his dinner."

"So they're just cute frogs?" I stepped closer to get a better look at the creature.

"Pretty much. I mean, I sell a lot to men who want to look like badasses. They just don't realize the little guys are all talk and no bite." He held the frog toward me. "Want to hold him?"

Laughing, I stepped back again. "No thanks. I'm more of a furry, cuddly pet owner. I'm here for dog food."

I pushed the cart back to the dog food aisle, thinking about Kent's tox screen. If the poison only came from the tree frog, and domestic frogs didn't produce the poison, how in the heck did he get that particular poison in his system? It didn't make sense.

Checking out, I watched Anne from the bank walk into the store. I waved her over. "Hey, what are you doing out of South Cove? I would have thought you were working."

She tilted her head like she couldn't place me, then a slight smile lifted her face. "I work Saturdays so I'm off on Mondays." Anne nodded to the dog food. "I guess you are running errands, too?"

"Emma's too big to miss many meals." I swiped my debit card and punched in my code. "Let me guess, you have a cat."

"Sorry to burst the single-woman-cat-lady stereotype, but I'm more into the amphibian creatures. Snakes mostly and a few frogs. I know, not what you were expecting. See you in South Cove." Anne headed toward the back.

The clerk handed me my receipt. "Thanks for visiting Pampered Pet Palace. Come back soon."

I loaded up the dog food in the back of the Jeep and headed to the grocery store. Was it a coincidence that Kent's spurned lover owned frogs? She didn't say she owned the type that secreted poison, but then again, she didn't say she didn't. I couldn't even mention it to Greg without admitting I'd read the report from Doc Ames.

Deeper and deeper, my investigation addiction was causing me to question my ability to be honest with the one person who mattered. I threw a package of steak into the cart. No, this time I'd 'fess up sooner rather than later. I'd tell him what I'd seen at dinner. Greg wouldn't leave a half-eaten dinner just because I snuck a peek at an official report. Except, knowing Greg, I could see him doing just that.

Too late to change the path. Time to bite the bullet. After shopping, I pulled into my favorite drive-in, grabbed a fish sandwich, fries, and a vanilla shake, and headed home. The Bluetooth in the car buzzed over the radio and a familiar number popped on the screen.

"Hey, Aunt Jackie, I was planning on coming to see you today. You're not in jail again, are you?"

The silence went so long, I worried I'd lost connection. "Aunt Jackie?"

"I'm here. Just not appreciating the gallows humor today. Where are you? I've been knocking forever." Even over the phone line, I could tell when my aunt was steamed. And her anger seemed to be directed at me.

"I'm turning off the highway now. Had to make a run into Bakerstown." *Again*, I added silently. Of course, the first trip I'd made yesterday had nothing to do with my aunt, so I guess I couldn't blame her for that one.

"I'm on your porch. Don't park behind my car. I'm not staying long." And then she hung up. No "good-bye," no "see you soon." Yep, I was in trouble for something.

I pulled into the driveway next to Aunt Jackie's car and climbed out. I grabbed the sacks with items that needed to be put into the fridge or freezer and left the back open. Climbing the steps to the porch, I held out my keys to my aunt. "Open the door for me."

She took them and did as I asked. "You could have said *please*."

I trudged through the living room and set the bags on the table. "Sorry, please and thank you. I have one more load I have to bring in, can you put these away?"

Aunt Jackie set her purse on the table and dug into the first bag. "You really shouldn't buy frozen French fries. You don't need the calories."

"My kitchen, my food," I grumbled as I headed back outside to get the rest of the food. I'd have to bring in Emma's forty-pound bag last. With my aunt in a snit, I might just take the one more trip to grab it.

By the time I got the dog food settled into the mudroom by the washer, Aunt Jackie had put away all my groceries and started a pot of coffee. I glanced at the clock: 2 p.m. If I drank more than a cup, I'd be up past my workday bedtime. I sank into one of the kitchen chairs, exhausted from the trip. Shopping took its toll, even though it was just walking around and putting stuff in a cart.

"So, why are you so invested in Mary's problem?" I grabbed a cookie off the plate I'd set on the table that morning. "I've already heard your excuses. And I get it, the guy is a scammer, but why are you acting as the avenging superhero in this story?"

Aunt Jackie sat across from me. "I know I stepped over the line on this one. You don't have to rub it in. Did Greg say when they'd be charging me?"

"The DA's out of town, so I guess you're on hold." I bit into the cookie. "You didn't answer my question."

"Don't talk with your mouth full, it's unattractive." She leaned back in her chair. "Mary bought an all-inclusive Mexican cruise package for her anniversary as a surprise to Bill. When she told me what she paid for it, I was suspicious, but I figured she just got in on a good deal."

I took another bite of the snickerdoodle and waited. Sometimes Aunt Jackie's stories took a while.

"Then she came to me last week in tears. The guy told her that was just her down payment and he wanted another eight grand for the trip or she'd lose her deposit." She shook her head. "Two thousand is a good deal, ten is highway robbery. We called the Better Business Bureau and they took a report. I guess they'd heard a lot of the same story and they suggested Mary sue the guy to get her money back."

"Which is where you came in?" I popped the rest of the cookie into my mouth and went to the counter to pour coffee. This was going to be an extended discussion. I might need to call one of my former coworkers to get Aunt Jackie legal counsel, but first I wanted to know the entire story.

"I figured she'd have a stronger case if we could prove he was tricking people. He ran an advertisement in the *Bakerstown Senior Times* paper. Who knows how many people have just paid the extra money, thinking it was legit." She pulled out the leather notebook I'd seen Mary give her yesterday. "And this proves it. Jill, he targets the elderly, makes notes about how much he 'thinks' they have in their accounts, then jacks the price based on their ability to pay."

I glanced down at the notebook. "You realize that's proof you were in his office?"

Aunt Jackie stared at the cover. "It's also proof he's been robbing people. Greg can charge him with that, right?"

Financial law hadn't been one of my stronger subjects in law school. What I did know was it was darn hard to make a case against someone for fraud. My aunt had lost nearly all her retirement savings due to a pyramid scheme. I understood her need to help a friend.

I shrugged. "I don't know. I think we need to call in the big guns."

I pulled out my cell and dialed Matt's private line. He was the first associate in our group to make partner and crazy good with all the financial stuff. When I explained my aunt's problem, he agreed to meet with us after a late lunch on Tuesday. When I got off the phone, I smiled. "At least Matt thinks he can spin a case with the DA to get you off the criminal charge."

Aunt Jackie refilled her coffee cup and pushed the book toward me. "I want Mary to get her money back. Hold on to this for me. I'd hate to have the guy show up and strong-arm me for the evidence."

Now I was worried. "You think he would do that? Maybe you should stay here with me until this is cleared up?"

"No need. Josh is having dinner with me and will watch me lock up tonight. No one is going to get into my apartment without him noticing. The guy is a security freak." She shrugged. "Did you know he had the same system the bank has installed in his building? He says we need to talk to this company and get our building wired."

She pushed a card toward me. I read the business card.

Stay Safe Security

Cheryl Paine

Regional Sales Representative

"Kent's ex-wife was the rep for the bank's security system? No wonder Greg has to deal with the auditors. What was he thinking?" I tapped the card on the table. "Can I keep this? I think Greg needs to know this."

Aunt Jackie stood. "As long as you consider the shop buying a system, too. Josh says Cheryl's very knowledgeable. And it's all high-tech stuff."

Which seems to go haywire at a moment's notice. I promised my aunt we'd talk more about buying a security package. I planned on talking to Cheryl, but I was pretty sure I'd take our business to another company, no matter what Josh said. The woman seemed to control too much of the South Cove security business as it stood.

After my aunt left, I called the number on the card and got an appointment scheduled for Cheryl to stop by tomorrow morning. I'd have the information before Jackie and I left for her lawyer visit. Glancing at the clock, I realized I needed to get the ingredients made for the kabobs we'd planned for dinner in case Greg could sneak away from the station.

I chopped up the steak and put it in a bag to marinate, then went to work on the shrimp and veggies. When I finished, I still had time for a quick shower, then applying makeup and blow-drying and curling my hair into submission.

When I returned downstairs, Greg was in the kitchen, drinking a glass of iced tea. "Hope you don't mind, I was dying of thirst."

"I gave you the key for just such an emergency." I kissed him on the top of the head as I passed by on my way for my own drink. "Should I get the kabobs out? How long do you have?"

"Just grab yourself something and come sit down. I want to relax for a minute." He reached down and petted Emma. "How was your shopping trip?"

"Interesting." I sat down across from him. "Did you know Pampered Pet Palace sells poison tree frogs?"

Greg didn't look up from petting Emma; she was loving the attention. "Really?"

"I ran into Anne from the bank. She owns snakes and frogs." He couldn't yell at me later for not telling him everything.

"Interesting. She seemed more like a cat person." Greg sipped his iced tea, now watching me.

My head bobbled like one of those ball player statues you get for attending games. "Exactly, that's what I told her."

"What else happened on your trip?" Greg was trying to make conversation and stay away from the facts of the murder. I could tell he was trying to lead me into a different conversation.

"Fine, I peeked at Doc's report and looked up the toxin. So sue me." I leaned forward. "But don't you find it interesting that Anne might own the same type of frog?"

"Might or does? Did you ask her?"

I shook my head. "I was checking out and she was going into the store. The conversation was kind of short."

"Do I have to say it?" Greg looked beaten down, and I felt guilty for even bringing up the subject.

"Stay out of the investigation. But you can't come back and say I didn't tell you what I knew. Like the girl sucking face with Kent the day he died." I tapped my finger on the table for emphasis. Not hard, but enough that Greg grinned. "I'm serious. You tell me to stay out of the investigation, then you complain that I'm not telling you what I know. You can't have it both ways."

"Well, I could, if you would just stay out of the investigation. But you're right about the beach meeting being important. It actually gave us a clue to follow. We got a plate off the beach security tape, but the car she drove was a rental. I'm talking to the rental agent tomorrow; they're back on shift then. So, point taken." He rubbed his temple. "This case is filled with angry, betrayed women; interviewing them all is giving me the hives. I just want to have a nice dinner with my girlfriend and not talk about finding a murderer. Who would have thought that South Cove was such a den for killers?"

I laughed at that and put on a fake accent. "But he was always so nice and quiet, you would have never known he was killing people right next door to our retirement home."

That made Greg smile. "Exactly. So can we change the subject?"

"Aunt Jackie came by."

He groaned. "Not exactly the change I wanted."

"Okay, but FYI, I'm taking her into the city to talk to an attorney tomorrow afternoon. Just in case you're looking for me." I stood and walked over to the fridge. "I've got to make a salad to go with the kabobs. Caesar or garden?"

"Garden. I'll help." He came up behind me and pulled me back into a hug. "I adore you, you know that."

"Back atcha." I leaned back into his arms and for a minute, the two of us were all that mattered in the universe. Emma barked, her ball in her mouth.

"Hold on, girl. I've got some cooking to do." Greg nodded to the door. "You want to go out to play while we get this done?"

Another bark and Emma went flying to the screen. After letting her out, Greg paused for a moment, staring out at the backyard.

"Hey, I thought you were helping?" I dug out the lettuce and other salad fixings, including the six bottles of different dressings I had in the fridge door. He walked back over, picked out home-style ranch, and pushed the rest toward me.

"What do you want?"

I smiled. "World peace, a chicken in every pot, and a good book to take me away."

"Nice, but I meant for salad dressing. No use leaving all these out." He glanced out the window again. "When did Gleason say they'd make a decision on the wall? I'd like to do some landscaping out back this summer if it's not the birthplace of South Cove."

Shrugging, I began to stick meat and veggies onto the metal skewers.

"This summer, I hope. At least that's what the last letter from the commission said. One way or the other, I'll be glad when it's over. Do you know how many townies ask me about it each week? I can't tell if they're rooting for me or seeing if I'm as crazy as they think."

While dinner was grilling, Greg's phone rang. He groaned and pulled it close to read the display. Answering, he shook his head at me. "Hey, Jim, what's up?"

Jim King, Greg's brother and the owner of the painting company whose crew painted my house, didn't care for me one bit. He was hard and fast on Team Sherry, even though Greg tried to tell me I was paranoid. Last Thanksgiving, the guy had come for the meal, but spent most of his time outside on the deck with Greg and the other men. I took Greg's glass into the kitchen to refill our iced tea and to give him some privacy for his call.

Greg met me at the door, phone call done. "You don't have to leave when he calls, you know."

I passed him his glass and sat on the swing. "I just like to give you some privacy."

He came and sat by me. "I think it's more than that, but I'll let you slide. He's taking us on a fishing trip next Sunday."

"Fishing? Where?" I wondered how far into the woods we'd have to go to find a lake.

Greg's face almost exploded, his grin was that wide. "The ocean, silly. We'll be pulling in the big boys, and we can stock that freezer of yours to the gills."

"Bad joke." I thought about our schedule. Sundays were typically our free day. We never planned anything without consulting the other. "I'll tell Amy we can't do breakfast. I suspect you'll want to leave at some ungodly hour."

"Nah, I told Jim we'd meet him at the dock at five." He peeked under the grill hood. "Grab a plate, they're done."

"Who goes fishing in the evening?" I reached through the open screen and grabbed the platter I'd set out. I stood next to him as he set the grilled kabobs on my plate.

He reached down and turned off the gas, taking the plate from me and holding the kitchen door open. "Five in the morning."

"On a Sunday? And you said it wasn't ungodly." I took out two dinner plates and handed him one. We didn't talk as we were dishing up the salad to go with the meat. Then we sat at the table in our regular chairs and started eating. Greg knew he could be called back to the station at any time. Which made me wonder why he thought he could get away for a full day of fishing. "Will the case be locked up by then?"

He wiped his mouth with a napkin. "Doesn't matter. I'm instituting a *No Work for Greg on Sunday* rule. I've missed too many football games this season. Now that we can get outside again, we're taking a day for ourselves." He looked at me. "Tell me you're on board."

"Actually, I love the idea. I don't want you to get your hopes up, though. You know how your job can be." I poured balsamic vinaigrette over my salad and broke off a piece of the French loaf I'd bought in town.

"I know it won't be possible every Sunday, but a guy's got to set some limits. Otherwise his woman gets lonely." He cocked his head at me. "Right?"

"Sometimes, but I get it. Your job is important. It's not like you work in an office or in construction. Although there's nothing wrong with those jobs, it's just not as critical as being a detective."

"We all have roles to play." He glanced at his watch. "Speaking of my job, I've got to go. Someone from the DA's office is coming over tomorrow to look over the case. Hopefully I'll have a solid lead before he shows up."

"Like what?" I smoothed some butter on the fresh bread.

He kissed me on the cheek. "Like who owns poison tree frogs in town."

CHAPTER 15

The next morning, I'd finished the commuter rush and was getting ready to turn the shop over to Toby when Cheryl Paine walked into the store. Her black suit framed her slender frame and her hair was fashioned into a sharp, professional look. A purple silk shirt peeked out from the black jacket, and the gold necklace around her neck was tasteful, yet reeked of expensive. She had a large black leather bag over her shoulder. She saw me watching her entrance and turned on the smile. Then she stopped walking when she recognized me.

"You were at the funeral home. Are you friends with that woman?" Her gaze turned cold on me.

I smiled and walked toward her, hand outstretched. "I'm Jill Gardner, owner of Coffee, Books, and More. And more importantly, I am definitely not friends with Sherry King."

Her shoulders relaxed and she took my hand. "Sorry, it's been weird since Kent died. The police are asking all kinds of questions, like they think he was murdered or something."

"You don't?" I motioned to a table I'd cleaned earlier. "We can sit here. I'm alone in the shop until noon."

Cheryl sat in one chair and put her bag in another. "You shouldn't be alone ever. Not every person who walks in your front door is a customer looking for coffee."

I let the comment slide. I was more interested in the question she'd dodged. "Did you get all the arrangements made? I haven't heard about a funeral date or time."

She pulled out her laptop. "Kent's wishes were very specific. We'll have a small family-only ceremony at graveside. Of course, you're more than welcome to donate in his name to the Cancer Cures for Kids. His mom was a big supporter."

I wondered if Kent knew a church full of grieving women wouldn't do anyone any good. Especially if they started comparing notes. I nodded and wrote the name of the charity down in my notebook. "We'll be sure to donate. Thanks for letting me know."

She stared at the laptop, like she could will it to boot up. Finally she looked at me. "I hate that we were estranged at the time of his death. I barely talked to him anymore. I think he felt more like my security client than someone I used to share a bed with. And when he started dating that woman, he became even more distant."

I decided to push my luck. "Did you know he was doing drugs? Maybe that's why he was distant?"

"That's a lie. A lie that woman is telling everyone. Kent wouldn't do drugs; he knew his body was a temple." Cheryl's hand began to shake.

"I guess I was misinformed. Let's get back to why you're here. Can you tell me what kind of system would work best for this size of building? I'll need a quote for the apartment upstairs, as well. My aunt lives there."

Cheryl sat straighter and blinked away the tears. "You're right. We should deal with today, right?"

"Exactly."

Cheryl took me through a list of questions, designed to lead me to what I suspected was a top-of-the-line system and much more than I needed. But I let her play her sales game. By the time she'd finished talking about all the advantages of installing one of her company's systems, I was almost sold, yet something was nagging at me. "What about all those security problems the bank's been having? I've heard it's the underground power lines or phone lines in the area that's been setting off the alarm? I don't want to be chasing after errors in the system."

"Oh, you've heard about those?" Cheryl focused on the computer screen again. I'd been with the girl for twenty minutes and I'd found her tell. She might not have been lying, but I knew when she didn't want to talk about something. "Every system can have a few glitches at first. I'm sure we've taken care of those here in South Cove."

"Too bad the bank was the test system. Seems like that would be the one place you'd want your system to be perfect."

Cheryl handed me a pamphlet that went over the cost of installation and the monthly service fees, along with her card. "Unfortunate, yes, but not unusual. I can almost assure you that there will be no further issues with the Stay Safe Security systems in the town of South Cove."

After Cheryl left, customers kept me busy until Aunt Jackie came in, dressed in a skirted suit that looked even more expensive and polished than Cheryl's had. She eyed my jeans and Yellowstone T-shirt. "You're not wearing that."

"I'm not the one in trouble, so yes, I am wearing this." I gave my aunt a kiss on the cheek and finished the book order for the week. I'd found a new mystery I'd already tucked into my purse to keep me busy while I waited for my aunt to talk to her lawyer.

Toby arrived and I went over a few pickup orders I had taken for that afternoon. A group of women were having a retreat over at Main Street Books and had ordered a selection of coffees and treats for their afternoon break. Mary had called in the order, apologizing for the lateness. She had told them she would do the additional break, but with the excitement the last few days, she'd forgotten to bake.

"She'll be here at two to pick up." I gave the list to Toby, who nodded.

"No problem." He picked up the flyer Cheryl had left. "You considering this company for the shop?"

"I talked to their salesperson this morning. Have you heard anything about the company?"

"Nothing good. I'll get you some names of a few guys who are housed out of Bakerstown. Stay Safe Security has a PO Box as a headquarters in Colorado and well, you know about the bank's issues. The auditors are insisting on the branch cancelling their contract and hiring a new provider." He lowered his voice. "I'm only telling you this to keep you from getting into the same problem."

"I won't tell Greg you said anything," I assured my barista.

Aunt Jackie came in from the back. "You won't tell Greg what?"

I hustled my aunt out of the shop. "Call if you need us." Although we wouldn't be in a position to help for hours. Maybe I should have called in Sasha for the day. She'd started taking classes at the local university, so she'd cut her hours from the full-time position we'd carved out for her after the end of her internship. I dialed the shop's number on my cell as we walked to my Jeep.

"Coffee, Books, and More, how can I help you?" Toby's baritone boomed through the speaker.

"I'm impressed. Usually you just say, 'Talk to me.'" I clicked open the doors with my key fob and climbed inside, waiting for Aunt Jackie to settle in the passenger seat.

"I saw you dial the phone out the front window. So what do you want?" Toby went back to being the smart aleck he typically portrayed.

"If it gets too busy, call Sasha. She doesn't have classes on Tuesday, so she might come in to help."

"No way. If she doesn't have classes, she needs to be studying. I can't believe the load she's taking this year. Did you know she wants to go pre-law?" Toby's voice was tinged with humor.

"I tried to talk her out of it, but she's stubborn. I just hope she doesn't become a police officer." I tapped Aunt Jackie's unfastened seat belt with my finger. She frowned but clicked the belt on, holding her hands out in a surrender motion.

"Nothing wrong with wanting to serve and protect. There are a lot worse jobs out there. See you tomorrow." Then my barista hung up on me.

"I guess he was done talking." I put my phone in one of the cubbies by my seat and started the engine.

"You mother-hen the boy. I swear, he could rob us blind and you'd still be hanging up his coat for him when he walked in the door." Aunt Jackie sniffed.

"That's not true." Well, it was a little true. I did hang the guy's coat up more times than not because he had a bad habit of throwing it on my desk when he arrived. I went with the safe response. "He's a police officer. He would never steal from us."

"Trust the person, not the role," my aunt muttered. Then she turned toward the window and watched the scenery as we drove into the city. I wondered if she was considering whether her act of kindness for a friend would get her ten to twenty. Part of me wanted to believe everything would be all right. The other side made my guts clench when I thought of the woman spending even a short time in jail. She wasn't made for rough living. Aunt Jackie thought camping was driving up to Palo Alto and staying in a bed-and-breakfast.

Finally, I thought of a subject that didn't lead back to her life of crime. "So, what's going on with you and Josh? At the Business-to-Business meeting it looked like the two of you were cooling the relationship." I turned down the stereo that had been blasting my all-Dixie-Chicks, all-the-time mix CD that I'd made last weekend.

"We're taking things slow. He's been hinting about making the situation permanent, but I've told him I have no interest in getting married again. Once was enough." Aunt Jackie didn't turn to look at me when she answered.

Whoa. That wasn't what I'd been expecting. The thought of calling Josh Thomas, uncle anything, made my skin crawl. Thank goodness my aunt was still sane and not leaning toward making it legal. "I thought it was just fun. You two don't seem to be compatible."

Now she did turn toward me, her gaze accusatory. "Now you're just being rude. Josh and I have many interests in common. Did you know he collects rare coins?"

"I didn't know you collected rare coins."

Aunt Jackie's cheeks bloomed pink. "Well, I always wanted to, and now I do."

"What else do you have in common?" Since she'd brought up the subject, I wasn't going to let her off with just a mutual love of sorting through change drawers to find a lost prize.

She waved a slender hand, her nails done in a classic French tip and small age spots dotting the skin weaved with visible veins. "We both enjoy antiquing. I mean, it's his job, but I've been very successful in finding several rare items in the last few trips we've taken."

"That sounds riveting." I turned the car onto the street where my old firm was located. I hadn't been back to the office since I'd cleaned out my desk that last day, and for a minute, I regretted not picking a more formal outfit. More upscale to show I had made the right decision to leave. But my clothes didn't signify my status, not anymore. Back when I was a lawyer, I spent hours getting the right brand of suits, the right shoes, and even the right briefcase. Now those hours were spent reading books, hanging with friends, and enjoying life. Yep, I'd made the right decision, no matter what my former coworkers thought about my worn but clean jeans.

After parking, we walked into the reception area. The young woman sitting at the desk with a Lady Gaga headset had been hired after I'd quit and was a stranger to me. When I explained who we were there to see, she nodded and asked us to take a seat to wait.

"You never would have guessed you used to spend eighty hours a week in this joint," Aunt Jackie fake-whispered. If the receptionist heard, she ignored the jab at what my aunt deemed a lack of hospitality.

"Shh." I picked up a magazine. *Business Journal* was doing a series on the trends of Generation X walking away from the rat race. I decided I didn't need to read the article since I'd been living it. Flipping through the pages, I wondered who actually bought and wore all the watches advertised. Phones had gotten smaller, but watches had become huge. Especially when they were matched with a huge price tag.

"Jill, how are you?" A man in an expensive black suit stood in front of me. My gaze traveled up the impeccable fabric and landed on the blue eyes of John Bristol. We'd both started at the same time, but John had rocketed upward to partner, while I'd worked as an associate for way too long. He pulled me up into a hug that lasted a bit too long and then looked down at my left hand. "No wedding ring, so I guess I still have a chance."

Bristol had always seen me, not as a peer but more like a quick roll in the hay. At least I didn't have to play nice with him anymore. "Hey, there." I stepped away from him, trying to rebuild my personal space bubble, and pointed toward my aunt. "I'd like you to meet my aunt, Jackie Ekroth. We're here to meet with—"

My introduction was interrupted by Matt Clauson, Jackie's new attorney. "Me. And we're on the clock, so let these ladies be, John, unless you want to pay for their time with me."

John put up his hands. "I know when I'm outmaneuvered. I'll call you sometime and we can catch up. Or better yet, I'll surprise you at that little shop you opened. When are you around anyway?"

Aunt Jackie looked at John and lied. "She works from one to four every day."

"Nice to see you." I took her arm and hurried after Matt. When we reached his office and I closed the door behind us, I whispered, "Thanks."

"The man has no manners. Besides, I get the impression he's a bully." She slipped into a chair in front of Matt's desk and I took the other one.

Matt laughed. "You sure can read people. I don't know what the other partners see in that jerk."

"He brings in a lot of business to the firm." I recalled seeing John's billable hours and new client listing each month on the report. Seeing how well the other associates were doing was intended to inspire you to work harder. For me, it just cemented the fact that I was smack in the middle of the pack. Too valuable to fire, not good enough to promote.

"His family brought their business to the firm when he was hired. They're kind of connected." Matt leaned back in his leather chair. "So what brings the two of you here today? You know I'm not strong in estate law."

"My aunt has gotten herself into a cucumber." I glanced at her.

She shook her head. "You mean a pickle. I swear, for as much as you read, you come up with the strangest sayings." She told Matt what she'd done and why, and then pulled out the book. "He's got everything written down right here. Mary and Bill deserve their money back or the vacation he promised. It's the only right thing to do."

Matt frowned, picked up a napkin from his desk, and took the book. "Did you tell the police you have this?"

"Are you kidding? As soon as I found it, I gave it to Mary and told her to sit in the car until I came back." She squirmed a little in her seat. "Then as I was closing up the office, the police came and took me to jail. He must have some sort of silent alarm set up in that place, I didn't even hear them arrive."

"How did you get in?" Matt laid the book on his desk, slowly turning the pages.

When my aunt didn't answer, he looked up from his studying. "As your attorney, I need to know the entire truth. If you need your niece to leave?"

"No." Aunt Jackie put a hand on my arm. "Stay. Okay, so I went in to the office earlier and pretended to be looking for a vacation. When I left, I had the extra office key he kept in his desk in my purse."

Matt shook his head. "You just happened to find the key?"

"Actually, Mary had seen him put it there when she was trying to get her money back. He'd given it to his secretary, and when she left for the day while Mary was in the office, she saw where he put the key." Aunt Jackie made the whole plan seem reasonable. Which made me even more worried. She'd had a plan; this wasn't a senior spur-of-the-moment action. She'd gone in knowing she was going to return and take the guy's accounting book before she ever left South Cove.

"I need to know where the DA stands on the criminal charges first." Matt put the book into an envelope and set it aside. "We'll keep this just in case. But, Mrs. Ekroth, you have to realize, if they decide to go ahead with the charges, you may not be able to use a piece of stolen evidence for any leverage to help your friend or the others the man swindled."

"Please, call me Jackie. I know it was a risk, but you have to press on, no matter what happens to me." Aunt Jackie sat taller, even more determined.

I took her hand and squeezed. "Let's let Matt do his magic and maybe he can find a way to keep you out of prison."

"That's the hope." Matt stood and reached out his hand. "I'm good at what I do, Jackie. Let's see if that's enough."

Aunt Jackie dug in her purse and pulled out a business card. "Mary Sullivan's private line. Please don't discuss this with her husband; he doesn't know about the issue."

As we waited for the elevator, I watched my aunt. She didn't look fazed at all, except a slight tremor in her hand as she patted her hair into place for the third time. "Bill doesn't know about any of this?"

"How could he? The trip was a surprise, and once the money was gone, Mary didn't know what to do. That's her inheritance from her late mother."

"I hope Matt can get it back for her." The elevator doors opened, and we stepped into the empty car.

"I'm counting on it," Aunt Jackie said, and our gazes met in the reflective surface as the doors closed.

CHAPTER 16

Amy sat on her regular stool, watching me prep the shop for the upcoming day. "I can't believe Jackie might have to go to jail for this. Did you tell her lawyer about the travel scams?"

I stacked a sleeve full of cups near the coffeemaker. "Believe me, he knows everything. And now, so do I. What in the world was she thinking? You can't solve problems by committing new crimes."

"You have to give her credit, at least her heart was in the right place. Jackie and Mary have become close over the last year. You'd break into a business to help me out, right?" Amy sipped her hot chocolate and watched me over the lid.

"No, I don't think so. And if I did, I'd bring Greg along with me to make the break-in a semilegal search." I laughed and poured my own cup of coffee, walking around to sit next to my best friend. "Who am I kidding? Of course I'd do exactly what Jackie did for Mary. What does that say about my character?"

"That you value your friendships over trivialities."

"Trivialities like private property and breaking-and-entering charges." I sighed, setting the coffee down untouched. "I'm worried, Amy. What if she has to go to jail? She's not a strong woman."

Amy touched my arm. "Your aunt is the strongest woman I know. Besides, she's not going to jail for trying to stop some lowlife from ripping off Mary. I have friends in the media. We can rally popular support for her. Just say the word."

"Thanks. That means a lot." I nodded at Amy's phone. "You talk to Justin lately?"

"Not for a couple of days. He's texted, but he took off work and went home for a short trip. His mom's really nice. She probably told him if he didn't show up at her house, she would come to his. He says she worries." Amy stared at the phone, and I could tell she was wishing it would ring. "I should have been more supportive, I guess."

"You didn't know how much finding Kent would affect him." I felt bad that I had made fun of Justin myself, but I wasn't his girlfriend.

"I guess." Amy straightened her back and looked at me, an idea forming in her head. "So what does Greg say about who killed Kent? Is he ready to throw the guilty party into jail?"

"Greg doesn't talk about suspects with me. You may want to hang around and see if you can charm some intel from Toby, though." I took a sip of my coffee. "Every time I think I might have a viable suspect for him, the lead peters out."

"Like Evelyn Baker?" Amy finished off her coffee. "Too bad we can't blame this on Mayor Baylor. He and Tina are gone on a week-long cruise, and you know she's going to want me to make up her scrapbook when she returns. Digital *and* print."

"Oh, the life of a small town city planner." I put the back of my hand on my forehead. "At least they are out of your hair. You can count that as your vacation, too."

"So true." Amy stood and headed to the exit. "Time to make the donuts."

I watched my friend slip out the doorway, just as Leslie, Anne, and a couple of the bank tellers I didn't know walked in the café. "Good morning. I just stocked the display case this morning with an assortment of cheesecakes and some brownies the bakery swears will replace your need for sex for a week."

One of the girls nudged Anne. "You better get a couple of those brownies now that your on-the-side guy is harassing the angels."

"Ruth, that's mean." Leslie put her arm around Anne and nodded toward the table. "You two go sit down, and I'll buy the coffee with an assortment of pastries. Deal?"

Ruth and the still unnamed woman claimed a table in a sunny spot in front of the window. I opened the display case and held up a pair of tongs. "What can I plate up for you?"

"Just give us four pieces, doesn't matter. And two large coffees, a large mocha, and a skinny latte." Leslie dug in her purse while I pulled out three cheesecake slices—traditional, pumpkin marble, and a new chocolate mousse that was heavenly. When I reached for a peanut butter pie, a hand stilled my movement.

"Dish up one of those brownies. Ruth may be crass, but she's right on one point. My body is missing Kent more than my mind." Anne's voice wasn't much louder than a whisper.

Not knowing what to say to that, I grabbed two of the brownies. "One on the house." Then I went to make the drinks.

"So glad the auditors showed up today for a vault audit." Leslie opened her purse. "We'll get paid for the time they're there, and then they'll reimburse me for the money I spent on this."

"Did you all get to leave?" Somehow I hadn't thought they'd kick out the employees while they counted the money.

Leslie laughed. "Everyone but the new branch manager they brought in from corporate."

"It should have been you. You did Kent's job for years without the recognition. Now with him gone, the job should have been yours. But no, they bring in some twelve-year-old who doesn't know a thing about management." Anne's voice was harder now.

I put the last coffee on the tray and ripped off my gloves. Ringing up the order, I shook my head. "I was a cubicle dweller for ten years before I dropped out and bought this place. Promoting the wrong person is a grand tradition in corporate law."

Leslie handed me the credit card. "No matter. I'm a few years away from retirement, they pay me well, and when the day's done, I get to go home to my husband. Kent put in too many hours at that job to make it look enticing."

"It's still not fair. You should sue the bank." Anne wasn't giving up, not yet.

I ripped off the receipt and gave the slip and a pen to Leslie. After she signed, she picked up the tray.

"I can deliver those." I stuffed the receipt in the drawer and reached forward.

Leslie moved faster than I'd imagined the larger woman could. "You didn't know I was a waitress for ten years, did you?" She smiled at me and the two walked back to the sunny table.

As I watched the women talk, I realized I'd missed a chance to talk to Anne about her frogs. I studied the woman. She'd lost even more weight since the last time she'd come in the shop. All over a man. She'd been in love with the guy and he'd just used her. Kent had a lot to answer for as he stood in front of Saint Peter.

The door flew open and Darla strolled in, directly toward me.

"Uh-oh." I let the words escape before I realized I'd spoken.

"Now, why do you look so worried?" Darla smiled as she climbed on a stool. "Pour me a cup of coffee and come sit with me. I've got an idea."

"That sounds ominous," I replied, but I poured her coffee and one for myself. Typically midmornings were slow and the bank crowd might be my only customers, especially on a Wednesday.

Darla sipped the black liquid and sighed. "No matter how I try, I can't make coffee as good as you do. What's your secret?"

"The beans. We have a magic coffee bean tree that sprouts at night in the parking lot behind the store. We pick our beans right before midnight for best results." I sipped my own cup and watched her.

"You're a funny girl. I should have given you a bigger part in the murder mystery play." Darla pulled a piece of bright pink card stock out of her satchel. "Put this up in your window."

I glanced at the announcement and frowned. "We're doing the dinner theater next week? Don't you think that's a little insensitive?"

"Then I won't invite his ex-wife or girlfriends." The edges of Darla's lips curled as she let the words register. I looked up in shock. "Don't look like that. I am a journalist, for goodness' sake. Did you and Greg think you could keep Kent's love life a secret?"

Memories of Greg's fury over Darla's front-page reporting of the murder tugged at my mind. He'd thought she had an informant on the police payroll. Could I figure out who was feeding her spicy tidbits by playing along? I decided being coy wasn't one of my strong points. "Whatever." I tapped my nail on the poster. "I don't know, we haven't even had a full run-through of the play yet."

"You're reading my mind." Darla glanced at the impromptu bank meeting near the window. She reached into the satchel, pulled out a notebook, and uncapped her pen. "Practice is tonight at seven. You think your guy will be available? Or is he chasing some hot lead?"

"Good try, but I'm not giving you anything." I amended my statement. "Even if I did know anything. Greg's been holding his facts close to the vest on this one."

"You mean his cards."

I scrunched my face, not understanding what cards had to do with a murder investigation. "What?"

"The saying is, he holds his cards close to his vest." Scribbling in her notebook, she waved me off. "Never mind. Just be at the winery at seven tonight. I'll buy the beer."

I watched as Darla picked up her coffee and strolled over to the table filled with the bank employees. I was too far away to hear what she said, but the group laughed and Darla pulled up a chair. I'd never seen her in action before, except when she was trying to needle me for information. I sat down on the couch to read until someone needed me, losing interest in Darla and her new friends somewhere around page 4 in the mystery.

When Toby arrived to take over, the shop was empty and I'd read about half of the book. "Research or marketing?"

Smiling, I slipped a bookmark between the pages and closed the book. "I believe I'll charge my time to research this morning." Jackie had set up a "slow time survey," trying to see who and when someone stocked the pastry display, completed marketing activities, or did research for new books and coffee delights. My reading fell into two of those categories, even if I didn't explain exactly how I used my time on her survey. I believed she had a clue, though. Toby looked tired this morning. "Rough night? Too many DUIs?"

"Nah, Greg had me reading through old case files to see if we could match the toxin he found . . ." He paused. "You're good. All concerned about me and then I'll spill a tidbit or two. You should go work with Darla at the newspaper."

"All I wanted to know was that you're okay." I grabbed my purse out of the office, ignoring the jacket Toby had thrown on my desk. "You're the one who went all detailed on me. Haven't you ever heard that when someone's asking about your health, nine times out of ten, they really don't care?"

"Aw, boss, don't go all warm and mushy on me. You'll give me false hope."

I paused on my way out the door. "False hope about what?"

"That you really have a heart." Toby grinned and started restocking the dessert display case, something I should have done instead of reading.

Walking back home, I called Greg, but then hung up the phone before he could answer. The way he felt about our parts in the mystery play, I'd better deliver this news in person. I entered City Hall through the side door, where the police station had its offices. They had a back door for officers and the occasional lawbreaker to enter, but this door took me directly to the reception area and Esmeralda.

"Jill, I didn't expect to see you today," Esmeralda chirped, then held up a hand halting my response. "South Cove Police Dispatch, how may I help you?"

I thumbed through the magazines on the rack, finding mostly old copies of *Guns & Ammo* and a few *House Beautiful* issues. I made a mental note to bring over some of my own magazines that had started to stack up on the floor of my office for when I had time to read them, which would probably be never. I watched Esmeralda handle the call and wondered about her greeting. Wouldn't a real fortune-teller know when she was going to see someone? Or was I thinking of a psychic? Could Esmeralda see the future? Or were her powers limited to the range of the crystal ball?

Smiling, I twisted these thoughts around until I heard my name.

"Jill, are you all right?" Esmeralda appeared concerned.

I dropped the magazine I'd been flipping through and walked back to the reception desk. "Sorry, I got lost in the article."

Her eyes narrowed and she grunted. "Right. You don't have to lie to me."

"Really. It was about a local hunting area." I dug my hole deeper and she continued to stare. "Whatever. Is Greg busy?"

Esmeralda pointed to the closed office door. "Barricaded himself in the office this morning with a pile of files that Toby gathered for him last night. I'm sure he'd welcome a distraction."

I stepped toward the door, but stopped when she continued.

"I don't need the crystal ball to see the future. Sometimes I just like to be polite and not freak people out."

I turned and saw she was smiling, but something in her face registered a feeling of sadness.

"Sorry, I shouldn't have . . ." I started.

She waved her hand toward me, mirroring my own response. "Whatever."

As I opened the door to Greg's office, I thought about Esmeralda and her life here in South Cove. And for the first time, I realized I'd never seen her with a friend or even on a date. I'd assumed my neighbor was a recluse by nature, but maybe she was trying to reach out. That would explain the campy friends song she kept repeating when she did my readings. Or it could have been a warning about Aunt Jackie.

My head hurt, so I pushed both ideas away and put on a smile I didn't feel for Greg.

"Uh-oh." He stared at me as I walked in. "What's going on?"

Slipping into one of his office chairs, I frowned. "Why does it have to be a bad thing if I stop to see my boyfriend on the way home from work?"

"Mostly because you have that smile on your face, which usually means you did something that I need to clean up." He studied me, then checked the clock. "You haven't been interviewing my potential suspects again, have you?"

"The day's early, but no." This time my smile was genuine. "Actually, I do have a favor, or really, just a favor you've already granted."

"Do I want to know this favor?" Greg's voice sounded gravelly, like he'd been drinking coffee and smoking all night. Except he didn't smoke.

"Were you working with Toby last night? He came into the shop all worn out and you look twice as bad as he does." My intuition told me there was something more going on than just reviewing files. I pointed toward the pile of manila folders on his desk. "What are you looking for?"

"A needle in a haystack mostly." Greg leaned back in his chair and stretched his long arms over his head. I thought he might tip the chair over. As he righted himself, he shrugged. "Look, I've got a lot to get through today. What do you want?"

I could have been offended, but I knew he didn't mean the words in a cruel way. "We have practice at the winery tonight at seven. And Murder Mystery Theater is back on for next Friday. Darla's already printed out the posters."

"Terrific. I'd planned on a night at the apartment with a beer, in my gym shorts, watching the Lakers on my big screen." He rolled his shoulders. "Okay if we meet there? I'll probably work up until then."

"If you make sure to eat, sure." I stood. "The nights have been warm, so I'll probably walk up to the winery. Can you drop me home?"

"Do you have any of Sadie's apple pie?" His eyes twinkled.

"Sorry, big boy, I've finished that off." I laughed when I heard his groan. "Although I might just have something else."

"You know I'd drive you home for a cookie." He stood and pulled me close. "We'll go away for a weekend just as soon as this case is wrapped. You want to go north or south?"

I thought about our options. We'd been talking about a short Mexican resort stay, just to see if we liked the area. "South, definitely. I'll pull up some choices, and we can talk about them over dinner this weekend."

"Don't forget fishing on Sunday." Greg kissed me, then sat back down and opened a file.

I headed to the door. "Can't wait," I said drily.

I heard his chuckle as I returned to the empty reception area. Esmeralda had put a sign on her desk. "On break, back in fifteen minutes," I read aloud.

I opened the outside door and took a deep breath of the salty air. The breeze was coming from the west and directly off the ocean. The smell centered me, and I made a decision. No matter what Pat said, or Sherry did, Greg and I were a couple until we weren't. And no one was going to change that. I'd just have to trust in us.

My steps were lighter as I strolled the rest of the way through town and back to my house. The sun was shining, my work for the day was complete, and I had a date with Greg tonight. What could go wrong?

CHAPTER 17

After running with Emma that afternoon, I'd spent the rest of my day reading. I kept ignoring the notebook lying on the kitchen table, a list of Kent's conquests still listed in Jackie's easy handwriting. After the run-in with Evelyn Baker, I was done with assumptions. Besides, Greg seemed like he had a handle on the case. I grilled a piece of cod, served it on top of a salad, and added a glass of white wine for dinner.

Then I went upstairs to shower and get ready. Instead of my usual outfit of jeans and a boy band or rock legend tee, I slipped on a favorite sundress Greg liked. I took clips and swept up the front of my hair away from my face, applied blusher, mascara, and lip gloss, and I was ready.

The best thing about California casual? You could find appropriate flip-flops for all occasions. I grabbed my jewel-bedazzled pair and went downstairs to put Emma out in the backyard. She hadn't eaten any of my designer throw pillows lately, but I didn't want to tempt fate.

I was almost into town when I realized I hadn't checked to see if Esmeralda wanted to walk in with me. So much for trying to be friendly. I made a commitment to talk to her at the play practice.

Diamond Lille's was packed with regulars, and through the window, I saw Carrie, my favorite waitress, carrying a loaded tray. Thoughts of Friday's fish and chips special filled my mind as I continued to walk to the winery. Loud voices broke my concentration.

"You know I can't do that. Nick is still at home. He needs me." Sadie's voice sounded less angry and more frustrated. I scanned the area for my friend. My gaze stopped in front of Dustin Austin's bike rental shop. Sadie stood in the open doorway, her back to the street.

I crossed the empty road and stood at the edge of the sidewalk. I didn't want to pry, but Sadie seemed upset. I was close enough to hear Austin's next words.

"I guess I know where I stand in your life. Thanks for making that clear before I made a huge mistake." He paused. "Good-bye Sadie."

At that, Sadie burst into tears and turned to flee. She didn't even see me before she was on top of me. "Hey, it's okay." I put my arm around her and led her away.

Sadie's body hitched. "It's not okay. I don't know what I was thinking. No one will come between me and my son. Not now, not ever." Her bravado broke into more tears. I led her away from the bike shop and toward the coffee shop.

"You just need to calm down. Sometimes in the heat of the moment, we all say things we don't mean." I took a peek into the shop, but it appeared empty so I opened the door and led her to the couch in the bookstore area. "You sit here. I'll get you a cup of hot coffee."

"Tea, please." Sadie sniffed, pulling more tissues out of her purse. The woman carried everything in that large bag, and right now, I was glad.

I approached the counter where Aunt Jackie was already making Sadie's tea. "Man trouble," I whispered.

"I didn't even know she was dating." She put the cup on a tray and added a brownie. "You look like you're on your way somewhere. You want me to handle this?"

I felt torn. I should stay with my friend, yet Greg and the rest of the cast was probably at the winery getting ready for practice. "Let me ask Sadie. But I'm sure she'd like to talk to you about the problem."

I'd never had a kid or felt like I had anyone to protect in a relationship besides myself. My aunt hadn't raised children, but she and Uncle Ted had had a long and happy marriage. Maybe she had some insight for Sadie that I couldn't provide. I took the tray and walked back over to the couch.

Sadie looked like she'd been told her best friend had died. I handed her the cup. She sipped the still-brewing tea and set it down. "Thanks for this. I didn't realize how upsetting the conversation would be. I should have just called him rather than coming to visit."

"What happened?" I still had time to walk the rest of the way to the winery and be there before seven. Sadie needed a sounding board.

"We just want different things. I mean, I knew a future with a man, any man, would someday turn physical, but I'm just not ready. Besides, Nick's still at home, and I can't tell him that premarital sex is bad while I'm spending the night with someone myself. How would he ever trust me?" Sadie tore a tissue into small bits while she talked. Her tears had dried, but I could tell her heart was still in pieces.

"He should understand. I mean, he must have dated women with children before, right?" I thought about all I didn't know about Dustin Austin, like had he been married, ever? Did he have his own kids? Since I'd moved to South Cove, I'd never seen him with anyone. I pushed the brownie closer. "These are amazing. Of course, you know that since they're yours."

Sadie attempted a smile. "Thanks, but I'm not hungry. Austin made it clear he wasn't interested in helping to raise a child. And we both agreed that Nick would be my responsibility, just like always. I wasn't looking for a father for my son. I just wanted some adult companionship."

"But your timetables are different." I understood the problem even if I didn't have the same experience as Sadie.

"Why couldn't we have started this next fall, after Nick went to college? I know my beliefs seem old-fashioned, but I know what's right. And this isn't right." Tears shone in Sadie's eyes. She took her cup and sipped the now-brewed mixture. She took in my dress and makeup and sighed. "And you're on your way to meet Greg."

"I've got a few minutes, but yeah, we have play practice tonight at the winery." I smoothed the skirt of the dress with my palms.

"Then you go ahead. I'll just sit here awhile and get my composure back so I can drive home." She took a deep breath.

"Maybe we could talk?" Aunt Jackie appeared with what appeared to be a steaming cup of coffee for herself. "I've had a few heartbreaks in my life."

Sadie nodded. "I'd like that. And I wouldn't feel like I was imposing on Jill any longer than necessary."

"You weren't imposing. We're friends." I stood and gave Sadie a quick hug. "Come by the shop in the morning and we'll talk."

Sadie squeezed me once and then let go. "We'll see. Thanks for rescuing me."

As I left the shop, I checked my watch. Five minutes to seven. I was pretty sure if I didn't show up soon, Greg would take the opportunity to leave and come find me. Then who knew if I could get him back to the winery. I lengthened my strides—and ran right into Josh Thomas.

"Watch it," he sputtered, spinning off-kilter with my weight. I watched as he went from crouching to sitting on his butt on the sidewalk, his camera swinging around his neck. He checked the display, then looked up at me. "I should have known. Can't you leave me alone?"

"I didn't intend to run into you. What are you doing anyway?" I straightened my dress and considered his camera. My eyes narrowed as I considered his angle. "Were you taking pictures of my shop? Of Aunt Jackie?"

Josh leaned forward and used his hands on one of my outdoor tables to push himself to a standing position. "Of course not. I told you at the meeting I've been tracking the issue of trash on our streets. Sherry King said if I got enough evidence, the council couldn't ignore my petition anymore." He glared at me. "She cares about what's going on in South Cove. Too bad our Business-to-Business committee doesn't seem to give a crap."

I thought about arguing, but knowing my time was short, I put that jab to my management of the committee to the side. "If you weren't snapping covert pictures of Jackie, then let me see the pictures." I held my hand out for the digital camera.

"In your dreams," he muttered, his gaze darting toward the windows of the shop. As dusk was falling, the light from CBM gave out a soft, inviting glow.

"I'll tell Jackie," I warned, not moving my hand.

He took the strap off his neck, clicked a button on the camera, and handed it to me. "Fine, I took a few shots. I've been worried about her since this whole travel scam thing. I don't want anyone hurting her."

I clicked through the pictures and saw a few with my aunt, smiling at a customer or to my amazement, reading a paperback when the shop was empty. "Caught you," I murmured.

"There is nothing inappropriate about those pictures. Your aunt is a lovely subject," Josh sputtered at my comment.

"No, these are great pictures. You should show her a few and tell her how much I enjoyed them." I was ready to hand the camera back when I saw one of the pictures Josh had given out during the last meeting. The one Greg had folded and put into his pocket. The picture showed the inside of a car, filled with bags with logos from my shop, Diamond Lille's, and more than a few of the fast-food places in Bakerstown.

But the food leftovers weren't what held my interest. It was the Baggie tucked inside the open glove box, which appeared to be filled with smaller Baggies of white powder. Josh had taken a picture of our local drug dealer's stash and hadn't even noticed. The antique dealer had perched his overweight frame on one of my patio chairs, trying to catch his breath from the exertion.

I handed Josh back his camera. "You should be careful taking pictures around town. Maybe hold off on the project for a few weeks. You said it yourself that Jackie might be in danger. What if the guy sees you when he's stalking her?"

"I'm not afraid of anyone." Josh's words didn't match the fear I saw in his eyes. "But you may be right that I should be more careful around town. You never know who's going to be angry when I disclose their dirty secrets."

"Exactly." I checked my watch. Five after. "Look, I've got to go. We'll talk tomorrow about the trash issue, and I promise the subject will be on the next agenda for the meeting."

Josh's eyes narrowed. "I'll believe it when I see it."

"Good night to you, as well." I took a last worried glance at the shop and started power-walking down the street. I'd call Aunt Jackie as soon as practice was over, just to make sure she was okay.

Greg was standing in the parking lot talking on his cell when I arrived. He gave me the look and then kissed me quickly. "No worries, Esmeralda. She just showed up. Thanks for checking."

"You asked my neighbor to see if I was still at home?" I pointed to my watch. "At ten minutes late? What would happen if I was twenty minutes late?"

"These days, you'd get a visit from whatever deputy was on duty. And probably a fun ride in the back of the squad car to your destination." Greg nodded to the barn where the practice was being held. "Darla's running late herself. We're supposed to grab a drink and mingle until she has everyone here."

"Good, I'm dying of thirst." We wandered toward the open bar, where Greg got a beer and I opted for an ice-cold bottle of water. I drank half of it down before we sat down at a table.

He considered me. "You want to tell me why you were late?"

"Sure. Sadie got in a fight with Dustin Austin, so I took her to the shop to calm down." I saw the worry in Greg's eyes. For all he said I should stay out of things, he sure took his job as the town's protector seriously. "No worries, she's talking it out with Aunt Jackie."

"What were they fighting about?" Greg sipped on his beer.

Laughing, I tilted my head closer to keep anyone from overhearing. "They are, I mean, were involved. I guess he pulled the old if-you-loved-me ploy."

Greg's eyes widened. "Austin and Sadie? Wow, I didn't see that one coming."

"Honestly, neither did I." I thought about the picture in Josh's camera. "But once I got her settled, I literally ran into Josh taking pictures out on the street."

Greg groaned. "I thought I told him to cool it."

"He thinks he's protecting Aunt Jackie along with the streets of South Cove from a mountain of trash." I finished my water.

"He's going to get himself hurt," Greg muttered.

"I saw the picture you took from the pile at the meeting." When he didn't answer, I went on. "Let me clarify—I saw what interested you in that picture."

"Jill, stay out of it. This is my job and part of an open investigation." Greg took my empty bottle. "You want another water or a beer?"

"You think you know who Kent's supplier was?"

Greg finished his beer, ignoring my question. "Beer or water?"

I stared. "Fine, beer."

"Good answer." He kissed me on the top of my head. "Don't move. Don't talk to anyone. Don't look at any pictures. Just be my girlfriend for one night, okay?"

"You know you love me the way I am. Curious, insightful, with mad investigating skills." I smiled but got a hard look in return. "Fine, you're looking at just Jill tonight."

By the time Greg returned with my beer, Darla had started rounding up the first act players. I waved at Amy and Justin, who stood in the front, ready to go backstage. Justin didn't see me, his gaze darting around the room, never sticking at one place. I saw Amy put a comforting hand on his arm and he visibly sighed and looked down at her.

"Poor Justin." My words were soft, but Greg, who stood by my side, answered.

He put his arm around my waist. "Some people have never had to deal with the reality of death before. From what I hear, even Justin's grandparents are still alive and working on that farm in Missouri."

"He had to have pets that have passed." I worried about Amy and how heavy the stress of Justin's emotions weighed on her.

"Animals are different. Justin's a strong guy; he'll get through this." Greg pulled me into a quick hug. "You ready for your stage debut?"

"Actually, I'm experienced." I stared up into Greg's baby blue eyes and for a second, forgot what I was saying. "You're looking at the star of the Liberty High School production of *Our Town*."

"I'm surprised Darla didn't give you a bigger part, knowing you were a celebrity and all."

I fluffed my hair. "Seriously, she doesn't know what she passed up."

The lights dimmed, and the curtains pulled back. For one second, I held my breath, hoping a body wasn't lying in the middle of the stage. I saw Justin and Amy enter the scene, and after a brief hesitation, Justin delivered his line: "Lovely night for a stroll."

An hour later, with practice done, the beer flowed with the conversation. Justin and Amy had joined us at our table, and the hesitancy had vanished from the surfing professor. When Greg and Justin left to get more drinks, I turned to my friend, who had sunk back into her chair.

"He's normal again." I nodded to the men's backs as they made their way through the crowd.

Amy's eyes glistened with unshed tears. "I had to drag him here, but now, it's like this is what he needed. You know how sometimes a disc gets stuck and plays the same thing, over and over? It's like he was in a loop and this knocked him out."

"I told you to give him some time. Why don't you suggest surfing this Sunday?" I sipped on my longneck. "I have to cancel our breakfast anyway."

Amy nodded. "That's a great idea. Wait, why are you canceling? The investigation isn't complete, is it? Are you guys heading out for the weekend?"

"I wish. No, Jim invited us on a fishing expedition. If I wind up as shark bait, you know who to blame."

"I didn't think you and Jim got along." Amy knew all about my hesitations about Greg's brother. "This is a good sign."

"I think Greg told him I was coming. I'm pretty sure Jim didn't suggest bringing a girl along on a fishing trip." If I knew anything about Greg's brother, he was traditional in his view of the sexes. Women stayed home and tended the fires while men went out hunting for food. "I would have backed out, except I know it's going to mess with Jim's head that I'm there."

"You'd rather spend a day being miserable fishing than let the guy win one?"

I saw Greg and Justin heading back to the table, so I answered quickly, "You got it, sister."

"You're evil, you know that?" Amy stretched an arm in front of herself.

"You're just now figuring that out?" Greg handed me a bottle and scooted his chair closer to me. "What were you girls talking about? Or do you want me to guess?"

I poked him in the side with my finger. "It's not what you think. We were actually talking about Aunt Jackie and Josh."

Amy choked on the sip of beer she'd just taken.

"And you are a terrible liar." Greg covered his side with a hand, faking a pain. "Now, no more hitting. I might have to call Toby and have him take you in."

"Pansy." I took a sip of my own beer, making eye contact with Amy, who rolled her eyes at me. I scanned the room. It was slowly emptying, as most people, including me, had an early wake-up call for tomorrow. "You really think we're ready for prime time?"

"As long as they serve plenty of alcohol before, during, and after." Justin held up his beer. "To the audience as well as the cast members."

"Anything for charity," Greg muttered. I leaned into his shoulder. "The next time you try to talk me into something like this, I'm holding out for a weeklong hunting trip with the boys. You deer-hunt, Justin?"

Even in the darkened room, I could see his face turn pale. "Not me. I'm more of a camera guy myself. Shoot and release." Even though Justin tried to joke it off, I could see he was thinking about finding Kent's body. Amy was right, Justin was better, just not totally healed.

As soon as the beers were finished, Greg and I said good-bye to Amy and Justin and walked toward town. "That was nice."

Greg took my hand and intertwined his fingers with mine. "This is nice. That was fun."

"You always have to have the last word, right?"

Greg chuckled, the sound seeming to echo in the empty street. "Just a clarification, not an argument." He brought the back of my hand up to his lips and kissed it. "You want to tell me that acting out some play is nicer than spending some one-on-one time together without anyone to interrupt?"

"Well, when you put it that way . . ." I leaned my head into his shoulder, grateful for the heat radiating from his body. The night had grown cool, and I'd left the house with only my light jacket. "Very, very nice."

We turned the corner and started strolling down Main Street. The lights glowed softly, making South Cove look more like an English village than a California tourist stop. As we passed by the recently re-planted flower pots, the floral smell mixed with the sea salt on the breeze. I leaned into Greg's arm.

"I kind of love it here," I murmured. When he didn't answer, I tilted my head to see his face. He was staring across the street. "What's got your attention? Some beach bunny in a bikini?"

My gaze followed his and landed on the bank. No one seemed to be around, but now Greg had stopped walking.

"What's going on?" I nudged him.

He stepped away from me. "Shh. Go to the shop and call Toby."

"No one's at the shop, Aunt Jackie closed about ten minutes ago." I peered closer at the brick building Greg was so intent on watching. I repeated, "What's going on?"

He turned toward me. "Listen to me without questioning, please. Go to your shop and lock the doors behind you. Once you're in the building, call Toby. Tell him to meet me here."

I froze beside him and felt his gentle push. "Go, Jill. It's probably nothing, but I'd rather be safe than sorry."

"Be careful," I whispered, then I started power-walking the short distance to my building, digging in my purse for my keys without stopping or looking in the large tote. My fingers grazed the cool metal, and I pulled the key ring out before I crossed the street.

My hands were shaking so hard, I kept missing the keyhole. *Get a grip, Jill.*

On the third try, the key slipped into the lock and I heard the opening *click* when I turned the key. As I was about to enter, a hand grabbed hold of the metal frame of the door and I screamed.

CHAPTER 18

"Sorry, didn't mean to scare you," a familiar female voice spoke right behind me. She stood so close, I could feel her hot breath on my neck. I turned to find Cheryl Paine standing there in jeans and a black silk shirt. She must have dressed for the weather as she had on one of those skiers' parkas, the ones with the mountain name emblazoned on the front.

A nervous laugh bubbled out of me. The keys jingled in my hands due to their violent shaking. "Well, apparently I scare easily. What are you doing out here in the dark?" I glanced around, but there were no other businesses open. I strained to try to see Greg near the bank in the gloom with no luck. The street, which had seemed so romantic a few minutes ago, seemed to have too many shadows. Even The Glass Slipper, a stained-glass shop that often had weeknight classes, appeared dark. Where had Cheryl come from?

"I ate a late dinner at the diner up the street and was trying to check in on the businesses I'd talked to earlier this week to see if they had any questions." She nodded to the empty shop. "Can we talk for a while?"

"Actually, we're not open. I'm waiting for the police chief to arrive; we have a safety survey he does every six months." She didn't need to know I was alone here until Greg and Toby figured out what was going on at the bank. I wasn't sure why I used Greg's position instead of his name, but something was off about Cheryl tonight, including her explanation of why she was on the streets.

Cheryl's eyebrows raised, an amused expression filling her face. "Interesting. Kent never mentioned any South Cove safety audits." She paused. "Maybe it's just because he's your boyfriend that your business gets special treatment?"

I twisted around to face her and closed the door partway, using my body to block the entry. "I don't like to advertise our relationship, especially to people I've just met."

Cheryl's eyes sparkled in the dim light. I'd yet to flip the switch that would bathe the shop in light, but I could still see her mind racing, trying to figure out what I was thinking. "Well, I guess I'll check in with you tomorrow. Do you know if Mr. Thomas is in his shop? He bought my best package last week, and I'd love to stop in and deliver a gift basket I have waiting in the car."

I craned my neck to the right, toward Antiques by Thomas. "Looks like he's locked up, too. Maybe you should come back midday. I'm sure you'll find him then."

I closed the door, not waiting for Cheryl's reply, and then flipped the locks. I watched as she walked down the street toward Josh's antique shop. Maybe I should call and warn him?

Then I remembered Greg's instructions. I found my cell, dialed Toby's cell, and repeated Greg's message.

"It's okay, Jill, I'll keep him safe." Toby didn't say good-bye, he just ended the call. But he'd known what I needed to hear. I said a short prayer for both of them and went to the bar to make a pot of coffee. Once they cleared the area, Toby and Greg would come to the shop and I'd probably get another ride in the back of the squad car. Although this time, I don't think I'd worry so much about my accommodations.

An hour later, Greg knocked on the door, and I jumped up from the couch to let him in. Toby followed right behind him. As he walked into the shop, I grabbed Greg and squeezed him, not worried about what anyone thought. Besides, only Toby could see me.

"It's okay, honey." He sniffed the air. "Great, you made coffee. I could use a cup."

Toby walked around us. "I'll pour us both a mug. Black?"

Greg turned me and led me to the counter. "Perfect."

I went back over to the couch and got my own cup for a refill. The pause gave me time to breathe and choke down the worry that had flowed out as soon as I heard Greg's knock. "So what happened?"

Greg waited for me to return to the counter and sit on a stool and for Toby to finish pouring the coffee and join us. "False alarm. There were lights on that shouldn't have been, so the place looked off. But the doors were locked, and when the new manager came, she said everything looked fine. She's doing a deeper look around tomorrow before they open."

"They need a real security system. That thing Kent bought is a joke," Toby growled. "You know he got a kickback from his ex for buying that piece of crap."

"The bank has a new system scheduled to go up in two weeks. I guess it takes some time to get all the paperwork cleared through the corporate world." Greg touched my cheek. "Cheer up, we'll actually be able to eat a full dinner without being called out to the bank for one of their glitches by the end of the month."

I rolled my neck, trying to release some of the tension. "Kent's dead and he's still messing with South Cove."

"Have you contacted a security service yet?" Greg sipped his coffee. "With all the stuff happening lately, I'd feel better knowing you were wired up here."

"Funny you should bring that up. Cheryl Paine greeted me at the door a few minutes ago wanting to know if I'd made a decision." I pushed away my full cup. My hands were still shaking from the shock she'd given me. "I'm surprised you didn't hear my scream at the bank."

"Why were you screaming?" Toby leaned on the counter, watching me. "And why didn't you tell me this when you called?"

I held my hand up to stop the lecture I knew was coming in stereo. "She was visiting the shops where she'd dropped off materials earlier this week."

Greg glanced at his watch. "At ten at night?"

"It was just past nine. Besides, I sent her packing." I tried to change the focus of the conversation. "Antiques by Thomas signed with Stay Safe Security." I watched the look pass between the two men. "Apparently Toby thinks I should buy my security services from a company based locally instead."

"I agree with Toby." Greg set his cup down.

I considered the two men. "You're not going to tell me what's really bothering you about Cheryl Paine and her company, are you?"

"Isn't it enough that we're telling you not to use them?" Toby filled a to-go cup with coffee and grabbed a few oatmeal cookies in a napkin. "I've got to go back to the station and write up the report. See you guys tomorrow."

I went behind the counter and emptied the pot of coffee into two more cups, then put lids on them before setting them in front of Greg. "You want a cookie, too?"

He shook his head, finishing the rest of the coffee in his cup. "I'm good. Let's get you home, then I'm crashing in my office for a few hours. I've got an early meeting."

I locked up the shop and we walked toward the end of town. This time, I felt more unease as I walked through the deserted town. As we approached City Hall, a car sped by on its way out of town.

"Did you see that plate?" Greg asked, pulling out the notebook he carried everywhere.

I stuttered, "No, I mean, I wasn't really looking."

I felt his hand on my back. "It wasn't a test." He jotted something down and closed his notebook.

At the front porch, he hesitated as I opened the door. "You coming in?"

He shook his head. "Not tonight, Jill. I've got some things to think about."

"Good night then." I kissed him quickly on the lips and stepped into the house, shutting the door after me. I watched out the side window as he stood, waiting for me to click the dead bolt. Then he stepped off into the gloom that had turned into a dense fog. For the second time that night, I prayed for his safety.

Thursday had gone splendidly—so far. My run with Emma had been amazing. The commuter coffee club had actually bought books as well as their daily hit of joe. And I'd had a good lull in customers, which meant more time to read. When the bell over the door jingled, I slipped a marker into my book and stood to stretch.

"Were you serious about putting the litter problem on the agenda?" Josh Thomas stood just inside my door, holding a manila folder.

Inside I groaned. On the outside, however, I put on my best fake smile and nodded. "Of course. But we've got weeks before our next meeting."

Josh blushed and thrust the folder toward me. "Not that long. Besides, I want the committee to be prepared. Can you make copies of this file for each member? City Hall should be paying for these administrative costs, not me."

I took the file that was stuffed with paper copies of digital pictures Josh had taken regarding the trash flowing through our lovely town. A rubber band held the folder together. "I may not be able to make everyone a full set of these, but I'll have several copies made so people can get the full scope of the problem."

Josh pursed his lips together, considering my offer. "I guess that will work." He glanced toward the back of the shop. "Is Jackie working today?"

"Five to nine, just like every other Thursday." I set the folder on a table. "Why? Are you two fighting again?" I didn't know what she saw in the man, but he worshiped her.

Josh sighed and I thought I felt a minitremor run through the floor of the shop. "I don't know. I mean, I've seen a man hanging around watching for her. He disappears when I make myself known. Is she dating someone?"

"Not that I know of." *Except you*, I added in my head. "But maybe it's the guy who scammed Mary. What does he look like?"

Josh huffed. "It couldn't be that guy. The person I'm seeing has impeccable taste in clothes and looks like he's rich. Exactly the type of guy Jackie should be dating."

Now I got it—Josh was feeling insecure. "Actually that sounds exactly like the type of man who could scam money out of unsuspecting travelers like Mary. Let me see your shots of him."

"Who said I took pictures?" Josh rubbed the edge of his black suit jacket.

I held out my hand for the digital camera that hung around his neck. "Come on, I know you took pictures. Just to torture yourself."

He stared at me for a few long seconds, then took the camera off his neck. He scrolled through a few shots, then held the screen so I could see the image. The man was casually leaning against a car parked in front of The Glass Slipper, like he was waiting for his wife to reappear after a quick shopping trip. But instead of watching the stained-glass store, his focus was on the business across the street—my shop. From the lighting, this shot was taken at dusk, right when my aunt would have been working. "You have other shots of this guy?"

Josh nodded. "I saw him a couple of days ago, but then yesterday, he was in town every time I went out to shoot pictures. I have a schedule. I shoot at eight, ten, noon, two, four, and six. That way the council can see the effect of tourists on the amount of litter."

The guy was taking his crusade seriously. "Take all the pictures of this guy to Greg. Maybe he can verify if it's the owner of the business where Aunt Jackie had her issues. It should be enough to get him brought in for questioning, I think."

Josh hiked up his pants and grabbed the camera. "If Jackie's in danger, then I'd better get this over to the police station now."

As I watched him leave, I decided it was time to do a well-aunt check. I dialed the apartment number. The phone rang with no response. I hung up, considering going upstairs, when Aunt Jackie flew through the swinging door to the back office.

"Someone's trying to get into my apartment." She ran over and locked the front door. "Lock up the back and call your boyfriend."

I swore as I dialed Greg's cell, running to the back office to make sure the door was locked. I even bolted the door that led to the steps to the apartment. If someone was out there, they'd stay out.

"Hey, sweetheart, I can't really talk right now." Greg's voice was low like he was in some meeting. "I'll call you back."

My nerves crackled. "Listen, you have to get over here right now. Aunt Jackie says someone is trying to break into the apartment."

"Where is she?" I could hear the commotion on the other end as he left his office.

"Downstairs with me in the shop. We've locked up, just in case, but Josh says someone has been watching her." I went back to the front.

"Did you see anyone?" Greg's voice sounded calmer than I wanted. But to his credit, he hadn't seen the pictures Josh had just shown me.

"Just get over here. Don't bring the squad car. I don't know if he's looking out the window or not." I watched my aunt sink into a chair, her hands shaking as she sipped from a glass of water. Not much got Aunt Jackie rattled, but this time, the fear had overwhelmed her.

"Stay put." This time, Greg's voice was hard. "If, and I mean if, there is something going on, I don't need a hostage." He paused and I knew he was thinking the same thing I was: *or worse.*

"Hurry." I ended the call and paced the length of the shop, trying to listen for clues of what might be happening upstairs. Aunt Jackie rose from her chair and walked to stand by the front door. And we waited.

When Greg arrived, she unlocked the door and I wanted to choke him. "What are you doing? Did you even check out the apartment?"

"Relax, I've got Toby out on her back porch. He says someone is in the apartment, looking for something."

I took a deep, shaky breath. "So what are you doing?"

"I'm going in the front, Toby's going in the back, but we're trying to go together. Give me the apartment key." When I pulled the key out of the drawer under the cash register, he stepped around me and headed to the stairway. "I think the guy just wants his book back. Unfortunately for him, he just went too far."

The book that Aunt Jackie had taken during her recent B&E event was safe with her attorney, not upstairs, which made her even more vulnerable. I sprinted to the front door, turned the lock, and flipped the *Closed* sign in the window. Two women were walking down the sidewalk and almost ran right into the locked door.

I called out, "Sorry, we'll be back open soon." Then I headed back to the bottom of the stairwell.

In the few seconds I'd been gone, Toby and Greg had entered the apartment. I heard yelling and then it was quiet. I watched as they escorted a man out the back door and down the steps into Toby's waiting cruiser. Aunt Jackie stood next to me. "I can't believe this is happening. I need a double shot of espresso. Or a shot of Jack Daniels."

I followed and started making her coffee. She frowned as she walked toward the front of the shop. "Why is the door locked? How are our customers supposed to buy our coffee?"

When the lock turned and she flipped back the *Open* sign, I tipped my head so she wouldn't see my lips curving into a grin.

CHAPTER 19

Greg flipped burgers on the grill for dinner that evening. Even though the investigation of Kent's murder was still in process, he'd carved out time to have dinner with me. I'd invited Aunt Jackie, but she insisted on working her normal shift with Sasha. "Your aunt was lucky today. Leaving the apartment was a smart idea."

I sipped on the beer and let the cool liquid flow down my throat. "I was a mess."

He closed the lid of the grill and came to sit by me. He brushed my hair back out of my face, then pulled me close and I laid my head on his shoulder. "That guy could have gone off on her, especially since she didn't have the book. Now he's trying to bargain with the prosecutor, saying that he'll drop the charges on Jackie if she'll drop the charges on him."

"Seriously?" I sat up straight. I wanted to kill the guy and he was going to walk away scot-free?

"I didn't say the prosecutor was taking that deal. Jackie's lawyer turned over the evidence after signing a we-don't-know-how-we-got-this deal. The worse Jackie will get is some community service, but I'm thinking she won't even be charged." Greg tucked me back under his arm. "The guy will get prison time for this, even if he pays back his marks."

"Like Mary? She'll get her money back?" I drank in Greg's scent. Being close to him always seemed to calm me.

"Maybe not all of it, and definitely not soon. She needs to tell Bill what happened." Greg tilted my chin toward him to look into my eyes. "You wouldn't hide something like that from me, would you?"

"Of course not."

Greg laughed. "Baby, you always hide stuff from me. If you think

I'm going to be mad when you're doing your investigation stuff, you just don't tell me."

"I've told you everything this time. At least, I think I have." I nodded to the smoking grill. "The burgers close? I'll open the potato salad I bought at Lille's and dump it into a pretty bowl."

"That's my Suzie Homemaker." Greg stood. "Grab me some cheese slices and a plate and we'll be ready."

After dinner, I made a pot of coffee and fixed Greg a thermos, packing a few cookies in a bag for him to take back to the station. I had a feeling he wasn't the only one who would be nibbling on the chocolate chip oatmeal delights that evening. Toby was on duty and they were his favorite, too.

I carried the sack and thermos into the living room and saw Greg paging through the pictures in the file. "Josh wants me to copy each and every one of those for every member of the Business-to-Business group. I told him I'd talk to Amy about making batches."

"Can I have a few?" Greg held up a few of the pages.

I set the bag of cookies and coffee down on the table. "You can have most of them, that way I don't have to explain to Amy why I'm using all of her monthly allotted paper for copies."

"Just these ten will be fine." He tucked the pages in his back pocket and picked up the coffee, holding it under his arm. He held the cookies in his other hand. "I'm hiding these from Toby. He'll eat them all before I get a chance."

"Sharing is caring." I put my hand on Greg's chest and moved closer, wishing he didn't have to leave. "Great, now I'm sounding like those 'fortunes' Esmeralda's been spouting off."

"You figure out if you're the key or the problem yet?" He kissed me on the forehead, then dropped down to my lips, keeping me from answering.

When he stepped away, I sighed. "I think I'm the shiny new friend she needs."

Greg frowned, not understanding. Then, glancing at his watch, he paused before he asked, "Whose friend?"

"Go to work. It's not a big deal." I walked him toward the door. "Will I see you tomorrow?"

"Probably not. I'll pick you up early Sunday morning for our fishing trip." He grinned when I made a face. "What, did you forget?"

"I was hoping you had." I tapped the pocket with the pictures.

"What's got you so interested in litter? Or are there more pictures showing illegal activities in our small town?"

"You never know what you'll find in the trash."

Sasha poked her head through the doorway to my office-slash-storeroom at the shop. "How am I supposed to code this free book coupon again?"

"What coupon?" I'd been updating the book sales spreadsheet Aunt Jackie had developed to track what types of books were selling. I thought the process was a complete waste of time, but she'd talked me into giving it a try. I liked my tried-and-true gut method. It made ordering more fun. I could experiment with new authors or even new genres. Apparently, numbers told a clearer story. *If* I could get the darn sheet updated. I kept typing, waiting for her response.

"She said she got it in the council's swag bag at Vintage Duds."

Now I knew why my aunt had taken my bag away from me, especially since I'd never approved the expense. Marketing to the other stores in South Cove was just throwing your money away. The people who owned and worked here would buy without a coupon. I glanced at the ceiling, wondering if my aunt was up for a few words. "Scan the book, then key the full price as a coupon. If they bought a drink, the only thing they should be charged for is the food."

"They're just getting the book, so the machine keeps wanting to charge them tax." Sasha leaned against the door. "I guess I could take the money out of the tip jar to even up the till."

During my shift, Sasha took home the tips as part of her wages. I wasn't going to let her make up the difference for the coupon my aunt had designed. "Just ring it up and write the tax on a piece of paper. Put that in the cash drawer and Jackie can do a write-off entry when she does the books tonight."

"You sure? I don't mind chipping in."

"I'm positive." I saved the spreadsheet and turned off the computer. Aunt Jackie could finish the data input this evening. Fridays were usually my day off, but I'd agreed to work in the office in case Sasha needed help. Toby would be here in an hour. I grabbed my purse and entered the café. I was surprised to see Sasha's customer. I didn't think Lille Ramsey had ever bought anything from me. When she saw me, her face turned beet red. I decided to listen to the good angel on my shoulder. "Picking up something to read over the week-end?"

"Carrie asked me to get this stupid book for her." Lille waved the historical romance at me like it was a flyswatter.

"I love that author," Sasha added. "She knows how to write a hot love scene."

Lille turned a deeper red. "I don't know anything about the book. I bought it for Carrie." She turned and skittered out of the shop, the bell on the door chiming hard when the door slammed shut behind her.

"I hope I didn't say anything to offend Ms. Ramsey. I enjoy eating at her restaurant." Sasha watched Lille through the shop's front windows.

"You'll be fine. She believes I sent her boyfriend to prison and she still lets me in the door." I glanced around the empty shop. "Will you be okay until Toby gets here?"

"This ain't my first shift." Sasha smiled. "The three of you baby me so much, I'm beginning to think you believe I can't do much at all."

I leaned on the counter and studied her. "If you're ready, I'll let you fly solo. You're on your own with the other two."

"If I get in trouble, I'll give Jackie a call." Sasha smiled. "I appreciate your confidence in me."

Walking out into the chilly air, I wondered if Greg was in the office. Last night, I'd gone through the photos that Josh had given me and discovered I had two copies of everything. Studying the ones Greg had been interested in, I realized they were all of the inside of the same car—Conner McBride's blue BMW if I had to guess. And in the middle of all the fast-food wrappers and empty to-go cups sat a plastic box filled with what looked like little Baggies. Little Baggies filled with something white.

Either Conner enjoyed baking and the powder was flour, or, more likely, Greg had found the most recent drug dealer for the South Cove area. And probably, Kent's supplier.

Even though Greg had told me the cocaine wasn't the cause of death, I had to wonder. What if it had been spiked with something to make the powder go further? But if that was true, why weren't others dying from Conner's bad product?

On a hunch, I called Information for the number of Pampered Pet. When someone answered, I started my story. "I'm interested in buying one of those pretty frogs, the poison dart frogs for my son. But I'm concerned about safety."

"Hold on a minute, I'll connect you to that section," the chirpy female voice said, then switched me to a recorded message about grooming appointments and the importance of spaying and neutering your pets. Getting closer to City Hall, I found a street-side bench and settled down to wait for a real person to return to the line. I took my notebook out of my purse and dug deeper until I found a pen.

"This is Jeremy, how can I help you?" a friendly voice spoke into my ear.

"My son is begging me for one of those poison dart frogs we saw in your store last week, but I'm concerned. Are they safe?"

"The frogs are just frogs, unless they eat stuff that has poison in them. So yeah, if you keep them on the suggested diet, they're perfectly safe in captivity. Now, I wouldn't go out into the jungles and take one as a pet." He chuckled at his own joke.

"Do you sell a lot of them?"

"A fair amount. The frogs can live up to twenty-five years if cared for, so you have to be sure you're in it for the long haul. Many people can't have dogs or cats in their rentals, so taking on a frog gives them that feeling of having a pet. We sell a lot to single guys looking for the coolness factor."

Jeremy was a wealth of information; now, if I could just get him to tell me one more thing. "Do you have any customers in the area I could talk to about owning a frog? Like what to look out for? Maybe there's someone who lives nearby me I could talk to or call."

"Hold on." The line was filled with *click*s. Then the voice came back. "There are five registered owners in the Bakerstown area. Of course, some buyers don't join our Pet Rewards program, so I wouldn't know those. Where do you live?"

I gambled. "South Cove."

"Love that town. My girlfriend and I bike down the highway and stop there for lunch in that diner." The sales clerk paused. "Hey, you're in luck. I show two owners real close to you. Do you know Anne Marsh or maybe Conner McBride? He's some sort of an artist. I think he's used the frogs as models for his paintings before."

"Actually, I know both of them. Thank you so much." And thinking I needed to give him hope for a sale, "Will you be available next weekend if we decide to buy?"

"We'll be open. We don't work on commission here, so anyone can help you." He called out to someone in the store that he'd be right there and returned to the call. "Anything else?"

"Yeah, what's the wrong kind of food to feed these frogs?"

"Any insects with a high alkaloid level can cause the frogs to become toxic. Like ants or centipedes. Don't worry, we'll send your frog home with a safe diet." He chuckled. "Wouldn't want to lose a customer over a bad diet."

"Literally, you mean." I said my good-byes and wrote a few notes down, then sat tapping my pen. The frogs only had poison if they were in the wild or fed the wrong things. Maybe Conner knew that, too. I decided it was time to tell Greg what I'd learned.

Reaching the station, I hurried into the reception area where Esmeralda was on the phone. I pointed to Greg's office and shrugged my shoulders to ask if he'd arrived yet. She nodded then covered the mic on the phone. "Go on in, he's alone."

Even so, I gently knocked on the door before swinging it open. Greg, too, was on the phone. He waved me in and I took a chair.

"Look, all I want is a search warrant. I know I have probable cause for a search, so just do your job." He slammed down the phone. "Judges should be shot and dumped into the ocean."

"Bad day?" I perched on one of his chairs.

Greg stood and came around the desk, where he leaned onto the front and took my hands in his. "Until now."

I raised my eyebrows. "I don't quite believe you, but it's nice to hear."

He ignored my comment. "So what brings you out on a Friday morning? I would have thought you'd still be in bed, sleeping."

"I went down to the shop to be close in case Sasha needed something." I rubbed my finger over his callused hand.

"She's going to rebel sooner or later like all good children do."

I shrugged my shoulders, watching the sun come out from behind a cloud. "That's basically what she told me. So I left."

"And came here to see me?" He pushed a stray lock away from my cheek. "I'm honored."

"Actually, I wanted to try out a theory on you." I pulled out my notebook and walked Greg through the steps that had to happen for Conner to have killed Kent. When I added in the part that Conner had a poison dart frog, Greg held up his hand, stopping my presentation.

"You know this how?" Greg picked up a pen and held it over his own notebook, poised for my answer.

"I called the pet store to see if anyone in the area owned the things." I shrugged.

"They just gave you out of the blue a list of their customers and what pets they had purchased? Did they let you know how much money the company made last week, as well?"

This wasn't going as well as I'd hoped. "Don't be silly. I may have led the sales associate to believe I was in the market for a pet for my son."

"You made up a son?" Now he was smiling. "What's the poor kid's name?"

I leaned back. "I didn't name the kid. Do you want to hear my theory or not?"

"Go ahead." He wrote down something, then tapped his pen on his notebook. "Hold up, was there anyone else your friend at the pet store mentioned who owns these crazy frogs?"

"One. Anne Marsh." I saw Greg write down the name, then he listened to the rest of my theory. When I'd finished he glanced at his watch.

"I've got to go. I'm meeting Toby before his shift." He walked around the desk, pulling me into his arms for a good-bye kiss. When he let me go, I stared at him.

"That's all you got to say? 'I'm meeting Toby'?" I put my hands on my hips. "This is a good theory. Can't you just check it out?"

Greg put on a baseball cap with the South Cove seal and then took his bulletproof vest out from behind the door. "What do you think I'm meeting Toby for?"

Walking home, I considered Greg's side of the situation. I was a private citizen, no matter how much I loved investigating. But still, you'd think that the guy could have said something during the ten minutes I'd sat there and told him everything he'd already known. Sometimes the man could be infuriating.

Instead of running with Emma, I took a frozen pizza out and put extra cheese on top before throwing it in the oven. Then I turned on the deep fryer and cooked some frozen fries for an appetizer. To round out the meal, I'd open a pint of Rocky Road for dessert. I poured a glass of zinfandel and took my fries and wine to the couch. I popped the first Harry Potter movie into the DVR player and settled in to enjoy. Emma stared at me from the corner of the couch. "Let Greg deal with South Cove's crime. I'm a bookseller, for goodness' sakes, not a private eye."

Convinced that I wasn't going to hand over a fry or two, she laid her head down and closed her eyes. When I finished the Harry Potter movie, I started on my romantic comedy collection. The phone rang during *Sleepless in Seattle* and woke me.

My eyes watered and blurred as I watched Meg Ryan climb into the closet with her corded phone. I laid my head back down on my pillow when my cell rang again. I didn't look at the display when I answered, "Hello?"

"Why didn't you tell me Greg had found Kent's killer?" a woman's voice shrilled in my ear. "Didn't I make it clear you should be reporting your progress back? Or did you even try? Maybe Greg figured the whole thing out without any help from you."

I sat up stretching my neck, which was kinked from my nap on the couch. "Who is this?" I held out the phone to try to see if the display showed a name, but nope, just a local phone number.

"Your worst nightmare. Now that I'm off the hook for Kent's murder, I'm going after Greg."

For a minute, I didn't understand her threat. This was crazy, why would anyone be telling me their homicidal plans? "You're going to try to kill Greg?"

"Ha, not unless I can get him so worked up he has a heart attack." The caller paused. "Are you stupid or something? I said I'm going to get Greg to come back to me."

Then I realized it was Sherry on the phone. But what she'd said initially kept echoing. "Wait, Greg arrested someone for Kent's murder? Who?"

"You really are worthless. Check out the local news station." Then the phone clicked in my ear.

The good news was I didn't have to help Pat prove Sherry's innocence any longer. The bad news was the girl didn't think I'd done squat, so her plans for the total destruction of our relationship was front and center on her mind. I paused the movie because I really wanted to watch the scene where Meg flies to Seattle and spies on Tom Hanks, and turned on the local newscast.

The weatherman—or meteorologist, as he liked to be called—was finishing up his weekend predictions. I held my breath, hoping Sunday would bring torrential rains or hurricane-strength winds. Instead, the day was going to be the first nice day in the entire month. Not what I wanted to hear. When he turned it over to the newscasters, I almost missed the short recap of a rumored drug bust in South Cove. We'd gone through this last year but Conner's arrest felt more personal. The guy was one of the Business-to-Business members, even though he rarely showed. Now I understood what had kept him away; he had a second business to run.

"Unconfirmed reports from sources who claim to have been close to Kent Paine, who died under suspicious circumstances a few weeks ago, say the arrest may close that case, as well." The blond newscaster read off the teleprompter, dropping her smile so she wouldn't appear uncaring.

"Bad business." Her co-anchor let his own smile drop as he shook his head.

"Very bad business," I repeated, finishing the last of the nearly melted ice cream. I sent a quick text to Greg, knowing that he couldn't talk, and went to bed.

CHAPTER 20

Except for a quick return text wishing me sweet dreams, Greg had been silent. I kept myself occupied, running with Emma before work, and then the shop had been busier than normal. Everyone wanted to talk about Conner's arrest. Had I known him well? He seemed like such a nice boy. And, of course, the ultimate question: Do you think he really killed that banker guy?

By midmorning, I felt overwhelmed. Part of me knew my happy place wasn't in the front of the house. I enjoyed working my early shift because we didn't get the crowds. As an introvert, the constant stimulation of people wanting to chat drained me. Maybe someday when the business was doing better financially, I could just have Sasha work the morning shift, then I could just do the office stuff.

I was still daydreaming about it when Toby arrived. He blinked at the almost-full tables and hurried to take off his coat. "Looks like you've had a morning." He chuckled as he washed his hands. Donning a clean apron, he started refilling the coffee cups. "Let me guess, they all want to know if you have insider information on the Conner arrest."

"I'm sure your shift will be busier, since they assume you're a better source than I am." I poured out the last of the strong coffee into a cup and started a new pot. "If Greg and I ever break up, my walk-in traffic is going to die."

"Not likely, you do realize the caffeine we serve is addicting. They'll keep coming, just to see how you're doing with the split. There's always a mini–soap opera going on in small towns. Didn't you know that?" Toby eyed the dessert display case and nodded his approval. "You've done all my prep work today. What, nothing to read?"

"I couldn't get settled. I kept hoping Greg would call." I collapsed on a stool in front of the counter, took a quick glance around the room, and lowered my voice. "Is it true? Did Conner kill Kent?"

Toby didn't answer right away. Instead, he poured himself a cup of coffee and leaned over the counter. "Greg says he's a person of interest. Conner swears he was out of town with some chick that day, but we haven't been able to find her to support his story. It could all be a lie, but the dude sounds sincere."

"A sincere drug dealer?" I sipped my coffee. "It would be nice to have this drama over."

"According to Conner, someone approached him about the same time Craig Morgan was killed last year. The shop had been struggling, so he thought it would be a way to keep his art studio going until he was discovered for his true talent." The bell rang over the door, and Toby's attention went to the new customer. "And that's all you'll get from me. If you want more, ask your boyfriend."

"Like I'll see Greg before next week," I grumbled. I felt a hand on my back and turned to look into his blue eyes.

"Ask and you shall receive." He kissed me and then looked up at Toby. "Four large coffees to go. The district attorney's coming in, and I'm not subjecting him to Esmeralda's green tea this morning."

"You could have called. I would have delivered these." Even after what I knew had been a long night, the guy looked powerful in his jeans and fresh shirt. "Did you get any sleep last night?"

Greg shrugged. "A few hours. Don't worry, I'll be fresh as a daisy tomorrow when I pick you up for our adventure."

"Five, right?" I tried to sound excited, but honestly, I'd thought maybe Conner's arrest would have put the fishing trip on hold. Like, forever.

Greg chuckled. "Wear layers. It can be pretty cold in the morning, but by midafternoon, we'll be getting a tan."

Toby put the last cup into a cardboard holder and grinned. "You want to add something sweet to this, just in case the guy's in a sour mood getting called out on a weekend?"

Greg took a ten out of his wallet for the coffee. "John can get his own breakfast." He kissed me again. "See you tomorrow morning."

I thought about mentioning Sherry's call, but we'd have time to talk tomorrow. Lots of time, if my memories of past fishing trips held true. I put my hand on his arm, squeezed, and lied. "I'm looking forward to it."

After Greg left, I updated Toby on the few tasks I didn't complete, then finished my coffee while wandering through the new releases on the shelves. I found a women's fiction from a favorite author that I hadn't remembered ordering, and headed home. Time for a few chores, then I'd eat a salad to make up for the junk-food meal I'd had the day before and dive into the author's world.

True to his word, Greg knocked on my door right at 5 a.m. the next morning. I unlocked the door and motioned to the kitchen. "Coffee's on and I have cinnamon rolls just coming out of the oven."

He followed me into the kitchen. "Smells wonderful in here. You didn't have to make anything. Jim ordered sandwiches and chips from Lille's. He's on his way there now and will meet us at the marina."

"That's lunch. I'm hungry now." I poured coffee into a carafe. "Does Jim take cream or sugar?"

"Nope, he's a simple man, just like me. Real men like their coffee black." Greg got three travel cups out of the cabinet. "Fill mine up now. Jim can pour his own once we're on the boat."

Once the coffee was set, the oven timer went off on the cinnamon rolls. "Sadie brought these over last night with specific instructions on how to bake. I love her to death, but sometimes I think she believes I've never turned on my stove before."

"You can get distracted." He held up the book I had set on the table when I let him in. "Like when you're reading."

I grabbed the book and tucked it into my bag. "Sue me, I love a good story." I placed the disposable pan into a fabric carrier Sadie had let me borrow to transport the rolls. "Coffee, rolls, napkins." I checked off my mental list. "What am I forgetting?"

"A hat and sunscreen if you have some." Greg eyed the rolls. "You think we should try one, just in case they aren't completely done?"

I slapped his hand as he reached to unzip the cover. "They're fine. You're just going to have to wait. And I've already packed a hat, sunscreen, and hand wipes." I nodded to the oversized bag I'd gotten out last night. The thing could carry a laptop, a couple of books, and still have room for a few bottles of water. "Should we bring bottled water?"

"Jim should be getting some, but it might not hurt." Greg went to the fridge and pulled out six chilled bottles. "You have a small cooler we can take?"

I pulled out a soft-sided cooler painted with a beach scene. "Amy gave me this last summer when she took me out for a surfing lesson."

"I would have paid to see that." He packed the water and took ice cubes out of the freezer to keep the bottles cold.

I ignored his comment and took a bone out of the cabinet for Emma. I gave my dog a kiss on the head and herded her outside. "See you tonight."

When we got to the marina, Jim was already on the boat waiting for us. "Took you long enough."

"We brought breakfast," Greg offered, holding up the rolls and coffee.

I could tell when the smell of the rolls reached Greg's brother because his frown disappeared—for two-point-five seconds. He turned and started untying the boat. "Well, get in and let's get going."

The sun was just beginning to rise over the mountains as we left the marina. I sat on a bench and watched the beach disappear as we moved out into open water. The gulls were flying overhead, arcing around our wake. Greg sat down next to me and put his arm around me.

"Nice, huh?" He leaned back, stretching his neck. "I needed this break."

Cuddling closer to break the chill of the wind the boat was creating, I put my head on his chest. "I'm glad you invited me."

"Made you come with me, you mean." He stroked my hair. "Sherry hated outings like this, so Jim and I usually went alone."

"No wonder he wasn't happy to see me." The marina lights were almost dots now. "Sherry called me Friday night to warn me she's taking you back."

"Typical Sherry." He pulled his head away and tilted my head up so he could see my face. "You told her to bring it, didn't you?"

I shrugged. "Kind of. She woke me up and I didn't know who had called for a while. I guess that ticked her off. Then when she said she was going after you, I laughed."

"Well, she visited me at the station yesterday. All dressed up with nowhere to go."

I pushed aside the bit of worry that hit my stomach. "So what did she say?"

"Oh, some sort of crap about rekindling our friendship even though we weren't together anymore." A grin curved his lips. "So I invited her to join us today."

"You what?" Jim stood over us. I hadn't noticed the boat slowing, but now we sat still in the water, the engine idling. "She hates anything outdoorsy."

"You don't see her here, do you?" Greg laughed. "I knew she wouldn't come. But the invitation got her out of my office and quick. She claimed she'd promised Pat they would go over the monthly accounts for Vintage Duds today."

"That doesn't mean she's giving up," I pointed out.

Jim scowled. "Marriage should be forever, but I swear, Sherry makes it hard for me to support her."

I turned to look at Jim and for the first time, I saw compassion for me in his eyes. Maybe this trip had been a good idea. I felt Greg's arm tighten around me.

"Don't worry, I'm a one-woman man." He laughed. "Jim, do you remember the weekend we took off to camp at Lake Tahoe?"

Jim sat on the bench across from us and poured a cup of coffee. "Yep. We got to the spot where we were pitching our tent and Sherry threw a fit. She tried to call a taxi to take her home."

"I didn't know national forests had taxi services." I smiled at the image.

"They don't. But she made our weekend miserable." Jim nodded to the pan of cinnamon rolls. "You mind if I have one?"

"I'll dish one up for all of us." I started to stand, but Jim waved me down.

"No need, I'll get them." He carefully unzipped the container and served us each a still warm roll. After he sat back down, he paused before he took a bite. "Elizabeth used to bake these every Sunday before we went to church. I haven't had one since she passed."

Tears sprang to my eyes. "I'm sorry, I didn't know."

Jim shook his head. "It's a good memory. No use apologizing for something that brings back the good times."

We ate our breakfast in silence. And when we were done, Jim stood and wiped his eyes. "Thanks for bringing food."

As he walked toward the cabin, Greg called out, "We fishing here?"

"That's what we came for," Jim called back as he brought back three poles.

I watched the men prepare the lines for each pole and thought about the power of food. It could bring back memories and maybe, just maybe, heal a pain. And for once, I didn't feel like Jim hated me for being the other woman. Maybe Greg's plan to get his brother used to me by proximity was working. All I had to do was get through the day. And learn to bait my own hook with what smelled like dead, rotten fish.

I put down my cup and went to watch the process, willing to learn.

Eight hours later, we were back at the marina. Jim and Greg, who had ignored my multiple offers of sunscreen, were red as a Maine lobster. My skin felt tight, but I hoped my repeated slathering of the coconut-scented lotion had allowed my winter-white skin to tan rather than burn. The last time I'd tried to douse my arms in the sunscreen, Greg had taken it away from me with the comment, "You smell like a woman working a tiki hut."

I figured that was a bad thing.

"Well, we weren't skunked." Greg kept his voice bright. There was one lone fish in the cooler. A tuna that had somehow landed on my line while the men got a few bites, but nothing sticking. Greg had been supportive, talking me through reeling the catch in, but I could see the looks they gave each other.

"Beginner's luck," Jim grumbled, but his lips had curved into a tiny smile. At least I hoped so. "I'll take it and get the thing cleaned and packaged up. I can drop it off tomorrow at the shop if you'd like."

"The store's closed so I'll be home. You can come by there." I dumped the leftover coffee from the mugs into the carafe and threw all of the items into a tote I'd brought.

"I'll take it to the station. Greg can bring it to you." Jim nodded at his brother and Greg took my arm, leading me to his truck parked in the marina's lot.

"He can stop by the store, but not my house?" I put the tote in the bed of the truck and climbed in the passenger side.

Greg started up the engine, turning to look at me. "Don't press your luck. He's warming up to you. Jim's old-fashioned in many ways. He's respecting our relationship by not visiting you at your home, thereby avoiding any hint of scandal."

"Wait, he thinks stopping by the house will cause me to throw myself at him?" I rolled down the window, enjoying the last rays of the beautiful day.

As Greg pulled the truck out onto the highway, he responded, "It's happened before."

Once he dropped me off, I spent a few minutes with Emma, who thought I smelt wonderful. I smelt my hand and gagged. Coconut-flavored dead fish and sweat. "Time for a shower, then we'll watch some TV and eat soup? Sound good?"

Emma gave me a short bark, which either meant *terrific* in dog language or *where's the rotten fish?* Either way, I rubbed the top of her head and went upstairs to clean up.

Before I turned the television off that night, I turned on the evening news. Not a word about Kent's murder investigation or Conner's arrest or even South Cove. The media had moved on and now a new problem had taken the limelight. A scandal in a local election. I smiled as I turned off the television. "Feels good to be normal again, right, girl?"

I slept the sleep of the dead that night. No dreams, no nightmares, no premonitions surrounding the friend song Esmeralda kept sending me through all-spirit-radio, the only channel her fortune-telling talent tuned in to.

I love Mondays. I'm probably the only person on the planet who does. Except for other shopkeepers like me. Mondays are my Sundays, when I relax with a book, handle chores like bank deposits or mailing packages, or shop for food. The great thing about being off work when everyone else is working is you avoid the Saturday crowds at the grocery store or the dry cleaners. The bad thing? Everyone else is working, so sometimes I craved company on my jaunts.

I'd finished my shopping in Bakerstown, put away all the groceries for the week, and even had meals planned by the time Aunt Jackie called.

"I forgot to make the deposit." No *hello*, no *how are you*. Just what she needed.

I wasn't playing her game, not today. I hadn't been able to fit any reading in yesterday, so the rest of my day was devoted to finding out if the new chef in town was going to be able to make a go of her Mexican restaurant. Fictionally, I mean. I made a managerial decision. "Then go to the bank and make it."

"Smart aleck, I would, but I'm in San Francisco and the deposit is sitting on my dining room table in South Cove. With all the craziness lately, I'm pretty sure you don't want that amount of money just lying around, do you?"

Dreams of sitting on the porch in my swing, sipping iced tea faded. I checked the clock. I had an hour before the local branch closed to commercial business. "You owe me."

A chuckle came over the line. "I would think you'd be grateful for such a dedicated employee who would call to correct one tiny mistake."

"Whatever." I hung up the phone and grabbed my purse and the shop keys. I carried an extra copy of the apartment key on my ring, mostly because my aunt kept locking herself out. Instead of walking into town, I fired up the Jeep and drove the few blocks. I swung into the back lot, left my Jeep running, and ran up the outside stairs. Whoever Jackie had gone to the city with must have driven, as her Escape sat in its normal spot. Thoughts of the last week bubbled in my brain, and I wondered if I should have been more inquisitive about her whereabouts. I shook it off. "She's a grown woman who can do what she wants."

I unlocked the door and saw the blue deposit bag right on top of the dining room table where she'd left it. My aunt had decorated the little apartment with high-end furniture and antiques. It looked like a miniature version of her city apartment before she'd been bought out when the building owners decided to renovate the brick structure into expensive condos. Ones that my aunt couldn't afford due to an unfortunate investment that had robbed her of much of the money my uncle had left. No wonder she'd felt so driven to protect Mary.

Sending positive thoughts my aunt's way, I locked the door and hurried to the bank, only slightly exceeding the speed limit. Most of the shops in South Cove were closed on Mondays, except for the bank and the tobacco shop across the street. I parked in front of the building and hurried into the bank lobby.

A portly man dressed in a security uniform held the door for me. He nodded in welcome, then went back to standing to the side, his hands crossed in front of him.

Leslie's line was empty so when I walked up with the blue envelope, she nodded to the doorway. "I see you noticed some of the changes around here."

"They really think they need a security guard?" I'd seen guards in banks before, but typically it was for the larger branches. "You don't get enough business to make it worthwhile to steal from here, do you?"

Leslie didn't look up from keying in the checks. "Beats me. Kent always said we were safer without a guard. He said people tend to act stupid around someone in authority."

"Well, I guess when a new manager comes in, he's going to make some changes." I watched Leslie count out the cash my aunt had so carefully sorted and rubber-banded together.

"She. The new manager is a she. Although from what I've seen, she's cold as ice. Kind of like that lady who wrote the tiger book." Leslie handed me my printed deposit slip and leaned closer. "I hear the audit last week had some issues. I guess Kent was dipping his wick into the company till."

No wonder the guy could afford all those fancy suits. "Seriously? Why would he risk getting caught?"

"Who would catch him? The bank's security system was run by that ex-wife of his. She's one of the reasons they got the guard." Leslie leaned closer. "She was caught on tape searching Kent's office just last week. I guess she set off her own alarm system and had to run before the cops arrived. Ironic, right?"

That must have been the night she'd shown up at the shop when I'd sent her away. Her face had been red, but I'd attributed it to the chill of the evening air. "What was she looking for, do you know?"

"No clue, but we're all on strict operating procedures. We can't leave our money drawer without checking in with a supervisor, even just to go to the bathroom." Leslie sighed. "Kent was a piece of work, but at least when he ran the branch, he didn't make you feel like a potential criminal."

"Maybe that's because he was hiding his own issues." I thought about Aunt Jackie's stalker, the travel scam artist, and his separate book of deals. "Cheryl could have been looking for a record of Kent's thefts. Probably anything that implicated her."

"I hadn't thought of that." Leslie pondered the idea, but was interrupted by a tap on her shoulder.

Anne stepped over behind Leslie. "Sorry, I've got to close my line. The boss just called me into her office. I guess it's my turn to get the pep talk."

"No worries, sweetie. We're close to closing up anyway." Leslie gave her a supportive smile. When Anne went into the office and closed the door, Leslie sighed. "That girl lets things get to her. She's always worried about something."

"You don't think the manager is letting people go, do you?" I stared at the closed door. When we'd had firings at the law firm, it always happened just before closing time. Even though most of the associates stayed long after official hours ended, the management and clerical staff left at 4:59 p.m. on the dot.

"If she fires Anne, the woman will have to answer to me." Leslie looked thoughtfully at the closed door. "She needs to remember what happened to Kent before she goes messing with people's lives."

CHAPTER 21

When I returned home, a convertible BMW sat in my driveway. I parked the Jeep on the other side of the car and locked gazes with Pat Williams, who stood on my porch. "Now what," I grumbled as I turned off the engine and climbed out of the car. Pat was in a sleeveless shift dress with a statement necklace to match. Her heels matched the color of the dress and had those platforms on the bottom that used to indicate a woman was in the oldest profession. Heck, I'll say it. The girl wore hooker shoes.

When I got up to the porch, her gaze dropped to my jean capris and worn I Love Napa T-shirt. I didn't have time or the desire for a fashion makeover, at least not from Pat. I leaned against the porch rail, my house keys in my hand. "What do you want?"

She glanced at the door, realizing I wasn't going to invite her in to tea, then steeled herself. "I wanted to thank you and apologize for Sherry's call. She'd been drinking that night, and I didn't realize until Saturday she'd gotten in touch with you."

"You mean to threaten me that she was taking back *her* man?" My words made Pat squirm just a bit. "Look, *you* didn't call me, so no need for an apology."

Pat understood my unspoken meaning. "Sherry can be a handful. Honestly, she regrets what happened between her and Greg. I think she's just trying to make up for what she did to ruin their marriage."

I held up my hand to stop the Sherry pity party. "This is so not my business. However, you can tell your friend this, I'm dating Greg now and she can deal with it or not. I don't want her to call me unless it's about an agenda item for the Business-to-Business meeting or an order from CBM."

"I get that you're angry"—she started, but I didn't let her finish the sentence.

"I'm not angry. I'm just not playing Sherry's game. If Greg wants to go back to that situation, that's his call, not mine. And until he tells me our relationship is over, I'm believing him."

"Good. I'm glad to see you're growing a backbone." Pat smiled at my confused look. "Sherry's my best friend, but she can be a steamroller. I just wanted to apologize for asking you to get in the middle of this. I should have set boundaries."

I wasn't quite sure how to answer. "At least Sherry's not a suspect anymore."

"Greg does hold his cards tight." Pat laughed. "So you haven't heard?"

I shook my head, not liking where this was going.

Pat stepped carefully off the step and onto my walkway's first paving stone. "Conner finally alibied out for the day of the murder. He was in San Diego with his girlfriend, and he has the receipts and pictures to prove it."

When I went into the house, I set aside the book I'd been planning on reading, and instead pulled out my list of clues. I hadn't been updating my notebook since Conner had been arrested, thinking the mystery was solved. Now I had to review the information I'd found out, including the fact that only two people in South Cove owned the poison dart frog. Or I only knew about two people. Maybe you could find the poison online, already packaged up in a nice little box ready to kill someone.

Okay, it was a long shot, but as I booted up my computer, I knew that Sherry hadn't killed Kent. All I had to do was convince my boyfriend.

My alarm woke me out of a dreamless sleep, and as I went about my morning getting ready for work, Kent's murder kept running through my head. As I ran Emma, I thought about the mysterious redhead in the car. With all the women Pat had given me as Kent's conquests, no one had the curly flame-red hair that I'd seen when I witnessed their make-out session in the car that afternoon. I knew it wasn't a wig, not the way they were going at it. I'd worn a wig for Halloween one year, and I never could keep the thing straight on my head.

No, the redhead was the key. I quickly showered and power-walked down to the shop. Today I was alone, since the morning shift got next to no traffic on a Tuesday. Sasha and Toby would relieve me at noon. If I hadn't been able to talk to Greg by then, I'd stop by the station on my way home.

My plan set, I opened the shop and set up for the day. By ten, I'd done the prep, updated the book order list, paid invoices, and set up payroll. I opened my laptop and started searching for Kent's name to see if he'd ever dated a redhead that showed up on Facebook or Google, when the bell over the door chimed.

Anne and Leslie marched into the shop. I flipped the cover of the laptop closed. Anne immediately sat at a table away from the window while Leslie headed for the counter. "Two black coffees, large." She took a ten from her wallet and threw it at me. "Bring them to the table."

No chitchat, no *please*, no banter. Something was up or they were trying to sneak a quick break from the bank. I hurried and poured the coffees and walked them over to the table. "I put these into to-go cups in case you want to take them back to work. Just let me know and I'll do a refill when you're ready to go."

"She fired me." Anne took the cup from me and set it in front of her. "That creep kept all the loan transactions but made it look like I was getting all the money, not him."

"Anne"—Leslie shot a warning look at her friend—"maybe we shouldn't talk about this here?"

"I don't care who knows. Kent set me up. He said he loved me and we'd never get caught." Anne started crying. "We were a modern-day Bonnie and Clyde, then someone went and killed him. Now I'm the patsy."

"Look, maybe you should be telling this to a lawyer. I can get you a name from my old firm." Leslie was right, Anne needed to be quiet or all this would be fair game when she was on trial.

"They're not charging me. That would be too big of a scandal for the bank. All they're doing is ruining my life." Anne traced the CBM logo on the cup. "How am I supposed to get a job without a refer-ence? Who would hire a crook?"

"Honey, we'll figure all this out. You just have to have faith." Leslie put her hand on her friend's arm.

"I'll give you some privacy, but if you want an attorney, let me know." I stepped away from the table and went back to the counter to add these notes to my list. Of course, Anne added another reason she was on the I-Killed-Kent short list, especially with the frog ownership working against her. Now her overgenerous spending made sense. She'd been making her own money along with Kent. No need to budget like a mere mortal, just add to your disposable income without taking a second job.

I'd just settled in with a coffee of my own when the bell over the door rang again. Looking up, I smiled. Claire LaRue, the fashion lady I'd met at Sherry's estate lot sale had made good on her promise. She was halfway to the counter when she saw Anne and Leslie and stopped dead in her tracks.

I could see her making a decision, but the need for coffee won over what appeared to be shyness—although she hadn't seemed shy when I'd met her. Maybe she knew the women. Anyway, I was going to welcome her into the shop. I needed all the repeat townie customers I could get. "Claire, I'm so glad you decided to come in today. You can tell I'll have plenty of time to chat." I waved my arm around the almost-empty shop.

Anne and Leslie turned and stared at the newcomer.

Claire hurried to the counter. "I'm on my way to work and thought I'd get a coffee to go."

"Sure, what's your poison?" I pointed to the menu board. "Mild, Medium, Hard Rock, or do you want something with a touch of flavor? The hazelnut's really good."

"Hazelnut is fine." Claire took out her wallet and shoved a card at me. She really was in a hurry.

I charged her order, then turned around to pour the coffee. "You'll have to come in soon when you have more time. I'd love to hear about your new house." After adding a sleeve and lid to the cup, I turned back around to find Leslie standing next to Claire, staring at her.

"You think you're so smart. I can't believe you fired her after all she did for the bank." Leslie's words were hard.

Claire took the cup in her hand but didn't lift it. "She stole money. She covered up for Kent. I had no choice."

"Oh, you had a choice, but all you big shots want is to protect the bank." Leslie's eyes narrowed.

"Look, I shouldn't even be talking to you about a former employee, but it seems like your friend has filled you in on the details.

She approved loans for people who didn't apply for them—heck, they didn't even exist. Then she and her boyfriend went on spending sprees." Claire's shoulders sank. "I know it was probably all Kent, but the bank didn't give me an option here."

"Rules are rules, right?" Leslie almost spit out the words. The bell rang again, and this time when I glanced up from the prizefight going on in front of me, I saw Anne dart out the door. Leslie saw her, too, and headed out after her. She yelled back at Claire, "I'm calling in sick."

Claire blew out a long breath, then took a sip of her coffee. "Man, I need this today."

"What's going on? You're working at the bank?" I motioned to a chair. "Maybe you should sit down. I'm shaky after that scene and I just witnessed it."

She sank onto a stool and rubbed her face. Then she took another sip of the coffee before she spoke. "I'm the new bank manager. I was assigned to audit the branch when all the security alerts were re-ported by the local police."

"You mean the security service?" I didn't think Greg had enough people to report everything that happened in South Cove.

"No, that was the problem. We realized early on that the security service wasn't reporting the alarms to anyone. And the system was getting less sensitive with every false alarm." Claire paused as I real-ized what she was saying.

"Cheryl was lowering the system's alerts to try to get it turned off altogether?" I shook my head. "But why?"

Claire laughed and nodded to the now-empty table where Anne had sat. "Another one of Kent's schemes, we believe. Of course Cheryl's not talking. He sure had his women trained. They would do anything for him."

When Toby arrived for his shift, I filled him in on the morning's drama while I ate an apple I'd packed for a midmorning snack.

Toby whistled. "Wow. I knew part of this, but I'd never dreamed Anne would go along with something like this. I knew her sister, Kate, in high school. Anne was a few years older than me, but she al-ways seemed cool at the games when she attended."

"Anne thought he loved her." I finished my treat and glanced at the double chocolate mud brownies in the case. "Maybe I should take a couple of those to Greg."

"So you can pump him for information?" Toby packaged up four of the brownies and handed me the Styrofoam container.

Taking the box, I grinned. "Nope, because I'm a good girlfriend and I know the way to a man's heart."

"Whatever. I'll see you tomorrow." Toby greeted one of his regulars who tended to walk in just in time to avoid ordering from me. I think the girl sat in her car, waiting to see when he started. She had it bad, even though Toby had been clear he was off the market. Hope can make people do funny things.

I zipped my coat as the fog hadn't quite disappeared from town yet. I hadn't told Toby I needed the brownies to remind Greg about dress rehearsal on Thursday night.

Esmeralda was on the phone when I entered the station. I laid one of the brownies on a napkin on her desk before knocking on Greg's door.

"Hey, you." He stood up and kissed me. I surveyed his desk. Piles of reports and file folders covered every empty space, along with coffee cups and candy bar wrappers. I handed him the box.

"Looks like I should have brought you real food, not another treat." I sat in one of the chairs.

He opened the box and groaned, taking out a brownie with his fingers and shoving the entire thing in his mouth. Once he swallowed, he sighed. "This will do just fine. You're the best."

"I know. But thanks for saying it." I picked up the candy wrappers and threw them in the trash can under his desk. "Seriously, when was the last time you ate a real meal?"

"Just before Conner's girlfriend showed up and blew my case out of the water. I had motive, opportunity, and method, but now, all I have are hunches." He ate a second brownie while he surveyed the piles on his desk. "It's all right there, I'm just missing something."

"Anne, Leslie, and Claire had a fight in my shop this morning." I leaned back, watching his face. "Claire says you called the bank to rat out Kent and his ex-wife."

Greg held up a hand. "That's not how it happened. Actually, the alarm went off on a weekend and Kent was nowhere to be found. And, funny thing, Cheryl was AWOL that weekend, too. So when I couldn't reach the branch manager or the security service, I called a buddy I know who works for the bank's corporate office. One thing led to another."

"So Kent was under suspicion before his death."

He nodded. "Why do you think he was meeting with the auditors the day Sherry hosted the Business-to-Business meeting? I hoped he'd be there so I could watch his reaction to the surprise audit."

"You're good at keeping secrets, you know that?" I thought about Sherry's phone call and how she'd known more about the situation than I had at the time. Of course, she'd gotten her info from the nightly news, not Greg.

"I only keep the ones from you that I have to. If I told you everything I was investigating, I wouldn't have a job." He stretched his arms and stood. "Can I interest you in lunch at Lille's? I'm buying."

I pursed my lips together, pretending to consider the offer. "On one condition."

He pulled me out of my chair and put his arms around me. Leaning down he whispered, "You're a pain, you know that, right? What do you want now?"

I slapped his chest. "I was going to remind you that dress rehearsal is Thursday at seven."

Greg tucked his head into my neck and groaned. "I'm not sure I'll make it. I've got meetings in Bakerstown all day Thursday."

"You'll make it." I moved us toward the door. "But don't worry about picking me up. I'll walk to the winery and you can drive me home."

"Sounds like a deal." We entered the empty lobby.

I picked up the sign that Esmeralda had left and read, "Back in five." My stomach growled as I said, "I guess we can wait."

Greg went back to his office and locked the door. "No need. If she says she'll be back in five, she will."

After we'd ordered our food, I decided to push my luck. "One more thing and we'll stop talking about the case."

"I didn't know we *were* talking about the case." Greg unwrapped the silverware that Lille's staff kept wrapped in a paper napkin.

"Okay, then I have one question. Did you ever trace the plate of that car I saw in the beachfront parking lot the day Kent was killed? Could she be the killer?"

Greg rubbed his face. "I'd forgotten about that. Tim was supposed to run up to Bakerstown and talk to the rental manager, but when we arrested Conner, I told him not to worry about it." He pulled out his phone and keyed in a short text.

I sipped on my soda and watched. By the time he'd finished, Carrie had dropped off our food. He put the phone in his pocket and dug into his French dip. "Thanks for stopping in, I was starving."

"No problem. A girl's got to eat, too." We ate in silence until Greg's phone beeped indicating a new text.

He glanced at the display and keyed a short answer.

"That was quick." I dipped a French fry into Lille's special sauce, which consisted mainly of ketchup and horseradish sauce, but I loved the stuff.

"He's on his way now." Greg smiled at me and stole a few fries. "Thanks for reminding me."

"My investigation addiction comes in handy at times."

"Sometimes." Greg picked up the check and nodded at my plate. "You done? I need to get back to the station."

CHAPTER 22

Emma and I spent the afternoon on the back porch reading. Well, I read; she napped. The fog had burned off during lunch, and now the sunshine felt warm on my feet. I tried to put the whole Kent thing behind me, but I knew the answer had to be with the redheaded woman. She was the clue to breaking this puzzle.

I went into the house and looked up the number for the Bakerstown car rental office. Dialing, I hoped Tim had been there and gone, or Greg was going to hear about this.

"Bakerstown Rental, how can we make your day?" A female who sounded way too chipper for anyone at a real job answered on the first ring.

"Can I speak with your manager?"

"Sure. Steve's available. Can I ask who's calling?"

Crap, I hadn't planned on this. I grabbed the first name that came to me, "Amy Westhouse."

The lie must have sounded plausible because in a few minutes, a male voice came on the line. "This is Steve, how can I help you?"

"Hey, I have one follow-up question from Tim's visit today to finish up the report." I shuffled papers like I was looking for something. "Hold on, I know his report was here somewhere."

"Tim, the police officer from South Cove?" Steve sounded interested now.

"Yeah, on the rental vehicle, were you the one who rented to the suspect?" I paused, letting the implication sink in.

"Now, look here, I told the officer that we followed all the procedures. The woman had a valid license and a credit card, so there wasn't anything that suggested she was a criminal." He flustered through the information.

"Okay, I see that, but the name on the license, Tim's notes are a little blurry, who rented the car?" I held my breath, hoping he'd answer.

"Jennifer Adams. Check the copy of the driver's license. She just lives down the street at 14 Highland. Why don't you call her if you have any more questions, I'm a little busy here with customers." Now Steve the manager just sounded mad. "Is that all, or do you want to ask me all the questions the officer asked again?"

"You've been very helpful. I don't understand why the officers can't just print out their reports, it would save me so much time and headache." I sighed, hoping he would buy my overworked clerical act.

"Well, I guess it didn't hurt anything. Have a nice day." Steve hung up on me. I hoped he was so busy he wouldn't even remember this conversation in a few hours. I considered driving into Bakerstown just to get a look at this woman, but I knew if I went alone, Greg would have my head.

Checking the clock, I dialed Amy's work number. "Hey, do you want to do dinner in Bakerstown tonight? I'll buy."

We made plans for me to pick her up in thirty minutes in front of the bike rental shop.

When she piled in the Jeep, she gave me a quick hug and threw her bag in the back. "So why are we really going to Bakerstown?"

"Am I that obvious?" I turned on my blinker and turned back onto Main Street, heading the long way out of town. This way I didn't have to drive past the police station and risk running into Greg.

"Crystal clear. Besides, you never want to drive into town just for dinner. You tend to bunch your chores together." She shrugged then turned on the radio. "You don't have to tell me."

I got on the highway, then turned down the music. "Fine, we're checking out another one of Kent's girls. This Jennifer Adams rented the car that was parked next to Kent's the day I saw him making out with a redhead."

"Uncovering Kent's habit of keeping more than one woman on the line doesn't mean she killed him."

I thought about this. Maybe Jennifer was just another conquest for him. "True, but the leads are all dying. If this girl is a redhead, she may be one of the last people to see him alive. And maybe she could tell us who he was meeting later that night."

Amy considered my reasoning, then nodded and turned the tunes back up. That's the joy of having a best friend who gets you. Amy would be the one sitting beside me in the jail cell laughing about how much fun we'd had.

"I'm still buying you dinner." I turned into Bakerstown and keyed the address Steve had given me into my GPS.

"I never had any doubt." Amy watched out the window as we drove deeper into the little town. The buildings turned from offices, to retail, and finally to residential. Then the houses got smaller and less maintained. Finally we were parked outside 14 Highland. Or what had been 14 Highland before the house had burned to the ground. If Jennifer lived here, she was pitching a tent as the actual house was demolished.

"Do you think you got the wrong address?" Amy peered at the blackened lot, filled with trash.

"I think she gave this address for a reason. Mostly because it couldn't be traced to her." I studied the street and noticed a group of young men on a porch up the road. We could stop, ask if they knew Jennifer, and keep following the clues. Or we could be safe and just go to dinner. Greg would be investigating this. No need to be the stupid girl who opens the door to the killer in the slasher movies. I put the car in gear and pulled away from the curb. "Where do you want to eat?"

Amy suggested seafood, and I drove us to the place where Greg and I had our first date. "Best food in town."

After a dinner of fish, clams, and scallops, Amy and I were on our way back to South Cove. Stopping at a light, Amy pointed to a couple of working girls standing on the corner and giggled. "There's your redhead."

I turned to look and did a double take. She was right. The woman's hair was long and curly and just the shade of red I'd seen with Kent. But with all the women he had on the line, why would he hire a "professional"? A horn beeped behind me and I realized the light had changed. By the time I reacted, the woman on the street had gotten into a car and left. Now the driver behind me laid on his horn and I reluctantly left the corner.

"What if that was the woman?" I asked Amy who had leaned back, her eyes closed in some sort of food coma.

"Kent wouldn't hire it out. It would make him feel like less of a man." Amy yawned. "I'm going to go right to bed after this. I can't believe I'm such a lightweight. I used to party all night, weekday or weekend."

"We're all getting older." I sped around a car whose driver had never seen the ocean before.

"Speak for yourself." Amy laid her seat back as far as it would go and put on her shades. "Wake me when we get to South Cove, okay?"

For the next fifteen minutes, with the car interior completely quiet, I thought about the paradox of Kent and the hooker. Finally I gave up. The only way he'd be with a prostitute was if he didn't know what they really were. The realization hit me so hard, I spoke the thought aloud. "Someone else bought her for him."

When I got home, I pulled all the pieces together under one name: Anne. She had motive, opportunity, and a burning desire to make Kent pay, even though she claimed she still loved him.

I wrote it all out and put my notebook into my purse. I'd stop by the station tomorrow after work—being sure to leave out the part about driving to Jennifer's false address.

Greg wasn't in his office the next day when I got off work. Esmeralda was at the reception desk, studying her tarot cards, when I arrived.

"You should have called. You just missed him."

"When will he be back?" I peeked at her cards, wondering why she'd bring them into the office.

"Not until Friday. He's got meetings in Bakerstown today and tomorrow. I thought he would have told you this." Esmeralda's eyes sparkled with humor.

Laughing, I shrugged. "I guess he did. I mean, I thought it was just Thursday."

"Confusion happens." She caught me looking at the cards. "The switchboard's a little slow today, especially with Greg and the mayor out. Do you want me to throw your cards?"

Besides totally not believing, it always made me a little uneasy to consider having my future read. What if I was told I would die in a year? Would my disbelief protect me from an early demise? Or would I change my life, which would cause the prediction to change, only I wouldn't know it had changed? See, this was why I didn't believe. It twisted my head into a confused mess.

"I don't know . . ." I stepped back. "Maybe I should just go home."

I guess I didn't move far enough away because Esmeralda caught my arm in a death grip, her bloodred nails digging a little into my skin. If I hadn't been freaked before, I was now. "Come sit with me and I'll walk you through the cards. Something's telling me you need to be read."

And something's telling me you're as looney as a parakeet. I sat down in the chair next to her deciding to humor her. Which seemed to work, as she released my arm. People thought the fortune-teller was a bit odd, but like most folks in South Cove, I knew she was just trying to get by. I didn't believe she had an open line to the other world, but the woman was amazing at reading people. And that was a skill I needed. She gathered the cards together and had me shuffle them three times. The cards were made of heavy cardboard and not easy to mix together, but I managed. I pushed the deck toward her. But she didn't touch them.

"Now cut the deck."

Thin to win, my grandma always said. The woman loved her blackjack. Finally, Esmeralda picked up the deck and quickly laid out the pattern. "This is a Celtic cross. I like to use it for a first reading. It gives you an idea of what each card and position means."

She pointed to the first card. Then her finger started shaking. "You need to avoid the friend, she's the one who's dangerous. Some are silver and the others gold."

"What?" I switched my gaze from the cards to Esmeralda's face. Her eyes were staring at a spot on the wall, not looking at the cards at all. The phone rang and she blinked, then answered, "South Cove Police Department, Esmeralda speaking." She smiled at me and picked up a pen, tapping it lightly on the paper. "Sorry, he's out for the week. Can someone else help you?"

The caller must not have liked the answer because I heard a string of curse words come out of the tiny speaker on Esmeralda's Lady Gaga headset. She pushed the button off and returned her attention to me. "Sherry's been trying to reach Greg all week, but he's put her on a no-call list."

"That was Sherry?" I asked, already knowing the answer. Thankfully Esmeralda pretended not to hear me.

"So that's your reading. You're going to be pretty lucky this week. Did you understand the cards?"

I wasn't quite sure how to answer. Apparently, Esmeralda had thought she'd explained the reading, but instead I'd gotten the scary voice singing the friendship song. Totally creepsville. Since she appeared to be waiting for an answer, I nodded and lied, "That was great."

Then I remembered my decision to be more friendly, more neighborly. "Hey, do you want to come over some night and watch a movie or something?"

"Why would I do that? I have a television, you just didn't see it when you dropped off Maggie." She looked at me, confused.

"I just thought maybe it would be nice if we did something together." I stumbled over my words.

"Oh, my dear, you're lonely. I have a terrific women's group I meet with on Wednesday nights to help them deal with being single. You could come with me, the girls would love to meet you." She leaned forward.

"No, I mean, I'm fine. I just thought . . ." I gave up explaining and stood. "Thanks for the reading, Esmeralda."

"I'll tell Greg you stopped by when he calls in. I'm sure he'll get in touch as soon as possible."

As I walked out of the station, feeling like a complete fool, the friendship song echoed in my head. Something was ringing true with Kent's murder and the stupid song, but for the life of me, I couldn't put my finger on it.

I took Emma for a long run as soon as I got home and yet my mind still didn't feel settled.

CHAPTER 23

Darla had called three times to make sure I remembered the dress rehearsal. The last time, I'd been in the shower when the cell rang. Thinking it might be Greg, trying to call off because of work, I stepped out of the water, my hair still soapy, and dripped over my wood floors to the nightstand to answer the phone.

"Oh, hey, it's just me. Did I already call you about the rehearsal?" Darla sounded distracted, worried.

"Yes, you did. Now, stop calling. Greg said he would be there, and he will do his best. You know he has an investigation going on, right?" I shivered as the water started to dry on my skin.

"What's going on with the investigation?" Now I'd woken the sleeping tiger. No longer did she sound distracted. Now it was all Katie Couric focus.

"I'll talk to you when I get there." I clicked off the phone and ran back to the shower, trying to stay on my feet on the slippery floor. Twenty minutes later, I was dressed in jeans, ballet slippers, and a South Cove Rocks T-shirt. I had plenty of time to walk to the winery. Emma lay cuddled on her porch bed, her foot on the new chew toy I'd given her before my shower. I grabbed the tote that held my dress shoes for the costume. The silver ankle strap pumps weren't my style, but for once, I'd play the shoe girl. I had to admit, they were cute. I'd look good even if I couldn't walk.

Coming into town, I spied Greg's truck parked in front of Vintage Duds. He must have come back early from Bakerstown, I mused. Walking by, I considered stopping in, just to find out what he was talking to his ex about, but I kicked the bad angel off my shoulder and kept walking. Greg was a big boy. If there was something going on between him and Sherry, he would have told me. He had the moral compass of a recently crowned Eagle Scout. And I could trust him.

I said that last part aloud, just to make sure I heard the comment. Man, I was really going to need a beer after this practice was over. The streetlights came on and I realized how dark the walk had been. Too late to take the Jeep, I kept walking. Besides, Greg would probably drive by at any moment and take me the rest of the way. But he didn't.

When I passed the bank, the lights were all on, and the door stood wide open. I stopped across the street, watching to see an employee come out, or the janitorial crew pile out of the building. But nothing, no one, came. I dialed Toby's cell.

"Hey, why are you calling me? Dontcha know I'm not here?" His message machine told me to leave a number and he'd get right back to me. Probably first thing tomorrow morning. I still left a message about how the bank was open for all to walk in and take what they needed. I dialed Greg's number and it went straight to voice mail, too. I glanced around the empty street. There was no one to help.

I took a step toward the bank building, then froze. A shadow crossed over the window. Someone was in the building. This wasn't just a prank. I turned and power-walked back to Sherry's store. Now, in the gloom, I could see the front shop lights were off. That was curious. The store appeared closed. I tried the door and it creaked open.

Stepping into the dark, I waited a second for my eyes to adjust, then headed to Sherry's office. I'd seen the dark wooden door with an honest-to-God nameplate stuck in the middle, her full name engraved in gold during the Business-to-Business meeting. The woman was nothing if not predictable.

I put my hand up to knock, but then heard voices. Angry voices. Swinging the door open, I stepped into the brightly lit room. "Look, I hate to break up this charming conversation, but we've got trouble at the bank." Both Greg and Sherry stared at me. They were both sitting on tall café table chairs, their arms resting behind them. But then I saw their arms weren't resting; they were tied. "What the heck?"

"Let her go," Greg ordered to someone standing behind me. Suddenly, I could feel a person's breath on my neck.

I turned around and faced Leslie Talman. The crafter-slash-bank teller-grandma stood a few feet away. With a gun pointed at my chest.

She waved it toward a third chair. "You are such a busybody, Jill.

You really need to learn to stay out of problems that aren't yours. From what I've seen, you need to get a tighter hold on your man, too. Unless you want to lose him to this hussy."

"I am not a hussy." Sherry stuck her chin out in what must have seemed like a position of power. It was just pretty hard to take her seriously with her hands tied behind her and a cord tying her waist to the chair.

I slowly stepped over to the chair. From what I had seen, we were out of options. There would be no cavalry saving us tonight. Darla would think I was skipping the rehearsal to avoid talking to her about Kent. She already knew Greg might be working tonight. Leslie had more than a day before anyone would miss us. Or maybe longer.

I climbed onto the third stool. All I could think of was what would happen to my dog. Amy's apartment was way too small for Emma, and she hadn't even stopped growing yet. For her sake, I needed to fight, to hold on as long as possible so someone could find us. So I jumped off the stool.

"What are you doing? Do you want me to shoot you?" Leslie waved the gun at me. "Get up on that chair, now."

"Not until you tell me how and why you killed Kent." I folded my arms, trying to look determined rather than shaking like a falling leaf.

"You killed Kent? Why? I know he wasn't sleeping with you." Sherry looked befuddled.

Leslie walked up and slapped her across the face. "Shut up. I should just kill you now and figure out a story later."

Trying to get her attention away from Sherry, I said, "You hired that hooker the day he died, didn't you?"

Leslie's face broke into a wide grin. "You figured that out, did you?" She did a slow clap, each time jerking the gun and making me twitch. "I'm impressed. Your boyfriend here has been clueless all along, but you, a coffee shop waitress, had an idea."

"You bought cocaine from Conner, then what? Sprinkled venom from the poison dart frog on the stuff, letting it dry before returning it to the Baggie Conner supplied?" Now I was just making things up, but from Leslie's reaction, I was closer than I'd known.

"Very good, you should be our town's police detective, not this idiot who can't seem to decide who he's going to take to bed." Leslie poked Greg in the leg with the gun. To his credit, he didn't react.

"I can't figure out where you got the poison, though. According to the pet store, those frogs are harmless." Hope kept me talking, but fear made my words run fast.

She stepped away from Greg, and my heartbeat slowed for a second. "You didn't do your research then. The difference between the frogs in the wild and in captivity was what they ate. All I had to do was feed Anne's frog some tempting delights and wait." Leslie focused on Greg again. "I don't know what you see in this guy. You could do so much better."

I took a deep breath and decided to play out the scenario and hope Leslie gave me an opening. "You see where he was, not with me, right?" I sneered at Sherry. "What he sees in that, I just don't get."

"You little tramp. I'm twice the woman you'd ever think to be." Sherry was hot. Apparently she hadn't gotten the memo. If I hadn't been playing with life and death, this could have been a little bit fun.

"Whatever. You couldn't keep Greg, then you couldn't keep Kent satisfied. No wonder he went looking." I watched Leslie nod in agreement.

"That's why she killed him." Leslie pulled out a piece of folded-up notebook paper. "It says so right here. She was tired of his philandering and had to stop him, one way or the other."

"You were going to set up Sherry," I whispered, understanding why Leslie was here and why she'd left the bank wide open. Any law enforcement type worth his salt would be safeguarding the bank, which gave her plenty of time to fake Sherry's suicide.

"I sent her that text, thinking she would be arrested when they found his body, but your boyfriend ignored her visit. This plan would have worked, too, but when I got her tied up, the hero had to walk in to save the day." Leslie rubbed her face with her free hand, the note flapping with the motion. "Now, how will I explain away the rest of you?"

"You could let me go." My words surprised even me. "I wouldn't tell anyone. Sherry deserves this, and well, I guess Greg made his bed, so he can sleep in it."

"Nice try, but I can't let you go. You'd tell that cute little barista-part-time-cop." Leslie leaned forward. "The girls say he's quite the playboy."

Before I could respond, Leslie grunted and her eyes widened as she began to shake, then drop to the ground. Toby stood behind her, a stun gun in his hand. When she fell, he ran toward her, kicking the gun aside. He rolled the incapacitated Leslie onto her side and hand-cuffed her. When he pulled her to a sitting position, he said, "*Re-formed* playboy."

I fumbled with the fabric belts she'd used to tie Greg's hands be-hind his back while Toby freed Sherry. Once I untied the knot, Greg pulled me into a hug. "I was so worried about you. The woman was crazy."

"She just wanted the person who hurt her friend to pay for his crime. In a way, I get her." I took a deep breath of the musky smell of Greg. "I'm glad this is over."

"Wait, I thought you were mad at him." Sherry pointed a finger at me. "You wanted to help her kill me."

"Wouldn't have been the worst idea," I mumbled. Greg shot me a look.

"Jill was keeping Leslie busy until Toby could get here." He con-sidered his deputy. "Why are you here and not at the bank?"

"Tim's at the bank. He called in Mrs. LaRue and she's down there now, figuring out if Leslie did any damage." Toby grinned. "When I saw your truck at Vintage Duds and listened to Jill's message, I fig-ured I'd better get over here and save you. I just thought Jill would have been the one beating you down."

"Thanks for the vote of confidence." With Greg's arm around me, I felt like I could do anything. I laid my head on his shoulder, thank-ful the night had turned out as well as it had. If Toby hadn't checked his messages, or if Leslie had shot without trying to figure out a new plan, the night could have turned out very differently.

"I never doubted you," Greg whispered in my ear.

I checked my watch and smiled. "We still have time to make the dress rehearsal."

CHAPTER 24

I'd just started pulling the tables and chairs into a conference setting when Greg arrived. He took a table I'd been struggling with and moved it with ease. "You get the chairs, I'll move the tables."

"Fine, go all Tarzan on me." I arranged a few chairs, then looked at him. "I don't remember inviting you to the meeting. You here for a purpose?"

"Bill actually asked me to come and talk about the neighborhood watch program we're thinking about setting up for the businesses. That way I don't always have to be the one rescuing you."

I pointed my finger at him. "I rescued you this time."

"Children, don't fight." Aunt Jackie brought over a rag to wash down the tables, again. "Greg, I wanted to thank you for helping Mary get her money back. You really are a blessing."

"No problem. When the guy figured out that Mary's transaction was the only one we could pin on him, he started talking like the whole thing was a mistake and his commitment to customer service was so important." Greg moved the final table and then arranged the last of the chairs around it. "Are you going to have enough spots? There must have been thirty people at the meeting Sherry hosted."

"You never know when to shut up, do you?" I smiled and put my arm around him. "Actually, Sasha called every business and got a head count. We have more than enough chairs."

Sasha set two carafes of coffee on the table. "Yeah, once I explained that we weren't paying businesses a hundred-dollar stipend to attend like Sherry had, several of the attendees were too busy."

"Wait, Sherry paid people to come?" Greg laughed. "No wonder she had such a strong turnout."

"Anything to show she's the better woman." I grabbed a sleeve of coffee cups and set several stacks on the table.

The bell over the door rang, and Darla appeared. "Hey, doll, I know I didn't ask, but can I have a few minutes on the agenda to talk about how much money we made for the women's shelter?"

"Of course." I glanced around the shop. Everything was ready for the Business-to-Business meeting to start. Aunt Jackie had set out plates of cookies we'd bought from Pies on the Fly rather than the typical cheesecake we had served in the past.

Darla claimed a chair and reached for a cup. "We should do that again. Everyone had so much fun."

"Not everyone." Greg poured her coffee.

Darla's face broke into a large grin. "Now, Greg, you were amazing as Jill's mobster boyfriend. You have a knack for acting."

"Well, let's do something physical for the next fund-raiser. Like a race." Greg grabbed a cookie as he turned a chair around backward and leaned over the cane backing.

"Funny you should mention a race. How about a 5K fun run/walk?" Aunt Jackie stood by the counter, reading a letter.

I walked over to stand next to her. "What's that?"

"You got this letter yesterday, but I forgot to give it to you. I assumed it was shop business so I opened it this morning." She was rambling, a habit she had when she was excited.

"And it says?" I prompted. Checking the clock, I saw we only had minutes before the group would be starting to arrive.

"Dear Ms. Gardner, since you are the newest member of the historical commission's preservation team with the new addition of the South Cove Mission Wall to the California rolls, we'd like you to sponsor this year's Mission Walk in June."

"Wait, does that mean the commission has approved the wall?" I grabbed the letter away from my aunt, but except for contact information and a list of prior Mission Walk sponsors, the letter wasn't very informative. "I need to call Frank."

The bell over the door rang again. Aunt Jackie took the letter away from me. "You need to run this meeting. Go play hostess. I'll call Frank Gleason and figure out what's going on."

Greg stepped closer, putting his arm around me. "Congrats. What do you do now?"

"Honestly, if it's true, I have no clue." I smiled at Darla. "You want to help me coordinate a fun walk?"

"We'll talk after the meeting. There are so many things we need to set up . . ." Darla pulled out a notebook and started scribbling. "This will be so much fun."

"Or something." I watched as the regulars piled into the room and took their seats. Bill and Mary entered the shop laughing at something Josh Thomas had said. Behind Josh, Kyle walked in, carrying the school desk I'd forgotten all about buying from the antique store. I ran over to hold the door and pointed him to the children's section of the store.

The desk looked perfect, but I still took a few of my favorite children's books and displayed them on top.

"All ready for a day at school." Kyle appraised the area. "At least the fun part of the day. I loved storytime."

"Thanks for bringing it over."

Kyle blushed and nodded. "No trouble at all. Got to run. I'm watching the shop this morning during your meeting." He dropped his voice. "All by myself. Can you believe it?"

As he disappeared out the door, Sadie entered, waving at me and holding hands with Dustin Austin. They'd had their first public outing as a couple at the mystery dinner, so I guessed they must have reached an accord about the speed of the relationship. Sasha poured coffee and greeted each newcomer.

Somehow the meeting I'd always dreaded had turned into a gathering of friends and family. And for once, I knew I could get through two hours without losing my good nature. Esmeralda's fortune for me had been spot-on. Friendships are precious, maybe not metal all the time, but still important.

Josh Thomas approached me. "I'll be expecting my check for the desk before I leave. One more thing, you did put my agenda items on this time, right? I faxed you an updated list last night. We really must do something about the speed limit . . ."

Maybe not all relationships were treasurable. I stopped listening to his tirade and took in the gathering around me. Yep, everything was back to normal.

Looking for more Tourist Trap mysteries?
Keep reading for a sneak peek at KILLER RUN,
the next stop in
Jill's adventures in South Cove
Available August 2015

CHAPTER 1

Modern wisdom says it takes twenty-one days to make a habit stick. Lack of exercise, eating too much, or even negative thinking are all habits that can disappear in less than a month. My problem is, I don't seem to get past week one. Oh, my intentions are good. My heart's in the right place, but then the proverbial stuff happens.

Like the current Business-to-Business meeting, where I sat eating my second slice of Sadie Michael's black forest cheesecake. The item was a new offering from her bakery, Pies on the Fly. Each slice had enough calories to nourish a small village for a week. However, Josh Thomas was off on a rant, and the creamy chocolate dessert was the only thing keeping my mouth shut and therefore not pointing out the flaws in his reasoning. Today, the owner of Antiques by Thomas thought we should do something about the ocean smell that permeated our little tourist town. His idea was to have electronic air fresheners installed on each streetlight on Main Street.

I guessed the fact that South Cove was located in central coastal California—therefore, the ocean—hadn't been included in Josh's memo when he opened the store last year. I glanced over at Aunt Jackie and raised my eyebrows, a signal that she needed to control her tubby boy toy before someone pointed out this fact to the clueless Josh.

She ignored me.

As I eyed the last piece of cheesecake heaven, Bill Sullivan, owner of South Cove Bed-and-Breakfast and our committee's chair, interrupted Josh's tirade. "I'm afraid I can't support this idea. Most of my guests book rooms with us specifically because of South Cove's proximity to the coast. In my mind, the sea air is a selling point, not a distraction."

"You don't understand how damaging it can be to my inventory. I'm always having to dehumidify my shop. If air fresheners were installed, at least the smell wouldn't enter with my customers." Josh looked around the table. "I'm sure others on the committee feel the same way."

I saw ten heads shake as Josh tried to make eye contact with the other business owners. Even this month's representative from the local art galleries failed to meet Josh's eyes. Of course, that could have been because they were asleep behind the dark shades. Artists loved the grant money that being a member of the Business-to-Business committee gave them, they just didn't like the actual meetings. Or helping with community projects. Or even having a freaking opinion.

"Well, it looks like we can table this discussion for another time then." Bill took charge and glanced down at the agenda. "One more item: the Mission Walk sponsorship. Darla? Do you want to present or is Jill handling this?"

The Jill he was referencing is me—Jill Gardner, owner of Coffee, Books, and More—or CBM, according to the new logo on our last cup order. I'm also the liaison between the South Cove City Council and the business community. Which means I'm responsible for setting up the monthly meeting, publishing the meeting minutes on our website, and any other crappy job the mayor decided to assign me.

I nodded to Darla Taylor, the owner of South Cove Winery and local event planner extraordinaire. "Go ahead, you're spearheading this event."

The Mission Walk was South Cove's first entry into the world of the California Mission Society. The charity focused on the preservation of historic missions throughout the state. Now that the small wall in my backyard had moved up on the list from application to possible historic landmark, I'd been invited to help sponsor this year's 5K Walk and Run fund-raiser. Darla had jumped at the chance to plan the event, and I blessed her every time I got a new e-mail from the representative of the professional company that the society had hired to manage everything.

I reached for the last slice of cheesecake, but Aunt Jackie slapped my hand, moving the plate off the table and onto the coffee counter. I refilled my coffee cup instead and sat back to listen to Darla's report.

"We're all set for next Saturday's run. The greenbelt has been measured, and we've got parking set up for the start and finish lines.

Greg hired off-duty police officers from Bakerstown to help with patrols that day. The only thing I need is a small group to walk the distance on Friday so we can make sure there aren't any surprises Saturday morning." She glanced around the table. "Who's going to volunteer?"

The room went quiet. I raised my hand. "You know Greg and I will be there, just name the time."

"Thanks. I'd like to do the run-through at five p.m. sharp. That way we'll know how long it will take our slower walkers so we don't leave anyone on the trail." Darla wrote down our names in her notebook. "Who else?"

"Josh and I will be there." Aunt Jackie stood to take the coffee carafe back for a refill.

"Jackie, you know I don't . . ." Whatever Josh had been going to say was blocked by the scorching look my aunt gave him. Sure, now he shut up.

"Perfect. Matt and I will start timing you at the start line and then we'll drive to the finish line to wait for you." Darla focused on me. "Do you want to ask Amy if she and Justin would join, too? I'd like some runners to see how quickly people can get through."

I held back my retort about me being chopped liver and nodded. Besides, if Amy and Justin ran, I could bring Emma, and Greg and I could have some quality time before the craziness of the weekend hit. We hadn't had much couple time lately between the shop and his annual training requirements for the local police department.

Yes, my boyfriend was the local detective for South Cove. Greg King had just returned to the area when my friend, Miss Emily, had been murdered. While he investigated her death, we'd started spending time together. I think he just wanted to keep his prime suspect close. He tells a different story. No matter what the truth had been, we've been a couple for over a year now. And we rarely, if ever, fought. Unless he thought I was messing with one of his investigations.

As Darla wrapped up the list of assignments for Saturday's run, the committee members filled their to-go cups with more free coffee and squirmed in their seats, ready for the meeting to end. Fortunately, Darla was enough of a bulldog that she'd filled the final few volunteer spots before she'd turned control of the meeting back to Bill.

"And that's everything." Bill closed the South Cove notebook cover where he kept the meeting notes. Mary, his wife and a market-ing maven, hadn't attended the meeting, but she'd been working with Darla this last month to analyze the effect of the run on the city's business community. The couple's bed-and-breakfast business had been booked solid for the last week with runners preparing for the event. He waved as he left the shop. "See you all Saturday."

"As usual, they leave all the cleanup for the meeting to us," Aunt Jackie grumbled as she started moving tables back to their normal places scattered around the shop.

Josh inched toward the door. "Sorry, I have to open in ten min-utes. Otherwise . . ."

We watched as Josh lumbered through the door, his next words lost to the wind. He scurried as fast as his close-to-four-hundred-pound frame would allow toward his shop next door.

"I'm shocked, I tell you, shocked." Darla laughed as she placed chairs around a table my aunt had just moved. "Seems that Josh al-ways has an excuse when there's actual work to be done. I don't think the guy has moved a box since Kyle started working for him."

"Being catty doesn't suit you, dear," my aunt chided Darla, her tone gentle. If I'd said that I would have gotten a lecture about being generous in spirit in my words. Darla just got a verbal tap on the hand.

My thoughts were interrupted when the door opened and a man and woman entered. To refer to the pair as Ken and Barbie would be too generous to the dolls. Both of the new arrivals were actor-level beautiful. We had tourist traffic that came up from Hollywood at times, but typically they came later in the day and dressed in clothes a bit more casual (but just as expensive).

"I told you we were going to be late, Michael." The woman tossed back her blond hair with caramel highlights as she watched us mov-ing the tables.

He sighed. "We would have been on time if you hadn't had to call your stylist about what outfit would be appropriate for a business meeting."

The woman smoothed down the blue jacket that hugged her curves. "Blame me for wanting to make a good first impression." She turned toward me and flashed a hundred-watt smile. "Forgive our bickering. I'm Sandra Ashford and this is my husband, Michael. We're the owners of Promote Your Event. We've been hired by the

Mission Society to assist with their fund-raising events. We're checking in to see if you all are ready for the walk on Saturday."

"I'm Jill Gardner. I own the land where the South Cove Mission was found." I held my hands up and glanced around the room. "As well as this coffee shop/bookstore. We've committed to be one of the sponsors for the event."

"Lovely." Sandra's gaze covered the shop's dining area and book department in less time than it took to read a road sign. A look of disgust flashed on her face for a second, her lip twitching like the smell was Stockyard Drip instead of Vanilla Bean Delight. Then her plastic veneer went back up, and I almost thought I'd imagined the negative assessment. Until she spoke her next words. "I guess it will have to do."

Darla stepped next to me and held out her hand. "Darla Taylor, South Cove Winery, and *Examiner* lead reporter." She grinned at me before adding, "And South Cove Mission Walk chairman. I'm so glad you took time out of your busy schedule for us. Come sit, I've got the event plan right here. I'd love to have you go over it to make sure I'm not missing anything."

Michael stepped forward and shook Darla's hand. "I'm sure it's grand. You know, these events never could get off the ground without the tireless effort of volunteers like you."

As Darla stepped toward a clean table, I heard a sigh come from Sandra's direction. "I swear, if I have to do any more of these one-horse-town events, I'm going to scream."

Michael grabbed her elbow and leaned closer. "Be nice. Or pretend to be nice. I know it's hard to act like something you're not." The couple followed Darla, and as I watched, Sandra shook off her husband's grip.

Those two have issues. I knew what it was like to be in a marriage that wasn't working. Between my law practice and my own failed relationships, I'd had plenty of examples. The Ashfords were definitely dysfunctional and on their way to a nuclear blowup. I just hoped they'd get through Saturday. The Mission Walk was too important to be collateral damage from a couple's disintegration. I stood by the table as they sat on both sides of Darla.

"Before we get started, can I bring you coffee? A carafe? Or something more decadent, like a cinnamon roll and a hot chocolate?"

"Bottled water." Sandra didn't even look up from digging in her leather tote.

"I'm good." Darla waved me to a chair. "Sit down and help me present our plan."

Michael turned toward me. "That cinnamon roll sounds amazing. Can you heat it with a little butter? And coffee, cream and sugar."

Sandra snorted. "No wonder you didn't want to go to the gym today. You were planning on blowing your diet."

"I'm not on a diet." Michael smiled up at me. "But I should have accompanied my wife to the gym. Sometimes you just want that extra sleep."

And time away from a witch from hell. I started to walk to the counter, but my aunt waved me away. "I can handle this. Just sit down."

By all rights, Aunt Jackie should have been the one involved in the discussion. She had a knack for marketing. I had just muddled through before she'd come to help me with the shop. I slipped into the last chair at the table and accepted a folder from Darla.

Listening to the plans and schedule, I knew that Darla had been the right choice to set this event up. She had thought of everything. As I looked through the maps, sign-up sheets, and lists of South Cove businesses she'd gotten donations from, I was impressed.

Aunt Jackie set a glass of orange juice in front of me and looked over my shoulder, pointing to an item on the list. "I didn't think Lille would be participating. That woman's always griping about giving away her profits."

Darla laughed. "When I told her you were sponsoring all the water stations and providing CBM cups, she decided she needed to do something. So she's hosting a small celebration circle at the end of the walk. Burgers and fries."

"Just what a health-conscious runner wants at the end of an exercise event. Sometimes I think the woman is clueless." Sandra snorted.

Michael dug into his cinnamon roll, holding his fork up to show his wife. "There's more to life than just health food."

"I hope you choke." Her response sent a chill through me.

Angela Brewer Armstrong at Todd Studios

USA Today and *New York Times* best-selling author, Lynn Cahoon is an Idaho native. If you'd visit the town where she grew up, you'd understand why her mysteries and romance novels focus around the depth and experience of small town life. Currently, she's living in a small historic town on the banks of the Mississippi river where her imagination tends to wander. She lives with her husband and two fur babies.

Guidebook to Murder

When Jill Gardner's elderly friend, Miss Emily, calls in a fit of pique, she already knows the city council is trying to force Emily to sell her dilapidated old house. But Emily's gumption goes for naught when she dies unexpectedly and leaves the house to Jill—along with all of her problems . . . *and* her enemies. Convinced her friend was murdered, Jill is finding the list of suspects longer than the list of repairs needed on the house. But Jill is determined to uncover the culprit—especially if it gets her closer to South Cove's finest, Detective Greg King. Problem is, the killer knows she's on the case—and is determined to close the book on Jill *permanently* . . .

GUIDEBOOK TO
MURDER

A TOURIST TRAP MYSTERY

Dying for a visit...

LYNN CAHOON

Mission to Murder

Jill Gardner, proprietor of Coffee, Books, and More, has discovered that the old stone wall on her property might be a centuries-old mission worthy of being declared a landmark. But Craig Morgan, the obnoxious owner of South Cove's most popular tourist spot, The Castle, makes it his business to contest her claim. When Morgan is found murdered at The Castle shortly after a heated argument with Jill, even her detective boyfriend has to ask her for an alibi. Jill decides she must find the real murderer to clear her name. But when the killer comes for her, she'll need to jump from historic preservation to self-preservation . . .

MISSION TO MURDER

A TOURIST TRAP MYSTERY

Don't miss the deadly landmark...

NEW YORK TIMES BESTSELLING AUTHOR

LYNN CAHOON

If the Shoe Kills

As owner of Coffee, Books, and More, Jill Gardner looks forward to the hustle and bustle of holiday shoppers. But when the mayor ropes her into being liaison for a new work program, 'tis the season to be wary. Local businesses are afraid the interns will be delinquents, punks, or worse. For Jill, nothing's worse than Ted Hendricks—the jerk who runs the program. After a few run-ins, Jill's ready to kill the guy. That, however, turns out to be unnecessary when she finds Ted in his car—dead as a doornail. Detective Greg King assumes it's a suicide. Jill thinks it's murder. And if the holidays weren't stressful enough, a spoiled blonde wants to sue the city for breaking her heel. Jill has to act fast to solve this mess—before the other shoe drops . . .

IF THE SHOE
KILLS

A TOURIST TRAP MYSTERY

NEW YORK TIMES BESTSELLING AUTHOR
LYNN CAHOON

Printed in the United States
by Baker & Taylor Publisher Services